# SUNSET HOUSE

D1566466

# SUNSET HOUSE

**A Novel**

## ROBERT JAXX

Waterstone Press

Sunset House

Copyright 2017, Robert Jaxx

ISBN 10: 0692974725

ISBN 13: 9780692974728

This is a work of fiction. Names, characters, and places are the product of the author's imagination, or used fictitiously, and any resemblance to actual persons, living or dead, events or locales
is entirely coincidental.

All rights reserved. No part of this publication may be reproduced or transmitted in any form
or by any means, electronic or mechanical, including photocopy, recording, or any information
storage and retrieval system, without express written permission from the author.

Library of Congress Control Number: 2017916827

CreateSpace Independent Publishing Platform
North Charleston, South Carolina

First Edition

Waterstone Press

Other novels by, Robert Jaxx:

*SPARROW'S GARDEN,* to be released Spring, 2018.

*THE CRACKED,* tentatively scheduled for release Spring, 2019.

For more information on Robert Jaxx's books, please visit *robertjaxx.com*

*To my parents, for the lessons learned*

*Better the devil you know than the devil you don't.*

# CHAPTER 1

My plan had been to kick back, drink a few beers, and watch the ballgame, content knowing my hectic week of pouring over evidence and preparing witnesses culminated with the defendant agreeing to plead to a lesser offense, putting a sudden end to the rigors of my trial preparation. And yet, not two bottles drained, my cell phone rang. It was an interruption I would've liked to ignore (particularly since I couldn't place the number splashed across the screen), but when you're an assistant prosecuting attorney for one of Michigan's largest counties, with an eye, I might add, at becoming top dog once the current top dog retires, it wasn't a luxury I could afford. So I picked up the phone, and without a hint of enthusiasm, said, "This is Andrew Rivers."

"Drew, it's me, D.C."

Danny Cranston, generally known simply as, D.C., was, like me, a seven-year veteran of the prosecutor's office. Unlike me, however, he used to be a cop and still had close ties to his former brethren, which meant he often caught wind of things before the rest of us. As such, it wasn't a shock to hear him say, "Hey, I'm with some of my old crew. I have some news."

"Where you calling from? I asked, not the least bit fazed he was likely going to tell me a crime's been committed. Hell, in my line of work it's the norm not the exception, so you pretty much expect it.

"Oh yeah, the phone," D.C. replied, as though a light just went on. "Mine ran out of juice. I'm using Johnny Batista's. You remember Johnny, don't you? I worked in the 3rd precinct with him."

"Yes, I remember Johnny," I replied.

"He's the tall and skinny bald one," D.C. added.

"I remember him, D.C. Now what's up? Why the phone call?"

"Okay, you ready for this?" D.C. returned, after a momentary sigh. "It looks like we may have a serial on our hands."

"A serial what?" I asked, pushing the hair from my eyes.

"Rapist. A serial rapist."

I slowly stood from the couch, my body drawing tense, and said, "I'm listening."

"White woman in her early to mid-thirties abducted in her driveway – beat about the head until unconscious – hands tied behind her back with duct tape…"

"And anal penetration," I offered.

"Yep. Just like the other one."

I peered out the window from my fifth story apartment and noticed the streets of downtown Barrington, a small, but upscale city awash with bars, restaurants and retail shops, were quieter than normal for a Friday night. "Who found her?' I asked. I then glanced at my watch and realized that at 9:30 the streets below had plenty of running room left.

"An elderly couple walking their dog found her early this morning."

"Where?"

"Red Run Park. Apparently the crazy bastard left her there to rot."

I pondered the scenario a few seconds, before asking, "Any chance we're dealing with a copycat?"

"Not a chance. The first victim, the lab results came back this afternoon. Apparently the sick fuck didn't use his dick."

"Okay, I don't know what that means, the sick fuck didn't use his dick. You want to elaborate on that, please?" I returned, the angst inside me becoming difficult to mask. "And no riddles, D.C. Just spit it out."

D.C. took a few moments to respond, and in that time I knew he was doing his best to quell his own angst. Finally, he said, "The victim, she was sodomized with a foreign object. Word here is they think the second victim was too. Obviously they're waiting for lab results, but I'm hearing it's more a situation of, what kind of foreign object, not whether it was a foreign object." D.C. paused again, before saying, "There's something else, Drew."

"Christ," I muttered.

"My last year as a cop... I dunno, nine, maybe ten years ago, there was an incident with similarities to these two rapes. Do you remember hearing anything about them?"

I shook my head, saying, "You forget, D.C., but my first few years out of law school were spent working for the legal aid society in Chicago. That would have been around that time, so no, I hadn't moved back here yet." I then sighed, adding, "What were the similarities?"

"Everything but the sodomy."

"So you're saying a foreign object was still used?"

"Vaginally, yes. Doesn't mean it's not the same guy though."

"Well if that investigation was never closed there should be a case file we can review."

"There should be," D.C. returned. "But you know how lax the police department can be when it comes to storing anything for any length of time."

"I guess we're gonna find out," I said, again pushing the hair from my eyes.

"Copy that," D.C. said, before the next several moments were punctuated by the uneasy silence of deliberate breathing and unspoken thoughts. Finally, D.C. mused, as though talking to himself, "Goddamn, I'd hate to think this animal has been roaming around out there all this time."

"Me too, D.C. Me too."

# CHAPTER 2

I've been riding these elevators nearly every day for the past fifteen years and rarely have I entertained the uninterrupted luxury of my own company. During the workweek, though regrettable, I understand. My law firm, along with four others, occupies three-quarters of the office building so there isn't a moment when lawyers, bankers, businessmen, and thieves, aren't buzzing around like flies. But on a late Saturday afternoon with autumn's chill pushing suitable limits, and tedious skies casting the perfect backdrop for a nap on a couch, I was lulled into thinking, *Yeah, maybe today.*

And then a brusque, "Hold the door! Hold the door!" jolted me back to the stark reality that weekend relaxation is no longer the rule. It's the exception. So I settled against the back wall and waited as a stout man rumbled inside.

"Thanks," he said. "I appreciate you waiting."

"No problem," I replied, though in truth I made no effort to accommodate him. The door simply closed painfully slow.

"Going to twelve, I see."

I sighed, before offering the man a trivial smile.

"I've got business here on the ground floor," he stated, his dark, deeply set eyes now firmly set on mine. "But I'm going to ride with you awhile."

I eyeballed my travel companion a few seconds. Then, "Do I know you?"

"You might've heard of me. Name's Frank Marino."

Indeed, I had recognized the name. I pretended otherwise. "Sorry, no."

"No matter," he said, abruptly shaking his head. "The important thing is that I know you, Mr. Rivers. Mr. Ethan Samuel Rivers."

"Well good. Score one for you, Mr... Mr. Marino, right?"

"Yeah, that's right, Counselor. Marino. Frank Marino."

"Okay, well, we're going to be coming up to the 12th floor pretty soon, Mr. Marino. So if you have a point to make, I suggest you make it."

Marino moved in front of the elevator door. His eyes then narrowed, and the color in his overindulged face dimmed, as though a shadow had engulfed light. "The point is, you represented that scumbag, Billy Maxwell, a few years back. Remember?"

Billy Maxwell was an enterprising kid who fought his way out of the streets of Detroit. Rumor had it he did so by selling crack – and lots of it. I never knew if the rumors were true, and frankly never cared enough to ask. My association with Billy came about because he was charged with first-degree murder in the shooting death of eighteen-year-old, David Ricci, the only son of Anthony Ricci, reputed mob boss for Southeastern Michigan. The long and short of it: I defended Billy, turning his first-degree murder charge into a manslaughter conviction. He was sentenced to fifteen years. With good behavior he would've been out of prison in ten, an outcome Billy could only pray for from the outset. Nevertheless, I then successfully appealed the manslaughter conviction, and Billy was set free after having served a mere two years. That was nine months ago.

"Yes, I remember," I said.

"Good. Now try remembering where the little scumbag is," Marino directed.

A few months back I had received an anonymous postcard from Jaco Beach, Costa Rica, thanking me for being a great lawyer. The postcard was typed, but I had a strong hunch it was from Billy. Nevertheless, I ignored Frank Marino's insipid directive, casually shrugged my shoulders, and said, "I have no idea."

"You're his attorney."

"Correction... was. I was his attorney."

"I know people who will pay generously for the information."

"What's the matter, Mr. Marino, your people couldn't get to Billy in prison, so now you want to bribe me for information I don't have?"

"I thought you didn't recognize my name?" Marino responded. He then snickered.

I snickered in return, saying, "It's all coming back to me now."

Marino leaned forward, and pointing his finger at my face, said, "Well you had better hope that scumbag's whereabouts come back to you too. And soon."

"Are you threatening me, Mr. Marino?"

"No, Mr. Rivers. It's a point. I'm making a point, just like you asked."

"Good," I countered, my chest swelling as I pushed away from the back wall. "Because I don't take kindly to threats." And with that, the elevator door slid open, Marino ambled out of the way, and I calmly walked off, though once exited I turned and stared at Marino staring at me until the elevator door slowly closed once more.

My office, a rich collection of handcrafted mahogany furniture and Post-Impressionism Art, once marked my stature within the firm. Today it stands as little more than a footnote to the success I have achieved over the years. Originally decorated by my first wife, Suzanne, a self-proclaimed interior designer whose sole experience was confined to my office, it was redecorated a few years ago by my second wife, Olivia, to include, most notably, two portraits, both of which hang on the inescapable wall behind my desk. The first is of Olivia and our then five-year-old twins, Leah and Liam. The second was actually reproduced from a photograph taken of me, my parents, and younger brother, Andrew, on my brother's 35th birthday, though I've never understood why Olivia chose that specific photo since my brother didn't look particularly happy to be in it. Then again, Andrew never had the good sense to learn how to hide his dour moods. If something's on his mind, you'll see it in his eyes. And if you see it in his eyes, you'll generally hear it in the sound of his voice. Perhaps that's why he's better suited to the guileless rigors of being a prosecutor. His job is not to create, posture, or perform. His job is merely to pursue, which, right or wrong, good or bad, Andrew is capable of doing with a good deal of spit and vinegar. Perhaps that's why it would also behoove me to stick him on that son-of-a-bitch, Frank Marino, harm's way notwithstanding. I chuckled to myself at the thought, and then turned away from the portrait, both portraits, and walked over to the wall of windows overlooking the afternoon traffic below, deciding any decision on Marino would wait another day.

Early on in my career I was offered an office overlooking the Detroit River in downtown Detroit, where our firm has been headquartered for longer than I care to remember. My father has his office there. I declined. Didn't want nepotism involved. My success would be my own. That's how I explained it at the time. But I had lied. Not about my eventual success, which I knew I'd achieve even if stationed on the moon. I just wanted space between me and the old man. So given the opportunity to create some, I did. And it's worked out well. I get to sit on the top floor in our suburban office, look out on the upscale landscape of a thriving city, and my father gets to take his bland energy into a broken city, drink martinis for lunch, and by dinner forget why he's still there.

Because my father graduated from the University of Michigan Law School, and remained a staunch advocate of everything Wolverine, it was pretty much a foregone conclusion that once Andrew and I were law school bound, we'd be heading to Ann Arbor as well. But that's where the similarities ended, for while my father and brother both performed admirably, neither distinguished himself, as I, by graduating at the top of his class; a feat which brought several job offers the moment I stripped off my cap and gown and strutted into the spring of my adult life.

The truth is, however, I was never going to move, regardless of how many, or how intriguing the job offers were. I was born in Michigan, I was comfortable in Michigan, and I never thought to live anywhere but Michigan. Besides, any suggestion that I was moving out of town, much less the state, would've incensed my mother, perhaps beyond reason, a situation I spent many years trying to avoid.

I suppose if I broached the subject now it wouldn't be met with the same hostility. Only now I've come to enjoy a status and lifestyle that would require far too much work to reproduce elsewhere. So why bother? Michigan, and the City of Detroit in particular, has more than enough culpability to keep me in gold for a long time, a reality once again reinforced when the firm's receptionist announced that Judge Beckett had arrived for our three o'clock.

When Richard Beckett first approached me about a meeting, I was, to say the least, a bit curious. I had known the man in his Judgeship for ten years, and even spearheaded a successful fundraiser for him during his last reelection. Yet, I did not know him all that well personally. I'd heard some rumblings about his lavish lifestyle, but never thought anymore about it, choosing instead to keep our relationship professional, if not cordial. But as he sat in my office, and said, "Ethan, I may be in a situation that requires your help," I sensed all that was about to change.

I nodded slightly, saying, "How so, Judge?"

Judge Beckett sighed, all but erasing his look of calm, before replying, "I never thought I'd be sitting in your office because I'm guilty of breaking the law."

I stared at the judge a few moments thinking the exact same thing. Finally, I asked, "Would you like something to drink, Judge? Water, coffee? Maybe a little single malt scotch?"

Judge Beckett dropped his palms to his thighs and pushed himself up from the chair. He sauntered toward one of my paintings with all the distinction of a perfectly coiffed, impeccably dressed man strolling through the Louvre Museum without a care in the world. It was a solid effort, but at this point I wasn't fooled. Still, I admired him for trying. "No thanks," he finally said. "I like a glass of cabernet in the evening. The rest I've given up. But listen," he quickly added, while turning to face me, "you go right ahead."

I ignored the suggestion, and jutting my chin toward the painting, said, "That's a Denisiro. Not a very popular painter, but I've always been drawn to his use of shade and color. He blends the two indiscriminately."

Judge Beckett offered the obligatory, "Yes, I see what you mean," before folding his arms, and asking, "do you remember the Van Bourne Development?"

"Of course," I replied. "It was only the largest land development around here in last twenty years."

The judge stared at me a couple of seconds but the uncompromising expression so often used to intimidate the lawyers in his courtroom was, to me, the look of just another criminal about to sell me his rationale. "Do you remember reading anything about the lawsuit filed by the township to stop the project?" he asked. Before I could answer, however, he added, "The Van Bourne group wanted Drummond Township to annex the adjoining City of New Haven. Some of their land was strategically located and needed in order for Van Bourne to maximize the development, and, in turn, their investment. New Haven wanted no part of it. They wanted a park, not, according to their lawsuit, a concrete jungle. But that kind of bureaucratic thinking would have cost millions and millions in lost tax revenue. Not to mention all the jobs at stake."

I pondered Judge Beckett's story a few moments – then, "What's your position in all of this, Judge?"

Beckett turned his palms up, and said, "Look, Ethan, I was likely to decide in favor of Drummond Township anyway."

"Let me guess," I said, with a trace of a smile. "The Van Bourne group made your decision that much easier."

"In a word, yes."

"Hmm. So how much?"

Beckett frowned, breaking his perfect Palm Beach tan into an indiscriminate blend of shade and color. "Is that information really necessary?"

I returned the frown, saying, "That information is the only reason you're standing in my office."

"You're right," Judge Beckett said after a few moments of apparent contemplation. He then dropped his eyes to his Farragamo loafers and sighed until his shoulders drooped. "A single payment of five million dollars," he muttered.

I leaned back in my chair and put my own Farragamos on the desk, thinking, not bad. Not bad at all. Finally, I said, "It's been a few years, Judge. Why the trouble now?"

Judge Beckett made his way toward my desk. Instead of sitting down, however, he gripped the back of a chair and leaned forward, saying, "Word is one of the Van Bourne principals is going to be indicted for bribing a county official on an unrelated development. If so, he's going to turn state's evidence."

"And you'll be given up," I interjected.

"Like a lamb for slaughter."

"What county are we talking about, Judge?"

Judge Beckett arched his eyebrows, the would-be wrinkles on his forehead hiding under an obvious skin-tightening, and said, "Your brother's county."

"Hmm," I uttered, while tapping my forefinger against my chin. A few moments later I pulled my feet from the desk and sat up in my chair. "How interesting," I finally said. "How very, very interesting."

# CHAPTER 3

Just like he did with my older brother, Ethan, when I graduated law school my father asked if I would be interested in joining his firm. He was a partner in Smith, Patterson, one of Detroit's ancient blue-blood, good ol' boy law firms specializing in everything big business. Unlike Ethan, however, the notion of representing the well-healed held no significance for me. Now granted, Ethan used the prominence of the old man's firm as a springboard to build a thriving criminal defense department, and, in doing so, become one of the most prominent and recognizable defense attorneys in the State of Michigan. But I did not want to be a defense attorney any more than I wanted to represent a bunch of well-fed, bourbon-soaked, middle aged white men who wanted nothing more than to perpetuate their coddled existence.

The truth is, when I graduated law school I wasn't sure what kind of law I wanted to practice, let alone be squeezed into some specialty at the old man's firm simply because they had a need for it. In fact, the only thing I knew for certain was that I would be following Marissa back to her hometown of Chicago. That had been our pact from the beginning – the first to get a job meant the second had to follow. And since Marissa only applied for jobs in Chicago, and I, in turn, never applied anywhere, it wasn't real hard to figure out where I'd be living after graduation.

Explaining the situation to my father, now that was another story. He liked Marissa and all, but his thoughts for her, and of us together, were simply overshadowed by his desire to have both his sons working in the firm. My mother, on the other hand, couldn't have cared less what I did, plotting her way through life with a concern only for her precious firstborn, the latest in fashion, and discovering the fountain of youth – though I'm not sure in what order. As for the precious firstborn... frankly I doubt Ethan remembered Marissa's first name, let alone that we were moving to Chicago with our sights set on getting married.

Fortunately, the marriage thing never took hold because we ended up going our separate ways not three years down the road. I had been working at one of the city's legal aid clinics representing indigent and bum alike, and yet, somewhere along the way the stature of my job, or, as Marissa would be inclined to say, "lack thereof," began to weigh on her. Marissa couldn't understand how someone with my pedigree could graduate from *The* University of Michigan Law School (as though it was the holy grail of universities), and be satisfied doing such menial legal work. The part of the equation she always left out was that the menial work came with a menial paycheck. But she couldn't toss that in my face, for doing so would have been an admission that money actually mattered to her – and having money, of course, was sacrilegious... until she started making some of her own.

That's okay, though. I had grown bored with the relationship anyway. The conversations had become redundant, the sex obligatory, our future together pointless. As such, I decided to move back to Michigan, where, after bouncing through a couple of random interviews, an old law school buddy, Martin Pines, suggested the prosecutor's office. "I'll put in a good word for you, Drew. I've got friends over there." When I didn't immediately do backflips at the suggestion, Martin added, "You'll like the job, Drew. You'll be working with good people. Plus, it'll play to your strengths." I'm not sure Martin knew my strengths, simply because I couldn't pinpoint them myself. What I do know is that I walked into the interview wearing my Sunday best, and walked out an hour later with a job offer.

Before accepting any position, however, I had promised my father I would discuss joining his firm one last time. It was a short discussion, however, for no sooner did me and the ol' man sit down for a heart to heart (me in all my nonchalant glory, and the ol' man, a model of decorum), when Ethan, and his matinee idol good looks, came prancing into the conference room like a strutting peacock, only to flaunt his recent accomplishments with the rat-tat-tat of machine gun fire. It was then when accepting the position of assistant prosecutor became a certainty.

But that was something my brother had no doubt planned all along. He was never going to share the stage with me. Nor was he going to share, what he believed, was his rightful stake in the old man's firm. And no better way for Ethan to shoo me away than by reminding me, no matter what heights I might reach within the firm, he would always be hovering, ready to pounce and suck all the oxygen out of the room at a moment's notice. He knew it, having rammed it down my throat from the time we were kids – I knew it, having choked on it from day one – and deep down, dear-old-dad knew it. But like most things, he wouldn't admit it to himself.

In my first couple of years in the prosecutor's office, I had established a 96% conviction rate, which got me bumped from prosecuting criminal trespass and simple assaults to those involving drug trafficking, armed robbery... even murder. Point being, I was assigned cases that received a good deal of media attention, just the kind to attract the likes of my brother, Ethan. But the opportunity to square off against him in court never presented itself, for it wasn't another two years down the road before I was asked to head-up, what was then, the newly formed sex crimes unit of our department (an assignment the local media has, on occasion, accused me of pursuing with reckless abandon). Yeah, well, screw the local media anyhow. They've never witnessed firsthand the devastation sexual crimes cause to victims and their families. They're too damn busy chasing stories to stop and realize that a crime against the body is also a crime against the soul – a dim reality now plaguing the lives of the two recent sodomitic rape victims.

Lauren Hill, like Patricia Stevens, lived in the sprawling, affluent township of Chestnut Hills (a hop, skip, and a jump from my brother's house, in fact). Unfortunately, the police hadn't discovered too much more about the rapes than what they initially knew. Both women were in their early thirties – both had been attacked in their driveways between 11:00 p.m. and midnight – both suffered bruises and lacerations to the head as each one was pummeled into submission – and both were bound and gagged with duct tape, before being sodomized with what we now know to be a plastic object of some kind. No prints, no DNA, no physical descriptions, nothing was left behind but the broken spirits of two women and their families.

It took D.C. the better part of a week to track down the file of the unsolved rape from ten years back, but it was worth the effort, as it provided enough information to indicate we were probably dealing with the same monster. The victim, 32-year-old, Sally Rutherford, was abducted in her driveway approximately ten miles from Chestnut Hills, the biggest, and perhaps only distinction from the recent attacks. In other words, she too was beat about the head, secured with duct tape, and taken to a remote area where she was subsequently assaulted with what tests showed at the time to be a wooden object.

Fortunately, she had provided a written statement, which victims Lauren Hill and Patricia Stevens have thus far been unable, or unwilling to do. In short, Rutherford believed her assailant wore rubber gloves, which had been subsequently confirmed by tissue samples taken from her lacerations. This also coincided with our recent findings on the Lauren Hill, Patricia Stevens' lacerations. Rutherford also managed to steal a glimpse of the sick-fuck before losing consciousness. He wore a ski mask, though it provided a big enough window to see that he was white. And lastly, she guessed him to be over six feet tall, though given that Sally Rutherford herself was listed as 5' 2", tall might be a relative description.

When I asked D.C. if she was still living in the area and available for further questioning, he somberly replied, "No. She hanged herself two years after the attack."

Over the next couple of days I scoured the computer for any unsolved rapes within a fifty-mile radius of Chestnut Hills, hoping to find something (anything, in fact, beyond the use of rubber gloves, a mask, and foreign object), that would help piece together a profile of the assailant. It was an effort in futility, however, for even going back several years didn't provide anything fruitful. And then, just like magic, Wednesday night rolled around, and I got another phone call from D.C. "You're not going to believe it bud," he said excitedly. "Random traffic stop not ten minutes from Chestnut Hills. Cop goes to the window to get a license and the smell of marijuana comes pouring out of the car like it was a chimney. Cop then searches the vehicle. He finds three ounces of weed in the glove compartment, an empty vodka bottle on the backseat and, you ready for this?" D.C. asked. Before I could reply, he says, "In the trunk he found a roll of duct tape, handcuffs, gloves, not a ski mask, but a mask someone might wear at a costume party, and photographs of naked women bound and gagged. Turns out, this guy in the vehicle, this Sonny Marx, he's a registered sex offender."

"No shit," I said, pulling my feet from the coffee table so I could sit up. "What'd he do?"

"Had sex with a minor when he was 30-years-old."

"Oh, nice. Sounds like a regular salt of the earth kind of guy."

"Oh yeah, a real saint," D.C. returned. "Meanwhile, the son-of-a-bitch is sitting in the can at the 45th District Courthouse. He's going to be arraigned Friday morning."

"Okay, I'm gonna be there for it," I stated.

"Yeah, I had a hunch you'd say that. You going to want company?"

"Not a chance. It's bad enough the head of the sex crimes unit is showing up for an arraignment on a minor league drug possession charge. And you know as well as me, all the judge is gonna do is give him a future trial date and send him on his way. Fuck, he'll be home in time for lunch," I said, the restraint in my tone belying my hastened pulse. "You showing up to assist me might just raise an eyebrow or two. And it's important we keep this shit close to the vest. At least until we find out what's going on with this freaky bastard."

"Point taken," D.C. returned. Then, "You going to work it out with Langford beforehand, or you want me to?"

"I'll talk to her," I replied, knowing the county's chief prosecutor would give me free reign in the matter.

The arraignment came and went just as I had predicted it would. Sonny Marx, a tall and pale-skinned 38-year-old man, with a scar just under a receding reddish-brown hairline that made the rest of his facial features appear gaunt, stood moot, while his court appointed attorney, Jerry Diggs, insisted that nothing found in the vehicle was proof of any wrongdoing, let alone that a law had been broken. When Judge Burrows peered over his reading glasses and inquired about the three ounces of marijuana, Jerry Diggs said something about it belonging to his client's friend, to which I promptly interjected. "Your Honor, the marijuana was found in a car registered to Mr. Sonny Marx. Now from all indications there was enough marijuana smoke billowing out of his car to form a small raincloud, but not quite enough to conceal the presence of another human being, or in this case, his client's friend. And that pretty well could be why Mr. Marx is listed on the police report as being the only occupant in the vehicle." I then winked at Jerry Diggs, adding, "I think it's safe for the court to go out on a limb and assign ownership of the marijuana to ownership of the car."

Judge Burrows smirked, before saying, "It's nice to see you my courtroom again, Mr. Rivers. It's been a long time. To what do we owe the honor?"

"It's nice to be here, Judge" I replied, acknowledging him by bowing my head slightly. "Scheduling conflict in the office, so I volunteered."

"No task too small. I like that," Judge Burrows said.

"Just trying to do my part," I returned.

"Too bad more attorneys don't share your attitude, Mr. Rivers."

"Your Honor," Jerry Diggs cut in, "I'm sure we're all grateful for Mr. Rivers' presence, but do you think we can get on with my client's arraignment?"

Judge Burrows pulled the glasses from his face, setting them beside his gavel. He then peered sharply at Jerry Diggs. "Ask, and you shall receive, Counselor. Now then, how does your client wish to plead on the drug possession charge, since it's quite apparent the drugs belonged to him?"

Diggs rolled his eyes at me, before looking back at the judge, and saying, "Not guilty, Your Honor."

"Okay." Judge Burrows concluded. "The court will advise you on a trial date, but we're probably looking at several weeks out. If a plea agreement is reached before then, contact my clerk so she can get it on the docket."

Jerry Diggs had the reputation of being a decent, but lazy attorney. Never one to work for a law firm, he has spent most of his career lugging his droopy frame from one court-appointed arraignment to the next, before handing off the remains of a case to another lawyer in return for a fee; the better the prospective case, the bigger the fee. Therefore, it didn't come as much of a shock when, after scheduling a meeting to discuss a plea arrangement for Sonny Marx, another attorney showed up in his place and stead. The shock came when I opened my office door and stood face to face with my brother, Ethan.

"You going to invite me in?" he asked, a condescending grin firmly in place. "Or you just going to stand there catching flies in your mouth?"

It took another moment, or two, before I moved from the doorway and motioned my brother inside. "Sorry. Wasn't expecting to see you."

Ethan set his briefcase down and then peeled off his coat, at which point he held it out for me to take. When it became obvious I wasn't interested in playing valet, he cracked, "You never were very welcoming," whereupon I grabbed the damn thing and tossed it over the back of a chair. "Satisfied, Mr. Etiquette?"

"Boy, I'm not here two minutes and the attack is on," Ethan said, his feigned distress a poor excuse for sarcasm.

"Whatever," I said, as I moved to fill the chair behind my desk. I then waited for my brother to finish looking around my office (as though it held enough distinction to really interest him), and take the seat across from me, at which point, I asked, "So how come I didn't receive any notice you were taking over for Diggs?"

"I just filed my appearance with the court," he replied. "I'm sure you'll get a copy in the next day or so."

"I know I'll get a copy from the court. I meant, from you. Why didn't you tell me?"

Ethan and I then stared at each other, one uncomfortable glare burrowing into another, until he abruptly dipped his head to the side, postured a look of curiosity, and said, "You know, it just occurred to me... you could use a haircut. Not a lot," he quickly added. "Just enough to take some of the wild out of the length. And maybe a little off the top, as well."

I hunched up my shoulders, saying, "What the hell are you talking about?"

"Nothing, forget it," Ethan replied. "And for the record, I did think about calling you. But then, the thought of seeing the look on your face when you saw me standing in the doorway got the better of me."

"Always putting yourself first, that's you alright."

Ethan swatted away my jab with an easy smile, and an affable, "Olivia sends her best. She says I'm to invite you to dinner so you can see the twins. She says it's been far too long."

"And how are Leah and Liam?" I asked, my voice tailing off as I sighed.

"How bad can they be, for god-sakes? After all, they have my brains and Olivia's good looks."

"Yeah, well, with any real luck, Ethan, they'll have more of her family's DNA, and less of ours," I returned, a statement that silenced my brother until I asked him if something was wrong?

"No, let's just get on with our business," he replied, the edge in his tone befitting the strained, invisible wall he can singlehandedly put up on a whim.

"Fine. I'm listening," I said.

"Sign off on 90 days probation on the drug charge," he directed.

"Why would I do that?"

"Because it's a first time offense, Andrew, and the court's not going to punish him anymore than that anyway. You of all people should know that."

"First time offense, nothin'," I returned. "What about his sexual assault conviction?"

Ethan scoffed. "What, that little incident with the minor? That's crap, and you know it. The girl was two days shy of turning sixteen, so the conviction was automatic – so was her willingness to sleep around with older guys, by the way. He got probation. End of story."

"Oh, so the probation suddenly makes it right?"

"Right or wrong doesn't matter," Ethan countered. "My client's prior has absolutely zero relevance to this penny-ante drug bust."

"Well if it's so penny-ante, why'd you take the case?" I queried. "Isn't it a little beneath you at this point in your career?"

Ethan grinned, and replied, "I suppose I could ask you the same thing, little brother."

"So ask," I said, dropping my palms open. "I've got nothing to hide."

"I would, but I already know the answer," Ethan declared.

"Well good, then if you know so damn much," I said, the snap in my voice an instant reaction to the pompous look on his face, "maybe you can tell me your client's whereabouts on the nights of the Chestnut Hills rapes?"

After a momentary pause, Ethan said, "So that's what this is about? That's why you showed up at Marx's arraignment."

"I thought you said you knew?"

"I had a hunch," Ethan replied. "But you just confirmed it for me." Ethan's derisive grin then slowly returned, where it remained, until he added, "For the record, my client had nothing to do with the rapes. He works in an auto repair shop on the Eastside. The gloves, the duct tape, most of the crap found in his car has to do with his work."

I spent the next several moments staring into the abyss of my brother's innocuous expression. It was an exercise I had plenty of experience with, knowing full well nothing would be learned, for it was, quite frankly, the tedium that defined our relationship. Finally, I let the chair fall forward, and said, "So let me get this straight… they use handcuffs and pictures of naked women bound and gagged where your client works? That must be one interesting auto repair shop. Maybe I'll even take my car in for an oil change. Is it open Saturday nights?"

"I'll say it again," Ethan deadpanned, "my client had nothing to do with the rapes."

"I guess we'll find out, won't we big brother?"

Ethan didn't respond, and no other words passed between us until he was about to leave, and I said, "You can have your 90 days."

The offer was met with the sound of my office door closing.

# CHAPTER 4

There are two types of people who live in my subdivision: those who have a lot of money, and those who make just enough to spend a lot of money, which, in turn, makes other people think they have a lot of money. Rumor has it, Gene Baxter, owner of a string of auto repair shops scattered throughout metro Detroit, is in the latter group. Frankly, I don't care either way, since I had never looked at him as anything more than just another unavoidable neighbor – a morning jog here, a weekend barbeque there, and as little contact in between as possible. Then one day a few weeks back, right after the Patricia Stevens rape, in fact, Gene pulled up my drive just as I was about to climb into my Mercedes. "You should let me detail that car of yours, Ethan," he said, after pulling his hearty frame from his own Mercedes. "I'll send one of my guys to pick it up."

"And do what?" I replied. "Walk to my office?"

Gene scanned my front yard. "Nah," he said, his bald head glistening in the autumn sunlight, his eyes squinting. "Take you an hour just to walk the length of your property. Say, here's an idea," he quickly added, a sardonic grin in tow. "Ya know that beautiful, vintage Porsche you keep locked up in the garage? Try driving it once in a while."

"I would, Gene," I responded, while offering up my own sardonic grin. "But it needs a new starter. Remember?"

Gene's haughty expression quickly dropped. "Shit. I was supposed to order one for you, wasn't I?"

Sardonic grin still in place, I simply nodded.

"I'm sorry, Ethan. Sometimes I'm a damn idiot."

"You'll get no argument from me."

"Seriously, I can't believe I did that," Gene continued, throwing up his hands for good measure. "I guess I've had more on my plate than I realized."

I snickered, saying, "Now we're getting somewhere."

Gene's otherwise beady brown eyes grew pensive. "What do you mean?"

"Let's just say I doubt you stopped by just so I could jog your memory." After a brief but laborious silence watching Gene look everywhere but at me, I sighed, and then added, "Why don't you just tell me what's on your mind."

It took Gene a few moments of posturing, before he finally uttered, "I um..." He then shifted his eyes back and forth, before repeating, "I um..."

By the third, "I um," I had edged closer, Gene's gaze had inched higher, and I said, "You um, what?"

Gene finally settled on the captivating, "I um... I have this employee."

The employee, it turned out, was Sonny Marx. Gene asked me to take him on as a client.

"Thanks, but I don't do pro-bono work," I replied. "And there's no possible way he can afford me otherwise."

"I'll pay all his legal fees," Gene countered. "I'll do whatever you need. Hell, I'll even throw in a new starter for your Porsche."

It was at that precise moment when I found myself with a new client. Better than that, I found myself with the distinct possibility of gaining leverage over my fat neighbor, who's nervousness bordered on desperation, and who's desperation screamed, *I have something to hide.*

As for Andrew believing I ended up with this case because that stiff, Jerry Diggs, brought me in... let's just say he doesn't need to know any more than what's necessary. I'll spoon-feed Andrew the facts as I see fit. First, however, I have to set the wheels in motion, which I decided to do after leaving my brother's office with the 90 days.

Simply stated, I don't know if Sonny Marx is a serial rapist, or not. What I do know is that my little brother can be so driven by what he wants to believe, the closer he moves toward the light, the less he sees it, which keeps him shrouded from the very reality he's in search of.

What I also know is that Marx's alibi needed work. Sure, I could've told my brother that Sonny had a night job, but at the end of the day such a boast without verification wouldn't hold water. As a result, I not only insisted on learning every detail about the job, I insisted on a tour of his place of employment. When Sonny resisted, I told him to find another attorney, a threat that spooked him into saying, "Fuck that. Gene says you're the best. But he's my boss. Get him to sign off, and I'll give ya whatever ya want."

Under the guise of that same threat, Gene not only signed off, he offered to play the part of tour guide as well.

*The Knight Owl Bar & Grill* sat just beyond the commercial district of Springdale, an old, but trendy city of renovated houses and retrofitted storefronts, located some twenty minutes outside the laden bowels of Detroit. As I discovered soon after arriving for my mid-morning tour, however, the bar Gene so fondly referred to as a favorite among the shot and beer crowd, wasn't even open for business the night of the latest rape.

"Then saying you were working that night isn't much of an alibi, is it?" I asked Sonny, rhetorically.

"Yeah, but I was doing stock work. Ya know, inventory… that kinda thing," Sonny replied.

"Bullshit," I sneered. I then peeled my eyes away from my shoulder-shrugging client and looked at Gene seated behind his desk. "And you had me meet you in this hole-in-the-wall to try and sell me a load of crap like that? What the hell is the matter with you?"

Gene leaned back in his chair, and resting his hands in his lap and his feet against the edge of his desk, nonchalantly replied, "Relax, Counselor, "I'm paying for your time."

I glared at Gene until I was sure he could feel the heat from my eyes, at which point I stood up from my chair, slowly, and said, "Should Sonny get charged then my brother is going to have a field day with you. But he's not going to beat me in the process, so I suggest you find Sonny another lawyer." I then turned to walk away, whereupon Gene announced, "The place was closed for a private party. Sonny was working the party."

"What kind of party?" I asked, without looking back.

"A party. You know, a party," Gene casually replied.

"No, I don't know," I asserted. I then turned and glanced at Sonny, who was biting his bottom lip, before fixing my eyes on Gene, who was trying to look calm, though his inability to hold a steady gaze underscored his obvious concern. "Was it your party?" I finally asked. "Someone's birthday party? Retirement party? Bachelor party? What?"

Gene twisted his head toward Sonny, who was still biting his bottom lip, then looked back at me and pawed his chin.

"Were invitations mailed out?" I continued. "Were they emailed out? If so, where is the evidence? What time did the party start? How long did it last? How many people were there? Do you have any of their contact information? Was the bar rented out? If so, by whom? How much did you charge? Was there a deposit? If so, was it paid by check? Was it paid by credit card? Where is the receipt? Was food served? Was liquor served? Did they pay by the drink or was it all inclusive? Where are the receipts? How many employees were working? What are their names? How much did you pay them? Where are your payroll..."

"Sonny was the only one working," Gene abruptly interjected.

"Doing what?"

"He started by doing an airport run for me. I sent him to pick up a friend of mine."

"And then what?"

"And then he helped with the party after he got back from the airport."

"What time was he at the airport?"

"The flight came in at 9:00 p.m. Sonny left here at 8:00, and was back by 10:00."

"Can that be corroborated?"

"What do you mean? Corroborated how?" Gene returned.

I ignored Gene, and instead tilted my head toward Sonny. "Did you park in the airport parking lot, Sonny?" Sonny looked at Gene, as though waiting for permission to respond, so I said, "I'm asking you, Sonny. And when I ask you, I expect you, and only you, to answer. Understood?"

"Okay, yes."

"Okay, yes, what? Yes, you understand? Or yes, you parked in the airport parking lot?"

"Yes to both," Sonny replied.

I leaned against the wall and gave Sonny the once over, his tired features minimized under the soft office lights. "How long have you worked for Gene?" I finally queried.

Sonny tugged at his shirttail for a couple of moments, and then said, "Few years, I guess."

"All at the auto repair shop?"

"Yeah."

"And you get paid what, every two weeks?"

"I do," Sonny replied.

"By paycheck?"

"Yeah, uh-huh."

"And what about when you work here at the bar?"

"What about it?"

"Do you get paid the same way?"

"Uh-huh."

"What about when you have private parties?"

"I don't get paid for the parties."

"Why is that?"

Gene bounced forward in his chair. "What the hell does that have to do with anything?" he asked.

I pointed my finger at Gene, and snapped, "If I'm Sonny's attorney, we do this my way. So sit there and be quiet. I'll let you know when it's your turn to talk." I waited for my neighbor to settle back in his chair, before turning my attention back to Sonny. "So?"

Sonny shrugged his shoulders, and said, "I guess cuz' I take part in 'em." He then slumped against the wall beside Gene's desk, as though weakened by the admission.

"Did you at least get reimbursed for the airport parking?" I asked.

"No. Not yet anyway," Sonny replied.

"But you do still have the parking lot ticket and receipt, correct?"

"Yes."

"Good. Give them to Gene, and he'll reimburse you with a business check," I instructed.

"Oh, so now you're going to decide how I run my business?" Gene chimed in.

"Listen, my not-too-intelligent-neighbor," I grumbled, "if Sonny's alibi is going to be he was working the night of the rape, then it would be helpful to have evidence so I can try and prove it. And so far the only corroborating evidence is the parking lot ticket and receipt. But if you don't reimburse him out of the business, it doesn't look very corroborating. Got it?" Then before Gene could utter a sound, I added, "Good. Which brings me to you." I watched a few moments while Gene shifted nervously in his chair, before asking, "So who came in, Gene?"

"A friend. I already told you."

"Yes, I know what you told me. What I want, and what you're going to give me, however, is a goddamn name."

Gene tried to stare me down, but his efforts sank under the weight of his own apprehension, and within seconds, he muttered, "Her name is Lola Jones."

"Friend of the family?" I asked, couching my sarcasm with an air of indifference.

"No."

"Did you buy the ticket?"

Gene rolled his eyes. "Of course I bought the ticket."

"Have you known her long?"

"Couple of years."

"Couple, as in two?"

"A couple, as in four," Gene said, before shifting in his chair once again.

"Must be the new math," I responded.

Gene scowled. "Very funny."

"So why the late night party?"

"Why not?"

"That answer's not good enough, so I'll ask you again. Why the..."

"Because Lola couldn't get here any earlier," Gene broke in. "And she was helping me host it."

"Where is she from?"

"C'mon, Ethan, does that really matter?"

I took a deep breath before pushing myself away from the wall and moving a step closer to Gene's desk. Then peering down at him, I said, "How many times do we have to go through this? If you want to play cat and mouse, then get Sonny another lawyer, and play with him. Otherwise, answer my damn questions."

"Fine," Gene conceded. "She's from California."

"And she'll no doubt be able to confirm that Sonny, not only picked her up from the airport, but that he escorted her back here, where they both attended your party, correct?"

"More than likely."

"What does that mean?"

"It means, I was tied up at the party with other things," Gene replied impatiently. "So I didn't see Sonny other than when he first got back from the airport."

I looked at Sonny. "Were you at the party long?"

Sonny shrugged, saying, "I wasn't feeling great that night."

I turned my focus back to Gene. "Like it, or not, I may want a list of everyone at the party. Depending on how the situation evolves, I may want statements from all your guests regarding Sonny's presence."

"Is this kind of thing going to get a lot of play in the news?" Gene asked, the words riding out on the tail of a long and solemn sigh.

"We're dealing with rape, Gene. What do you think?"

"Some of my guests are married, Ethan. This could be embarrassing to them," Gene replied. He then buried his head in his hands, and groaned.

"What's to be embarrassed about?" I asked.

A few moments later Gene uncovered his face, though the strain he apparently felt had taken root in his expression. "There wasn't any prostitution going on here," he quietly remarked. "That's not my thing."

"Then what is it that may prove so embarrassing to your guests?" I asked.

Gene hemmed and hawed, so I repeated my question, to which Gene promptly dropped his hands to his desk, and said, "C'mon, I'll show you," a proposition which led me to understand, Gene did not purchase *The Knight Owl Bar & Grill* for its libationary appeal. He purchased it because the building had a large basement – what he impassively referred to as, "Master Gene's Dungeon."

It wasn't until we descended the stairs, however, and Gene pointed out the whipping, spanking, and bondage stations, that I realized, Master Gene was a sadomasochist, and his dungeon was home to S&M parties. That was also when it first occurred to me, my neighbor, Master Gene, did not know the incriminating information he was passing my way was not privileged. He had yet to draw the distinction between paying one's legal fees, and being the actual client. And quite frankly, it was not a distinction I planned to explain, particularly since the information may one-day prove fruitful for me.

In fact, the only thing I did explain came just prior to my leaving, when I said, "If the situation requires it, then the story is going to be that you had a private party in the bar, and Sonny was paid in cash. If need be, you're going to testify to that, Gene, and my brother will have little choice but to believe you. You are, after all, a law abiding, and respected businessman around town."

I then winked at my fat neighbor, and left.

# Chapter 5

Michelle (Mickey) Langford has been the Chief Prosecutor of Miles County, not to mention my boss, for as long as I've been working in the prosecutor's office. She's also, by anyone's estimation, an excellent trial attorney, though she spends more time catering to the nuances of public office than she does going to court. That does not mean she doesn't occasionally take the reins of a case, however. Now she just happens to wait until one comes along and the blemish of losing is more than her office can endure, particularly if it stunts her reputation as being hard on crime, or worse, hinders her chances at reelection. Sure, the situation reeks of political bullshit, and yeah, it thrives on self-serving energy, but when you've got dozens of people pulling you in dozens of directions, your time is not your own. As such, you've got to pick your spots in order to be effective. Sometimes the spots are good, as was the situation when Mickey successfully prosecuted members of a local drug ring responsible for the overdose deaths of seven teenagers – and sometimes the spots are bad, like the one and only time she faced my brother in court.

Jeffrey Lewis was a self-described entrepreneur, known mostly, however, as the son of William Lewis, a wealthy owner of high-rise office buildings, whose own fame reached a highpoint when he spearheaded the purchase of a string of dilapidated buildings in downtown Detroit and turned them into affordable, but profitable housing; erasing a section of city blight in the process. Jeffrey, on the other hand, possessed neither the skills, nor foresight of his father, relying entirely on his family's name and connections to start a multi-million-dollar investment fund, with the stated purpose of investing in start-up internet companies. The only investments made, however, were in Jeffrey's lavish lifestyle, and as easily as the money was raised, it was squandered, prompting a few bankruptcies, a host of lawsuits, and one charge of Solicitation of Murder for Hire.

Lee Bean, a successful chiropractor until he was indicted for insurance fraud, spent two years in prison, whiling away his time reading, and trying to understand, The Divine Comedy, which he did not find amusing, and obtaining a mortgage broker's license, which he did. After his release, and using whatever monies the Feds had been unable to confiscate from his insurance fraud days, he started a mortgage company, selling inflated mortgages to people who could not afford them, and, in the process, foreclosing his way to a healthy real estate portfolio.

One such individual who rarely got within four months of making timely payments was Dante Glover, part-time junkie and fulltime saxophonist for a popular local jazz band. One other thing about Dante – he had two priors. One for assault and battery, and another for felonious assault, though both were several years before he purchased his home, got married, and saw his wife give birth to a baby boy. And therein was Dante's problem, because for all his faults, past or present, he was, first and foremost, a proud family man, prepared to do anything to keep his wife and child in the house, the only stability they had ever known.

As such, it was not a giant leap when Lee Bean, so utterly incensed that he lost his investment, approached Dante with a proposition: kill Jeffrey Lewis, and the house is yours free and clear, to which Dante agreed. What Lee Bean had not anticipated, however, was Dante Glover having a subsequent change of heart, and agreeing to turn state's evidence in the process. At that point, Lee Bean's guilt was sitting on a silver platter and all Mickey Langford had to do was tie a bow around it and present it to a jury.

What Mickey had not anticipated, however, was Dante lying comatose the morning of trial, the result of being reintroduced to heroin the night before. And with no other witnesses to tie Lee Bean and his murder plot together, his freedom was all but assured. All Lee's attorney had to do, in fact, was make a motion to have the charges dropped, which Ethan did without hesitation.

"The worst part of the whole thing," Mickey said to me later that afternoon, "I mean apart from that scumbag walking free, is the way your brother looked at me on his way out of the courtroom… like he knew something I didn't."

"Believe me, Mickey, I know the feeling. I grew up with that fucking look."

"Yeah, but I don't mean he was just being smug and patronizing, Drew. I mean, let's face it, that's pretty much your brother's reputation, isn't it?" she asked, the rhetorical spin of her question punctuated with a spirited smile that quickly dissolved, when she added, "This was different. I can't explain it. I just felt like he was hiding something."

"Like what?" I queried, after momentarily stroking the shadow of my day-old beard. "You mean like evidence?"

It took Mickey a couple different starts and stops – her legs crossing and uncrossing the first time, her arms folding and unfolding the second – before she finally said, "Like maybe he knew Dante Glover wasn't going to show for trial because he was going to O-D all along."

Since I've never been one to put much past my brother, particularly when it comes to advancing his own interest, Mickey's declaration was hardly heart stopping. Nor was it something anyone would ever be able to prove. What it was, and, more importantly, what it did, was provide Mickey with a reason to view my brother differently than she did before, and, by virtue of our link, perhaps me, as well. To that end, I looked at her, and calmly stated, "I'm not Ethan," to which she fashioned a warm smile before retreating to the hustle and bustle of her job.

Beyond typical business pleasantries, it would be several more days before Mickey and I would speak at length again, and only then because I happened to walk into *The Blue Swan,* a quaint, dimly lit bar not far from our offices, and found her sitting in the company of an empty martini glass.

I walked up behind her, and said, "Sitting with all your friends, I see."

Mickey turned, not the least bit startled, and responded, "Less arguments that way." She then smiled, and added, "And you've got quite the posse there yourself."

To say I've never noticed how attractive Mickey is would be an out and out lie. But she was my boss, so the thought of dwelling on the way her long black hair accentuated her searing green eyes, or how the glint in those eyes softened anytime she smiled was as ludicrous as getting lost in the rhythm of her perfectly shaped hips walking down the office hallway. Not to mention, she was smart... really goddamn smart. But like I said, she was my boss, so when I offered to buy her a drink, I only did so because I figured it the gentlemanly thing to do.

"Why not," she replied, "I'm celebrating. And come to think of it, you should be too."

When I didn't pursue Mickey's response with anything more than a puzzled look, she explained that she finally got the budgetary approval to open the sex crimes unit she had been pushing for from the time she first took office. Then before I could congratulate her, she nonchalantly added, "And I want you to head it up."

It was an offer I could not dismiss. Then again, I couldn't dismiss the other bits of news she revealed – that she and her husband of eight years were childless – that her husband, Dr. Derek Langford, had not practiced medicine since being terminated by the hospital for gross negligence – that the gross negligence was nothing more than a glorified excuse for his alcoholism – that her husband has since taken off for parts unknown – that she hasn't seen or slept with him in longer than she cared to remember – that she had just turned forty, only to realize she was in love with a man five years her junior – that the younger man was... whoa... me.

So, what started with a martini, has, in the few years to follow, evolved into a full blown love affair. As such, no one bats an eye when she walks into my office and closes the door behind her, leaving us a few uninterrupted minutes to relive the night before, or plan the night ahead. Seldom have we discussed legalese in such a way, reserving that kind of chatter for the weekly staff meetings. That's why I was somewhat surprised when Mickey walked in today just to inform me Judge Richard Beckett, one of a handful of circuit court judges that preside over the sexual assault cases my team brings to court, was under investigation for bribery.

Of course, the surprise went right out the window when she said, "Rumor has it, Ethan's representing him."

# CHAPTER 6

I never contemplate the lives of my neighbors, content in the belief that so long as they don't intrude on my time and space, they are free to do as they please. And I seldom, if ever, retrace the steps of my own life, content in the belief that memories are better suited for the devoid, dying, and feint of heart. But having passed Gene Baxter's house on my way to the office, I sensed a commingling of the two convictions.

To wit: the relationship between Gene and his wife... what is the nature of it? Does Peggy know her husband has an underbelly, so to speak? If not, then how would she react if she were to suddenly discover the life and times of Master Gene and his S&M Dungeon? Would she care? Would she join in? Or does this proverbial housewife and carpooling mother of four have her own underbelly to hide? And what about all my other upscale neighbors? Are they as happily married as their pearly white smiles would seemingly indicate? Or do they too have some scandalous stains they cover in pretensions just to appear normal? Of course, these are the questions which led me to scan pieces of my own life, beginning with the brief and ugly reality of my first wife, Suzanne.

An otherwise attractive woman with enough intelligence to string a sentence together, Suzanne (like so many others, in fact), made herself available during my senior year in law school, once my future success as an attorney grew from likely to a simple matter of time. For her part, however, Suzanne at least tried to hide what was otherwise so transparent. She also had the good sense to curb her voice for mine, substituting any desire for personal achievement or individuality with a complete willingness to succumb and please, a characteristic that quickly set her apart from the others. It was also a characteristic that began to erode soon after we traipsed down the aisle. In fact, once Suzanne wrapped her hands around the marriage license, she apparently assumed a lifetime dye had been cast, triggering, in turn, an overt desire to lay the groundwork for my future, pushing and prodding me, as though I was clay to mold. Interestingly enough, I never understood the delusion, for I did nothing to fetter my own intensity or prowess. Either way, it wasn't something I was put on this earth to debate, or tolerate. As such, I gave Suzanne her walking papers eighteen months after saying, "*I do.*"

A couple of years then passed, during which time I randomly saw other women, though only when the urge to be in their company proved overwhelming. Otherwise, I spent the majority of that time solidifying my footings within the law firm. First, by taking on, and winning, a handful of high profile cases involving, shall we say, the corrupt and well-healed. And second, by negotiating a generous bonus package as a result, which included being named head of the firm's criminal defense department. It was, to be sure, a time most attorneys would celebrate. Yet, I did not look upon myself as most attorneys. Ergo, I did not celebrate. I did allow myself one transgression, however. I took an afternoon off work and walked the quaint, but exclusive art galleries of Barrington, hoping to find a painting, or two, for the expansive house I intended to soon purchase. What I found instead, however, was the woman who would become my second wife.

Olivia Chandler was standing in front of The East Park Gallery's showcase wall, touting the watercolor virtues of Earl Biss, a Native American painter who, over the years, had gained a measure of distinction for his ancestral landscapes (even though I often likened his work to a child with a poster-board and box of crayons). Nevertheless, the possibility of earning a commission by selling one of Biss' works proved enough to keep Olivia's attention on her audience of one. Therefore, I promptly made it an audience of two, meandering my way between her delicate beauty and her would-be customer, looking into her radiant blue eyes, and saying, "I'd like to make a purchase of the artist's work."

The purchase turned out to be for three paintings. More importantly, the purchase was followed by dinner, which, in turn, led to breakfast the ensuing morning. But in between, I had not only discovered a woman whose smile embraced like the warmth of the summer sun, and whose voice whispered like the autumn wind that soothed it. I had discovered a woman whose unblemished beauty and docility, I swear to this day, was sculpted by the God of Porcelain Dolls.

Now several years and a set of twins later, my only pause for concern is the distant relationship I have with my children. For this, a smattering of reasons persist, beginning with the old adage, I was born old. That is to say, ever since I was young, I aligned myself with adults. As such, I never thought of myself as a child, never wanted to be a child, and therefore, never really connected with children – then, or now. Needless to say, there's also my prohibitive work schedule to consider. Out of the house by 7:00 a.m., only to return some twelve hours later, a weekday visit is a rare occurrence. That leaves the weekends, but given that I'm generally at my office on Saturdays, while Sundays are best suited for church, and rest, weekends are not significantly better. Then again, the entire situation may boil down to me taking a page straight from my father's book and passing it along. Put another way, perhaps I am inclined, unwittingly so, to forge the same sort of relationship with my children that my father forged with me and my brother, Andrew. Fortunately, the twins are young so there remains ample time for the matter to evolve. Fortunately, too, Olivia has never been troubled by any of it, satisfied just knowing that I provide a very secure, if not altogether extravagant lifestyle for all concerned. Yet, that edict begs another question: if extravagance breeds satisfaction, does that automatically mean it breeds happiness as well?

Unfortunately, the question would have to wait, for just as I steered my Benz into my office building's sparsely occupied parking lot, my focus promptly shifted from our extravagant lifestyle to the extravagant black limousine parked in a few of the spaces otherwise reserved for specific members of my firm – including mine.

Naturally I was prepared to direct the driver to promptly move his vehicle, but just as I got out of my car, the passenger door to the limousine opened and out climbed Frank Marino. He spent a couple of deliberate moments brushing his pants and suit jacket, before looking up, and saying in as gruff a tone as I remember from our first encounter, "I have someone here who wants to talk to you."

"Good," I quickly countered. "Then have them call my office and set up an appointment."

"I don't think you understand, Counselor."

I snickered to feign indifference, before saying, "On the contrary, Mr. Marino. I don't think you understand." A moment later, I sarcastically added, "It is Marino, isn't it?"

Marino smiled, though it hardly put a dent in the sneer he was wearing, and said, "Don't go overboard, Mr. Rivers – loving husband to Olivia, and father to twins, Leah and Liam."

Rather than give Marino the satisfaction of knowing his tactics were anything more than dramatic flair, I merely sighed, and said, "What is it you want, Marino? I have a meeting with a client in a few minutes and don't have time for your nonsense."

Just then a smoke-tinted window powered down and a voice from inside the limousine called out, "Is there a problem, Frankie?"

"No. No problem, Tony," Marino replied, his steely gaze set firmly on mine. "Just having a friendly conversation with Mr. Rivers here."

At that point I assumed the voice inside the limousine was that of Anthony Ricci, reputed mob boss of Southeastern Michigan, and father of the late David Ricci, whom my one-time client, Billy Maxwell, shot dead. A few moments later my assumption proved accurate, as a well-dressed, ruggedly handsome man in his mid-fifties, stepped out of the limousine and introduced himself as one and the same.

"Yes, I know who you are," I replied, mindful not to display any sign of trepidation. "And I'm Ethan Rivers."

Anthony Ricci nodded, saying, "I know who you are too, Mr. Rivers. I think it's fair to say I'm familiar with your work."

"And I, yours," I returned.

Ricci manufactured a smile, although it wasn't long before his cold and calculating eyes narrowed and the smile disappeared, whereupon he said, "Touché."

At that juncture a light mist began to fall from the hovering gray skies, prompting Marino to glance at Anthony Ricci, and ask, "You want I should have Alvie get you an umbrella?" Yet, before Ricci could reply, Marino had barked, "Say Alvie, bring Tony an umbrella."

But Ricci waved off his driver before he even stepped out of the limousine, glaring at Frank Marino in the process. He then peered at me, his well-groomed features somewhat humbled in the early morning mist, his perfectly coiffed hair, no longer perfectly coiffed, and said, "I like this type of weather. It cleanses the body and soul. Don't you agree, Mr. Rivers?"

"Actually no, I don't," I abruptly responded.

"Is something wrong, Counselor?" Ricci asked, fabricating an air of concern. "You seem anxious."

"I'm far from anxious, Mr. Ricci," I replied. I then sighed, before adding, "I am, however, getting wet, which, for the record, I don't intend to do for much longer."

"I understand," Ricci said, nodding his head. "Inclement weather, like life, isn't for everyone."

I chuckled, before saying, "No, it's just that some of us know when to come in out of the rain. Figuratively speaking, of course."

Ricci glanced at Marino, who looked as alive as a block of concrete, then back at me, his expression a contorted mix of suspicion and frustration, and said, "Why do you think I came to see you, Counselor?"

"Frankly, I don't have the slightest idea," I said, posturing a look of ambivalence.

Anthony Ricci took a deep breath, exhaling the cool, early morning mist like a stream of smoke, before saying, "Then take a guess."

"Okay, fine," I said, after simulating a few moments of contemplation. "Because Marino here is retiring and you'd like me to take his place."

With palms open, Anthony Ricci hunched up his shoulders, and said, "I came here in good faith. Why the disrespect?"

I met Ricci's bewildered look with one of amusement, when I said, "You call sending Marino to lean on me for information a sign of good faith?"

"Oh, that wasn't leaning," Ricci advised. "Not by a long ways."

"Interesting," I countered. "Then what would you call it?"

"Negotiation," Ricci replied. "I call it negotiation." He then grinned.

"That may very well be, Mr. Ricci. But we have nothing to negotiate. So sending Marino to see me was a waste of time, just as you coming to see me is. Now, if you have something else to say, say it. Because I have business waiting for me in my office."

"I beg to differ," Ricci cautioned, his finger wagging in my direction. "You have business, right here, right now. And we're going to negotiate. Right here. Right now."

As if on cue, Frank Marino then took a step toward me. I didn't so much as flinch, however. Rather, I glared at Ricci, and said, "If your monkey takes another step toward me, I'm going to stick my foot so far up his ass, it'll take you a month to find it."

"Take it easy, Counselor, take it easy," Ricci implored. "I didn't come here to do violence. I never go anywhere to do violence." Ricci then proffered a sheepish grin, adding, "I only came to negotiate." His sheepish grin then slowly disappeared behind a veil of guile and treachery, as he continued with, "You have information I want, Counselor. Information regarding the whereabouts of that scum who murdered my boy."

"Stop," I interjected, while flashing Ricci the palm of my hand. "I've already been through this with your monkey over there. I don't represent Billy Maxwell anymore. And I don't know where he is. Now if you choose to believe me, fine. If not, I'm sorry, but that's just the way it is."

"As I was saying, Counselor, before you so rudely interrupted me... you have information I want. Now if you don't have the information presently, I think you can get it. I also think you're a very well-known attorney, with, I would imagine, some very good, very powerful contacts. That means, if I were to kill you, or if some strange accident were to befall you, or even members of your family, I'd be turning a spotlight on me. I don't like spot-lights, Counselor. I also don't like violence. But maybe we can avoid all of that by doing a little business. You do like doing business, don't you Counselor?"

"What's your point, Mr. Ricci?"

"My point is, get me my information. In return, I'll grant you any favor you want. And just to prove I'm a man of my word, I'll grant your favor first. So, if you have to get dirt on someone… if you need to gather evidence and can't do it legally… if you have an enemy that you want to hurt, or make go away… you tell Marino, and I'll make it happen. But I want my information. That's the negotiation. Beginning and end. Understood?"

I said nothing to Ricci before we parted ways. Nevertheless, I understood.

# CHAPTER 7

" I had this friend growing up – Stevie Lars was his name. Nice kid, but he had a stuttering problem, so the other kids would often make fun of him. But it wasn't the kids in our class, per se. It was kids two, three years older, taunting him until he would have this complete fucking meltdown and end up on the ground in a fetal position just wailing away. And then one day Stevie's older brother showed up out of nowhere to walk him home from school. Didn't matter. Some stupid kid figured he'd taunt Stevie anyway. Yeah, well, I don't know if a minute went by before Stevie's brother just up and smoked the kid to the point of tears. His brother caught a little hell for it, but he didn't care because Stevie never had another problem because of his stuttering.

The point is, that's what I always thought having an older brother would be like. You know, a helper, a protector, someone to actually mark the path so when little brother shows up it's not as difficult to walk. But Ethan wasn't like that. He was so involved with being Ethan, nothing, and I mean, nothing else mattered. And my parents didn't do a damn thing to change the culture. In fact, it was probably more like the opposite.

I mean, in the one corner you had my mother, dear, sweet, Evelyn… Miss Cat Fangs, herself, stroking my brother's hair and heaping praise on him like he was the second coming of… whatever. Shit, to hear her tell it, Ethan didn't just set the gold standard in the looks department, he was also the smartest kid and best athlete this side of the Rocky Mountains. Now granted, my brother may have grown up flirting with a positive quality or two, but c'mon,

Stephen Hawking and Michael Jordan, he wasn't. Still, it was the moniker my mother sewed to his chest at an early age, and it's the moniker he continues to wear today.

Then in the other corner, you had my father, Arthur – Old Faithful in the flesh. His input in curtailing Ethan's self-absorbed world was, shall we say, misguided altogether. Ya see, Ethan was off limits to him, and since there was no way he was going to piss off my mother – a situation he's gone out of his way to avoid for as long as I can remember – he wasn't gonna stick his nose into the situation anyway. Instead, Big Daddy figured he'd throw just enough attention my way to counter the burgeoning weight of my brother. The problem was, he worked all day and was rarely around, and unless my mother was out shopping, she rarely left the house. So, by and large, it was a losing proposition from the start.

Fortunately, there was a four-year age gap between my brother and I. As such, Ethan started college just as I started high school, so he was no longer home every day sucking all the air out of the house. I think that gave me enough breathing room, so to speak, to grow into my own skin. The other thing that probably worked in my favor was that a lot of this crap took place when I was a little kid, so I didn't know any better. Ethan being an asshole became normal to me. And the fact my parents let him get away with it… that became normal too. And by the time I was a teenager, I was more interested in hanging out with my friends anyway, so I didn't really give a shit anymore. It was only after graduating college when I came to grips with just how lopsided… okay, that's way too diplomatic… with just how fucked up my family's dynamic truly was. And that," I said, after taking a deep breath, "is my story in a nutshell."

"Wow. That's a pretty ugly description of things," Mickey said, her eyes narrowing, her tone settling. She then bit her bottom lip and looked away in silence.

I remained quiet as well, content to watch the wavering light from the fire we'd made toss uneven shadows across the room. Finally, she turned back to face me. "How do you deal with it?"

"Mostly by ignoring it," I replied. "And that's exactly why we didn't go to my parent's cocktail party, which, from the outset, sounded about as inviting as a rattlesnake bite."

"And they don't care? They're not going to give you any grief about it?" Mickey asked, the curiosity hanging from her questions muted by my own indifference to the answers.

"Doesn't matter. My mother gets to parade Ethan around to all her hoity-toity friends like he's her date. My father will explain away my absence as unavoidable, which, in many ways is true. And Ethan will do whatever Ethan wants, which will include, I assure you, pumping his chest and talking about his exploits to anyone with an ear."

Mickey snickered. Then, "Can I ask you something else?"

"Ah, ah, ah," I said, playfully wagging my forefinger at her. "The deal was one nutshell story about our lives and one question afterward. You've asked like three questions already."

Mickey winked, adding, "I'll make it worth your while, cowboy."

"Well now, little lady," I replied, "you put it like that, and you got yourself a deal. What's on your mind?"

"What was Christmas like?" she asked, her tone quickly turning somber, as though expecting a somber reply.

"What do you mean, did I get presents like Ethan?"

Mickey nodded.

I smiled, saying, "You want a blow-by-blow, or will a sample-size do?"

"A sample-size," she said, with a smile.

I rolled a few thoughts around, before settling on, "Okay, so one Christmas, about a month before Ethan turned 16, he got the keys to a brand new Mustang Convertible."

"And?"

"And what?" I returned, feigning ignorance at what she wanted to know.

"C'mon, Drew, what'd you get?"

I waited until Mickey asked a second time, whereupon I offered up a dejected shoulder shrug, and said, "I got a gift certificate for an oil change."

Mickey did her best to keep a straight face, but it wasn't long before her laughter mingled with my own.

"After I turned fourteen," Mickey began, "my parents decided I was finally old enough to stay home alone on Saturday nights. Believe me, I was prepared to babysit myself ever since I was like ten, but my parents wouldn't have any part of that. So my older sister, Maddy, was forced to stay home with me. She'd complain because she always wanted to go out herself, especially if she had a boyfriend at the time. In the end, though, it was never really an issue because the two of us got along so well together.

Anyway, this one time Maddy had been asked out for some Saturday night and she instantly said yes because this boy was, according to her, "The coolest guy in school." The problem was, she forgot to check with my parents, who already had plans to go to a wedding, so the *yes* essentially turned into, *I'm sorry, I have to babysit that night,* which then turned into an invitation for the coolest guy in school to come over, strictly against my parents babysitting rules.

His name was Jarrod Jenkins, and when I opened the front door he just stood there and smoked his cigarette. No *hello*, no *how are you*, no *my name's Jerrod...* nothing but the detached glare of someone trying way too hard to be cool. Back then, however, I didn't realize that he was just a Halloween version of James Dean, so I opened the door, and said, "Hi. I'm Maddy's sister, Michelle, but you can call me Mickey. Come on in."

Unfortunately, once inside, Jerrod Jenkins wouldn't leave – not when my sister pushed him away after he managed to paw her shirt open – not when my sister slapped him for continuing his unwanted pursuit – not when she punched him after he threw her against the wall and pressed himself against her – not even when I came running out of my bedroom with the baseball bat I kept hidden underneath my bed and hit him in the back of the knees. Although at that point he couldn't walk, let alone leave, making him an easy arrest target for when the police arrived. Jenkins was ultimately charged with two random misdemeanors, and one count of Sexual Battery, for which he received the grand prize... a year's worth of probation. I, in turn, was charged with Aggravated Assault. Apparently, after I knocked the little weasel to the floor with the first swing, I wasn't supposed to take a second swing to keep him there. Because of my age, I also received one year's probation, the judge telling me that had I been charged as an adult, I likely would have received some jail time."

Mickey abruptly shook her head. "Uh-uh, not yet," she said, after sensing I was about to interrupt her. "The story's not over."

I offered up a faint smile, which Mickey returned, before continuing with, "Now fast forward two years. I'm fourteen, it's a typical Saturday night, and I'm home alone watching T.V. when suddenly a voice behind me, says, 'Hi Mickey.' I jumped out of my skin and turned around all at the same time, only to find Jerrod Jenkins standing there. "I was gonna knock," he said, with this fucked-up, cockeyed grin on his face. "But the backdoor was open, so I let myself in."

I tried to run, hoping to get to a bedroom so I could lock myself inside, but he was obviously bigger and stronger, and had me cornered in a matter of minutes, if not seconds. And once cornered, he punched me in the face so hard I got woozy and fell down. Next thing I knew, I was sitting in a chair, bound and gagged, and he was ransacking the house. At that point all I kept thinking was, take what you want and just leave me alone. I got half of my wish. He took my mother's jewelry, but he didn't leave me alone. He spent, what seemed like an eternity, putting his hands all over me, and all I could do was sit in the chair and shake uncontrollably. Fortunately, my parents pulled into the drive before he got any of my clothes off.

The long and short of it is, Jenkins ran out the backdoor with my mother's jewelry in hand, but the police caught up with him about an hour later. He was hit with a handful of felony charges and spent seven years in prison. By the time he got out, my family was long gone. We had moved to Michigan because my father accepted an engineering position at GM. And that," Mickey said, after taking a deep breath, "is my story in a nutshell."

I'm not sure if I was stunned into silence because of the story itself, or Mickey's tough-as-nails attitude in telling it. Either way, it took a few moments before I picked my jaw up from the floor to ask, "How come you've never told me this before?"

Mickey smiled at me, and said, "The same reason you never told me your story before."

"Okay, now I'm confused," I remarked, and by virtue of the expression digging into my face, I'm sure it was quite obvious.

Mickey's smile lingered a few more seconds, before she replied, "Lover of mine, we spent the first two-and-a-half years of our relationship in the bedroom. We only just started talking this past year."

"Oh," was all I could manage, before I pushed myself from the couch, landing in Mickey's embrace.

Getting a phone call from my brother at 7:00 a.m. is no way to start a Sunday morning. "What?" I snarled into the phone.

"Didn't see you at the folks' soiree last night, little brother. Got kind of worried. Everything okay?"

After assuring Ethan that everything was fine, I asked him why he would call so early, other than to bother me n' Mickey (which he knew he was doing), and he replied, "Because we need to have a talk. I'm thinking early next week. Maybe Tuesday, Wednesday at the latest, depending on your schedule."

"About what?" I countered.

Ethan didn't reply right away, and since I was in no mood to play his typical game of cat and mouse, I said, "Either tell me what it's about, or say goodbye."

"Boy-oh-boy, someone pee in your Wheaties this morning?" Ethan asked caustically.

Then before I could respond, or hang the phone up altogether, he said he wanted to discuss the bribery investigation Judge Beckett was facing, declaring the entire situation, "A bullshit witch-hunt."

"Well if it's a bullshit witch-hunt, what are you calling me for?" I asked. I then winked at Mickey as I took the cup of coffee she was offering.

"It's really very simple, little brother. Somebody is setting Beckett up. And since he's a sitting judge in your county, you might have access to information that could help us find out who – maybe even find out which agency is spearheading this thing."

Before I could thank Ethan for inviting me to interfere with a federal investigation, or tell him to take a long walk off a short pier, he said, "In return, I have some info you might find interesting about your rape investigation."

Since I had nothing to lose, especially since I had nothing to offer Ethan, I told him I would check my schedule the following morning, and give him a call regarding time and place. I then tossed my cell on the bed, peered at Mickey, and said, "Talking to my brother always gives me a headache."

# CHAPTER 8

Jack Francis has been a P.I. ever since I plucked him from the front lines of the Michigan Academy of Private Investigations at the ripe old age of 28. That was some eight years and a myriad of cases ago. I'd first met him, however, after he'd been arrested for stealing some unsuspecting fool's credit cards, along with his identity, before going on a ten thousand dollar shopping spree.

Originally brought into the case because he was cousins with one of the firm's secretaries, I was instantly attracted to Jack's unflappable sense of bravado, not to mention his mendacious talents, both of which were on full display when he pick-pocketed the prosecutor's wallet during plea negotiations, just to prove to me he could. Fortunately, the prosecutor never realized what had happened because Jack was just as deft in returning the wallet as he was removing it. Fortunately, too, the prosecutor owed me a longstanding favor, as I once came to his defense over his handling of a murder trial. Of course, truth be told, I didn't come to his aid to help silence his critics, notwithstanding that being the obvious and immediate result. I came to his aid because I wanted him to keep his job. After all, he did, in fact, have poor trial skills, which made him easy prey anytime we squared off in court.

In any event, I convinced the prosecutor, who in turn convinced the judge, to recommend a three-month probationary period for Jack, so long as, the judge boisterously added at the time, Jack paid a small fine and made full restitution of the monies he'd stolen.

And therein began the start of a long and meaningful business association between myself and Jack Francis. You see, Jack was essentially broke, so paying restitution and a fine was not going to happen without some outside assistance – mine, to be exact. By that point in time, however, I had come to the realization that with a subtle, yet steady hand to shape and guide him, I could turn Jack's wily skill set into an asset for the firm, and, in particular, me. As such, I loaned Jack the necessary funds with the understanding that he was to pay me back by going to the Academy. "Not to become some run-of-the-mill P.I.," I assured him. "But to work for my law firm, which is no run-of-the-mill firm. You'll have constant work, credibility, and cachet. And believe you me, cachet takes a backseat to very little."

Naturally Jack's initial reaction was one of gratitude. Within seconds, however, his buoyant expression had turned to a look of uncertainty, when he said, "If I can't afford to pay restitution, Ethan, then what makes you think I can pay my way through the academy?"

"That's all part of the loan," I assured him. I also assured Jack that in addition to making a success of himself, he'd have the type of job he'd seldom find tedious – one that would underscore his daring and guile, not belie it. That being said, I don't believe Jack ever imagined he'd be thrust into the middle of a chess match with a reputed mob boss. But if the notion bothered him, he never showed it. On the contrary, after I summoned Jack to my office and explained my parking lot confrontation with Anthony Ricci and his grease-bucket henchman, Frank Marino, he fostered a spirited look, and said, "Sounds like my kind of party."

I leaned back in my chair, and then stretching my legs until my feet crossed the edge of the desk, said, "Might get interesting, that's for sure."

Jack nodded, before pulling his sinewy frame from the couch and walking toward my office bar. "You want something?" he asked, the poise in his stride and tone of voice, snippets of a demeanor masterfully cultivated over the years.

When I did not answer, Jack glanced my way, the glare emanating from his dark, sunken eyes, the perfect complement to a jawline scar and the perpetual weeklong stubble which did little to hide it.

"Thanks, no," I finally muttered.

After Jack downed a healthy shot of 12-year-old Kentucky Bourbon, skillfully suppressing the fiery collision between liquid and gut, he turned his brooding profile toward me, and asked, "So what is it you want me to do?"

I rubbed my chin a few moments, as though contemplating what I had already concluded, before replying, "I want you to go to Costa Rica. Jaco Beach, to be exact."

Jack's eyes narrowed. "Costa Rica? What the hell is in Costa Rica?"

No sooner did I finish conveying my hunch between my one-time client, Billy Maxwell, and the unsigned postcard I received from Jaco Beach, when Jack said, "When do you want me to leave?"

"Soon. There's still something I may need you to do here first."

"Such as?" Jack asked, while fastening his hands to his hips.

I smirked, and then said, "That girl you brought to the office Christmas party last year, Monica I believe was her name… are you still seeing her?"

Jack cautiously nodded.

"Are the two of you serious?"

Jack cautiously nodded his head once more.

"Does she ever ask you about your work?"

Jack frowned, saying, "Where are you going with this, Ethan?"

"Come on, Jack. Does she ever ask you about your work?"

It took a few moments before Jack's expression softened, and he replied, "Not anymore."

"But she used to, is that it?" I asked.

"To the extent she knows what I do for a living," Jack replied.

"And you, of course, never divulge any information to her, correct?"

"Give me a break, Ethan. You know better than that," Jack countered, clearly irritated by my question's intimation.

"I'm only asking, Jack, because I have to be particularly careful with how I play this Costa Rica situation."

"So what does that have to do with Monica?" he returned, his tone still flirting with irritation.

"Because I need to play it very close to the vest. At the same time, I think it would be best if she went with you. Let's just say, I'm playing the odds."

"I'm not following, Ethan."

I pulled my feet from the desk and let my chair lurch forward. "For appearances sake," I said. "Billy may be apt to run if he senses someone is looking for him. If you're with a woman there's a better chance he never reaches that conclusion. More importantly, I don't want Anthony Ricci to ever know you went to Jaco Beach alone. He's too smart not to figure out why. If you go with your girlfriend, however, it looks like a vacation. Nothing more. Nothing less. The fact Monica may find you doing some work while there is, I believe, insignificant collateral damage... especially since she never has to know the particulars of the work."

"Okay, but Ricci doesn't know me, so how would he ever find out?"

"I don't have the answer to that, Jack. I just know it wouldn't take long for Ricci to find out you do investigative work for me. So I think it's something he could put together. Either way, it wouldn't be prudent to underestimate Ricci's abilities. And I refuse to leave the situation to assumptions or chance. Not when so much may be riding on it."

"I suppose that makes sense," Jack said, his tone measured.

"It's intended to minimize risk," I asserted.

Jack ran his hands over his short, cropped hair, in what looked to be an attempt to groom what was too short to groom anyway, and then said, "Okay, so as it applies to finding Billy, I assume you'd like to know his living situation, work situation, and where, and with whom, he spends his free time. Does that about cover it?"

"If you can get all that information, fine," I replied. I then held up my forefinger, and said, "But not at the expense of giving yourself away. I prefer Billy doesn't know I'm trying to locate him. At least not yet. That being said, if you feel you have no choice but to throw my name into the mix, so be it. Otherwise, silence is best."

Jack hunched up his shoulders, the palms of his hands falling open at his sides, and said, "Ya know, there's a good chance he's changed his appearance."

"Indeed. There's also the distinct possibility he goes by another name." I then grabbed the manila folder from the top drawer of my desk, and said, "The last photograph I have of Billy is in here. I've also included his original mug shot, a list of his vitals, two writing samples, and some general information about Jaco Beach."

"Why two writing samples?"

"Because, Billy's ambidextrous. He can write with either hand. It's not something I recall him making a habit of. But he can do it," I said, handing off the folder.

Jack gleaned the contents a few seconds, and without looking up, said, "Apparently Jaco Beach has a population of some 10,000 people."

"What does that tell you?"

"That it's a small place."

"What else?" I asked, ignoring Jack's sarcasm.

"That an English speaking white-boy will stand out like a sore thumb," Jack stated.

"Then just imagine how it might appear if one sore thumb engages the local population to aid him in his search to find another sore thumb," I added.

"Just some guy looking up an old friend," Jack suggested.

"Maybe. But I've been to islands that small. And the local police generally hear every word the locals whisper. So a word of caution: be careful who you approach, and who you show Billy's photograph to." As Jack nodded his head, I said, "Something else. Billy used to like to fish. I presume he still does. So maybe you can make some headway along the marinas and docks."

Jack squared his eyes on mine, and said, "Okay, so I guess the only things left are for you to tell me when I'm leaving, and what you need me to do here before I go."

"When and for how long can your girlfriend get time off work?" I queried.

After Jack explained that flexibility wasn't an issue because his girlfriend was between jobs, I instructed him to leave in a week, and plan on staying for two. "If you don't locate Billy within the two weeks, we'll reevaluate," I said. I then instructed Jack to book a suite at the Villa Caletas, "Because it's supposed to be the nicest resort in Jaco Beach. So take time to enjoy it." Lastly, I told Jack I would know within the next 24 hours if I needed him to do some surveillance before he left the country. "It depends on the conversation I have with my brother," I noted, before Jack left my office, closing the door behind him.

Talking to Andrew never fails to expose the unsettled current that's run between us for more years than I can remember. It's as though for every word spoken, there remains another word unspoken, hurling every conversation into a chasm of doubt, or, dare I say, mistrust. It's a situation I learned to accept long ago, whereas my brother seems to be in a never-ending struggle with finding that unspoken word. Unfortunately for Andrew, when such a conversation takes place in person he is at a constant disadvantage, for he wears much of the search on his sleeve. In fact, while Andrew is busy trying to decipher what remains unsaid, his facial expression is off in another direction – one which paints a portrait of a man who has abandoned the moment, revealing, in turn, his vulnerability. It is precisely the reason I chose to have the conversation with my brother over an afternoon drink, and not over the phone.

As I have come to expect, Andrew arrived some ten minutes late, shuffling into the fashionable *Barrington Grill* like the quintessential poor man's lawyer he was. "I'm going to buy you a suit for your next birthday," I said, as he pulled out a chair from our corner table.

"Why? What's the matter with the one I have on?" he asked, while giving himself a quick once-over before climbing into his seat.

"Does the word drab have any place in your vocabulary?" I asked.

"Sorry, Ethan. We can't all have your sense of style," Andrew countered.

"How about any sense of style?" When Andrew responded with a disdainful squint of the eyes, I called out to the bartender, "Harry, bring my brother a Budweiser."

"You got it, Mr. Rivers," came the prompt reply.

"Very funny, Ethan," Andrew muttered.

I swirled the olives around my martini, watching as my brother fidgeted in his chair. After a few disquieting moments Andrew's beer was finally delivered, whereupon I held up my cocktail, and said, "Cheers."

Andrew tapped his mug against the stem of my glass, and said, "Okay, so why the meeting?"

After taking a healthy sip of my martini, the taste of vermouth languishing just a tad longer than I would've preferred, I said, "The last time we talked, I mentioned to you that I was representing Judge Beckett. I was looking for some information about an unfortunate situation he's found himself in."

Andrew shook his head, saying, "No, that's not the way the conversation went."

"Oh really?" I returned. "Well then perhaps you can tell me the way it went, little brother."

Andrew set his mug down. "You asked me to think about making a deal," he said. He then laced his fingers together, resting his forearms on the table. "You wanted information on Judge Beckett, assuming I had any. In return, you were going to give me information on the Chestnut Hills rapes. That's what I remember."

I watched as Andrew leaned back in his chair, momentarily pulling his hands from the table, before just as abruptly leaning forward again to latch onto his beer. I waited until he finished draining a quarter of the mug, and then responded, "As I was saying… the last time we talked, I mentioned that I was looking for some information on Judge Beckett. I was also going to say that I am prepared to give you a little nugget of information on this rape investigation of yours. Unfortunately, I wasn't able to finish my thought without you interrupting me."

Andrew sighed, and then drained some more beer, acting as if what I had just said was secondary to quenching his thirst. But Andrew's sudden indifference was the result of poor acting, not a nonchalant attitude. Nevertheless, I played along. "The thing is, I'm prepared to offer you this information without asking for any in return."

Andrew's eyes briefly widened in apparent surprise. He then drew the mug away from his mouth, asking, "Why don't I believe you?"

"Because, little brother, you don't want to believe me," I asserted. "You never do. It's either that, or you're so busy over-thinking that which requires very little thought in the first place, you lose sight of the very issue staring you in the face." I then massaged my forehead in feigned contemplation, before adding, "Look, what relevant information about Judge Beckett could I possibly get from you that I can't already assume? What, are you going to tell me a grand jury has been convened to look into the matter? Or, better yet, your office is working with the F.B.I. in its own investigation?"

Andrew remained stoic, though when he glanced away the instant I mentioned the F.B.I., I got my answer. The F.B.I. was apparently bearing down on my client. Fortunately, I had enough time to reach out to my contacts inside, which meant, in turn, rectifying the judge's situation remained a distinct possibility.

As for the nugget of information I promised Andrew — I told him to check out *The Knight Owl Bar and Grill*, knowing if he found the sex dungeon, he'd think it far more relevant to Sonny Marx's guilt than it realistically was. I also told Andrew the information I gave him was to remain between us.

Now it was just a matter of time to see if he would keep to his word, or get a search warrant and send in the troops. Either way, Andrew was certain to take prompt action, so I figured to know within a week. As such, once my brother and I parted company, I called Jack Francis, and said, "That surveillance we discussed? It's in play."

# CHAPTER 9

There are two prominent reasons why Ethan's, 'little nugget of information,' bordered on irrelevance. One, because the assertion came out of Ethan's mouth, and two, see reason number one.

The point is, Ethan never gave away anything in his life without expecting something more in return, let alone divulging information that might prove harmful to one of his clients. As a result, it wasn't hard to deduce that his *little nugget* was going to take me in the very direction he wanted it to go, detouring me from the conventional approach I generally adhere to in criminal investigations – let the police gather physical evidence, conduct witness interviews, and otherwise complete their work before handing the information off to the prosecutor's office. Thereafter, our office personnel decide what, if any, charges to bring. It can be a slow, painstaking process, and it's by no means a foolproof system, but it does provide enough checks and balances to facilitate successful prosecutions. That's not to say we're immune from chasing down the random lead, however. We just don't want to run off in fifty directions at once. As a result, unless the lead comes from a credible source, which, in this particular instance I do not consider Ethan to be, we tend to air on the side of caution.

Nevertheless, and notwithstanding my brother's *nugget,* Sonny Marx remains the only person of interest in the Chestnut Hills rape investigations. But that's due to the items initially found in his car. Additional evidence, be it physical or circumstantial, was necessary if we had any hope of establishing a direct link between Marx and the victims, or, in the alternative, Marx and his ability to commit the act of rape. Either situation would work so long as it gave us enough to bring him up on charges. Unfortunately, the police investigation had slowed to a crawl so I wasn't expecting the emergence of physical evidence to help establish a direct link anytime soon. As a result, I turned to the alternative, instructing D.C. to find out everything he could about Marx's past, in the hope we get lucky. "Because if we don't find something soon," I concluded, before D.C. left my office, "we could be looking at a dead-end situation. And as fucked up as it is to say, at that point it might just take another rape to jumpstart the investigation."

Of course, it never dawned on anyone that Sonny Marx, in all his moronic glory, would get arrested for assaulting a woman not halfway through his probation, at a bar not five minutes away from Chestnut Hills. The story goes like this:

On an unseasonably warm November night, under red and green Christmas lights strung across the crowded streets of Barrington like strands of rubies and emeralds, Mickey and I were in the midst of what had become our traditional holiday pub-crawl. The first year we didn't skip a bar, though we also didn't get very far before the liquor convinced us to call it a night. The second year was somewhat better, but only because we added food to the mix. Still, we didn't make it much past midnight. This year, however, we decided to confine our crawl to our favorite places, the goal, not just to eat, drink, and be merry, but also to remain standing and reasonably coherent as long as our last stop remained open, which, for the record, is easier said than done when the adventure kicks off at 8:00 p.m.

Yeah, well, any thoughts Mickey and I weren't going to make our self-imposed witching hour were dispelled the moment D.C. called to tell me, Sonny Marx had been arrested for assaulting a woman at a bar near Chestnut Hills. Okay, so maybe our conversation wasn't quite as smooth or matter-of-fact as that. But I was knee-deep inside a noisy bar and could barely make out one word from the next, so what the hell would you expect? The point is, I had to walk outside and call D.C. back, only to hear him ask, "Can you hear me now?"

"Yes, D.C., I'm outside. I can hear you fine."

"Are you sure? Cause if you can't, just find a good spot and call me back again. I'm not going anywhere."

"It's okay, D.C., I can hear you fine," I assured him.

"Okay, good. So where'd I leave off?"

I rolled my eyes, and said, "Not sure, D.C. I was having a hard time hearing you, remember?"

"So you didn't hear anything?" he quizzed.

After another eye-roll, I shook my head, saying, "Why don't you just start from the beginning."

"You got it," D.C. returned, followed by, "So Bull Davis and his rookie partner were dispatched to a bar called *The Hot Comet.* You remember Bull, don't you? He's the one..."

"Yes, I remember Bull," I quickly interrupted. "He's the one with no neck and big arms. I get it, D.C. Just tell me the story."

"Okay, I just thought you'd want to know the players involved," D.C. posed.

I sighed, before saying, "D.C., I'm with Mickey. She's waiting for me inside a restaurant. I'm trying not to be rude."

"So why didn't you just say that in the beginning?" D.C. asked.

I sighed again, before responding, "So anyway, Bull and his partner were dispatched to *The Hot Comet.* Go on."

Between D.C. carrying on about *all things police,* coupled with my efforts to manage his excitement by occasionally instructing him to breathe between words, it took a few minutes, but I finally got the full story.

In essence, Sonny Marx stumbled into the bar at approximately 9:30 p.m. By 10:00 o'clock he was back outside talking to a woman named Sadie, and by 10:15 he was trying to push Sadie into his car. When she broke free of his grasp, which D.C. described as a bear hug, he backhanded her across the face, sending her to the pavement, where she ended up with a nasty cut on her head. Marx then gets in his car, but before he can drive off a bouncer yanks him back out. But this wasn't just any ol' bouncer, no. According to D.C., this bouncer was about the same size as Bull, although D.C. was certain he wasn't near as strong. After all, Bull was one of the strongest, if not the strongest guy in the department. In fact, he had been the arm wrestling champ five years running.

Anyway, the bouncer wrestled Marx to the ground, where he remained securely pinned until the police arrived to arrest him. Before the cops could get cuffs on him, however, Marx takes a swing at Bull's partner, who just happens to be a female. That's when Bull stepped in and knocked him out cold. "One punch," D.C. emphasized. "One punch."

D.C. ended by saying, "The boys, they knew we had this guy on our radar, so they called me as fast as they could."

After thanking D.C. for delivering the news, I walked back inside the restaurant, grinning, and repeating, "One punch... one punch," stopping only to order a bottle of Champagne, which Mickey and I drank while I repeated the story.

Unfortunately, what should've been the perfect way to end our night took a nasty turn for the worse, for no sooner did Mickey and I leave the restaurant, when I saw my mother across the street, walking arm in arm with a man not named Arthur Rivers.

# Chapter 10

In the days following my afternoon meeting with Andrew, two things became increasingly clear about my younger brother. One, he was no longer the angst driven little boy who reacted to every word I said, and whose behavior was so easy to predict as a result. If he was, he certainly wouldn't have yawned at the prospect of investigating the sexual exploits taking place in the basement of *The Knight Owl Bar and Grill*. And two, he postured a stoic sarcasm I failed to previously recognize, or simply chose to ignore. Either way, it was quite apparent when he phoned me just as my family was getting ready to leave for church, and, after our obligatory greetings, nonchalantly stated, "Any deal you were hoping to work out for your client, Richard Beckett, will be an effort in futility."

The assertion caught me by surprise. Nevertheless, I managed to retort, "Is that so?"

"Yes, Ethan. At this point I think it's fair to say it's a done deal."

"And why is that, little brother? Why is that?"

"Because," Andrew replied, "he's been found hanging in his bedroom."

A moment of silence ensued, before I uttered, "Excuse me?"

"You heard me correctly."

I took a deep breath but otherwise continued my silence, until Andrew asked, "You still there, big brother?"

"When?" I queried.

"Likely sometime between Friday night and Saturday morning."

"Who?"

"Who, what?"

"Who found him?" I asked, my tone growing impatient.

"His maid did, Saturday afternoon. Apparently she's worked for Beckett for years. She has a key to the house."

"And you're just calling to tell me about it now?"

"Hey, it's not like I'm part of the wire service," Andrew countered. "I heard about it an hour ago. I'm telling you now."

"Suicide?" I asked, after taking another deep breath to steady myself.

"It's still too early to say," Andrew responded. "I'm told there appeared to be signs of a struggle, but nothing concrete."

"Is there going to be an autopsy?"

"Yes. As far as I know it's scheduled for tomorrow. But I likely won't be privy to the findings."

"What does that mean?"

"It means, unless the findings are made public, or his family consents, you're going to have to do your own dirty work to find out the results." Andrew then sighed, before adding, "I'm not sticking my beak in, Ethan. There's just no upside."

"His entire family consists of two ex-wives," I stated.

"I know," Andrew calmly replied. "And they don't count."

"Boy, you're a regular master of the obvious, aren't you?"

"Oh yeah, one other thing," Andrew said, ignoring my sarcastic remark. "In all the Beckett commotion, I forgot to tell you the other reason I called."

"Now what?" I snarled.

"Your client, Sonny Marx... he was arrested last night for assaulting a woman outside some bar in your neck of the woods."

"Christ," was the only word I remember muttering before tossing my cell phone to the couch beside me.

I was not surprised at how quickly news of Richard Beckett's death had spread, for he had been a high-profile judge for many years. I was surprised, however, to find a handful of reporters waiting for me as I pulled my Mercedes into the office parking lot early Monday morning, particularly since the judge was never formally indicted on anything (much less taking a five-million-dollar bribe), and I was not, in turn, formally representing him. As such, there were only a few people who could possibly know I had been meeting with the judge at all. And aside from my brother, they were all employed by my law firm.

Nevertheless, I was now confronted with, "What can you tell us about Judge Beckett, Counselor? How well did you know him? Why were you representing him? What kind of trouble was he in? Did he commit suicide? Was he murdered? Who was he involved with? C'mon, Ethan, talk to us. Did he have enemies? Was it someone he sent to jail? Was it someone he was planning to send to jail?"

I offered up a polite, but firm, "I have no comment at this time," and made my way inside the office building where I promptly disappeared into the solitary confines of the elevator, all the while wondering who brought the reporters and their incessant questions to my doorstep? Did my brother have his hand in the mix? Or did someone in my office leak information?

It was difficult to cast doubt on the few employees who knew of my connection to Judge Beckett for the simple, but unequivocal reason, I personally hired each one of them. To second guess their disposition now, especially since they've consistently rewarded the firm with quality service, would be to foolishly second guess myself, as well as my abilities to evaluate the character of others.

That conclusion, however, painted a quandary with Andrew. One the one hand, if my little brother had no intentions of, 'sticking his beak in,' because, 'there's just no upside,' and I had no evidence to doubt the veracity of his self-serving, albeit chicken-shit remark, shouldn't I exonerate him just as quickly I did my employees? On the other hand, maybe my brother's unfettered indifference to helping me help the judge was merely staged. Maybe Andrew's contrived lack of interest in the judge's situation was an attempt to see how far I would press him – how far I would bend the rules to further my client's interest. Perhaps he was even attempting to see if I would break the law, thereby compromising myself, giving him, in turn, the proverbial upper hand in any and all future dealings.

Then again, I mused, as the elevator doors opened, maybe our relationship had deteriorated to the point, Andrew simply gave the reporters a heads-up because he wanted to surprise and embarrass me – put me on the spot, if you will. A bleak display of brotherly love to be sure. Yet, I suppose it's no bleaker than my willingness to cast doubt on him in the first place.

Although I told my secretary of ten years that I did not want to be disturbed, it wasn't long before she tapped on my opened door, and said, "Ethan, a letter just arrived for you."

"Little early for the mail, isn't it Barbra?" I asked, without turning away from the window.

"Judge Beckett's clerk just dropped it off," Barbra replied.

As I turned to face my secretary, I could feel the rigidity in my expression narrow into a look of consternation. Barbra, a slender, middle-aged woman, with discerning taste and intelligence, proffered a dubious look of her own, before shrugging her shoulders, and saying, "I'll put it on your desk."

"That's fine," I replied, my own shoulders rising and falling in the process.

"Your mother also called. I told her you weren't in."

"Keep it that way when she calls back," I directed.

"Is there anything else? Would you like me to bring you some coffee?" Barbra asked, while moving toward my desk.

"No thanks. Just close the door when you leave," I said. I then waited a few moments before retrieving the envelope, whereupon I promptly opened it to find two additional envelopes – one containing a set of keys, and the other, a letter, which read:

*'Dear Ethan,*

*My clerk was instructed to deliver this letter to you in the event of my untimely death. And unless natural causes are deemed the culprit, rest assure, I've been murdered.*

*As you know, I've sent many men to prison in my time and no doubt have many enemies as a result. Names of some might be bandied about by the press, but that's just the media being reckless. None were involved in my death. Of this I'm quite certain.*

*I'm also quite certain that you don't know the full set of facts surrounding the bribe I took in the Van Bourne Development case. Yes, I explained that one of the Van Bourne principals was likely to be indicted for bribing a county official on an unrelated development. And yes, rumor had it that if an indictment was handed down, he'd turn state's evidence, which, as you know, meant there was a strong possibility I'd be giving up the bench for a prison cell.*

*What I didn't tell you, however, is the manner in which the Van Bourne Development was funded. The Van Bourne's consist of brothers, Peter and Clark. When they run into trouble funding projects because they're tapped out at the banks, they either raise money through a series of limited partnerships, or, more frequently, turn to their childhood friend, Anthony Ricci. For his part, Ricci wants to wash all the dirty money he can get his hands on. This money is put into various trusts so that his name is never associated with a project, and the trusts become the actual partners in the various developments. But trusts, or not, Ricci takes a personal interest in every project he invests in, especially when his invest-ment includes a 5 million dollar bribe.*

*Anyway, when word got out Peter Van Bourne was going to be indicted for bribing that other county official, Ricci wasn't concerned that Van Bourne would give him up. Ricci was concerned that Van Bourne would give me up, and I, in turn, would give up Ricci. But Ricci needed Van Bourne's expertise to run the project. After all, there were millions and millions of dollars at stake. So if that meant Van Bourne needed to turn state's evidence against me in order for him to stay out of jail, Ricci was all for it. It just meant that I became collateral damage.*

*That's why I hired you. I needed to have the potential indictment against Van Bourne disappear before he made his deal. I just figured, between your brother being a prosecutor in the county where the indictment would be handed down, and your skills as an attorney, I'd have a chance. Apparently, I just didn't have enough time.*

*As for the 5 million – I spent it religiously. However, I still have 2 million tucked away in the wall safe in the lower level of my house. The enclosed combina-tion, along with the enclosed key, will get you into the safe. It's located behind the Horacio Hawthorne painting hanging on the opposite wall of the T.V.*

*Should Ricci suspect that I've given you a rundown of his interests in this project, and he may well, there's a chance he comes after you. Since I have no family to give the money to, nor friends deserving of it, I thought perhaps the money could be used as a negotiating tool should you find yourself in a bind. Hopefully I have not put you in harm's way. If I have, then I hope your luck is better than mine.*

*Richard Beckett'*

After reading the letter a second, and then a third time, a handful of thoughts started to creep in: Did Ricci already know I was representing the judge? Was tipping off the reporters his way of telling me I can't hide from him? Did Ricci hang the judge, not just to silence him, but to intimidate me into giving up the whereabouts of his son's killer? And if I don't give him the whereabouts, am I to presume Beckett's death is a prelude to my own? Yet, if that's the case, why did Ricci make it a point to grant me any favor I wanted in return for the information? Don't I have to be alive to receive the favor?

If that's not enough, what if Beckett's death is ruled a suicide? The press will seize on the premise, he was distraught because he got caught taking a bribe. Hell, Ricci can even plant the story himself. And that'll give Ricci his perfect murder, his perfect out.

I suddenly laughed at the pathetic reality that when I needed answers most, all I could come up with were more questions, a trend I was not used to, did not appreciate, and certainly needed to change. Of course that thought summoned up one more question. How?

# CHAPTER 11

Let's face it, Sonny Marx getting arrested for assault (not to mention resisting arrest), was surefire proof he should've been whiling away his time on a dummy-farm. Instead, he now gets to spend a few days warming his ass in a jail cell, courtesy of breaking the terms of his probation. Better than that, however, his inebriated stupidity... scratch that, his unadulterated stupidity might have singlehandedly provided the ammo needed to propel him from person of interest to Chestnut Hills rapist. It was by no means the smoking gun I was looking for, but I do believe the chances of getting charges filed against him, and me, in turn, making them stick, were on the upswing.

Maybe it's because the items found during Marx's initial arrest, i.e., duct tape, a mask, vodka bottle (which certainly qualifies as a foreign object), and photographs of naked women bound and gagged, are a little too curious to be associated with a job in an auto repair shop – maybe it's because D.C. discovered that Sonny Marx was temporarily put into a foster home at the age of nine while his parents were investigated for sexual abuse – maybe it's because *temporary* became permanent when the allegations proved out, terminating his mother and father's parental rights in the process – maybe it's because many experts believe children of sex abusers are so filled with hate and rage, they're statistically prone to continue a cycle of abuse, whether by lashing out at their own children, or a stranger walking down the street – maybe it's because Sonny Marx is already a registered sex offender – maybe it's because the Chestnut Hills rapes stopped the moment Marx knew he was on our radar – maybe it's because the remorse Marx has shown to date has been, shall we say, underwhelming – maybe it's because I simply believe that when you mix all the pieces together, then sprinkle it with the fairy dust of Marx's recent assault... voila'! You have all the trappings of a rapist.

Whatever the reason(s), I also believe my brother will do his best to make any such charges my office brings disappear like a fart in the wind. As such, I had no intention of resting on my optimism. Instead, I would look for one more nail to put in Marx's coffin – a nail I hoped to find at *The Knight Owl Bar and Grill.*

I first met Gene Baxter many years ago at my brother's house, having just moved back from Chicago. Ethan and my sister-in-law were hosting one of their annual poolside summer barbeques; a catered, but casual get-together of the neighborhood's friends and foes – some glib, some glam, but all tucked and pointed, primed and painted, and ready to go. All except one: Gene Baxter, a round and sweaty bald man, who, in the years since, didn't seem to change one iota. Then again, apparently I didn't either, because when D.C. and I found him leaning against the bar, he cocked his bulbous head to the side, gave me a slow once over, and uttered, "Andrew Rivers... Ethan's brother, right?"

I nodded, whereupon Baxter said, "I never forget a name or a face."

"Pretty good memory," I offered, as though I actually gave a shit.

"Well, in your case it's easy. You've got the Rivers look. Plus you still have the long hair," Baxter said while extending his hand, which I reluctantly shook, thinking, *I don't know what and the hell the Rivers look is.* I then introduced him to D.C., who probably thought he was staring at a fatter version of himself, sans the sweat. "So what brings you to Springdale?" Baxter asked, after D.C. grunted hello. "Or should I say, what brings you to *The Knight Owl?*"

I scanned the bartender, a full-figured, middle-aged woman who needed to wear less makeup and looser fitting clothes, then returned my attention to Baxter, and said, "Is there somewhere we can talk in private?"

"What about?" Baxter replied apprehensively.

"Certainly nothing that concerns the bartender," I said.

"No, of course not," Baxter responded, after glancing her way. "Let's go to my office," an invitation that found me perusing local sports memorabilia and cheap wall-art, while Baxter situated himself in the overstuffed leather chair behind his desk. "Have a seat," he finally suggested.

"I'm good here," I stated. I then leaned against a patch of dark wood paneling, while D.C. opted for a chair beside me.

"So what's this about anyway?" Baxter quizzed. Before I could respond, however, he looked at D.C., and asked, "I take it you're with the prosecutor's office too?"

D.C. nodded, saying, "I am," at which point Baxter nervously returned to, "So what's this about anyway?"

"An employee of yours," D.C. offered.

"I have lots of employees," Baxter asserted a few moments later, his bravado returning on the heels of the angst he slowly exhaled, the result of our apparent disinterest in him. "Is it an employee here, or at one of my auto repair shops?"

"You tell us. His name is Sonny Marx."

Baxter leaned back in his chair (the chair groaning its discontent), and then folded his hands across his belly. "I had a feeling that's who you were going to say," he replied, his peering eyes jumping from D.C. to me.

"And why is that?" I responded.

"Oh, I don't know," Baxter said with a tinge of sarcasm. "Maybe because he's now been arrested twice in less than sixty days."

"So then you're aware of the recent assault?"

"Why wouldn't I be? The guy works for me for Christ sakes. Not to mention, his lawyer told me."

"You mean Ethan, right?"

"As opposed to who, Attila The Hun?" Baxter countered.

"Hey, for all I know there's another lawyer involved."

"Nope, just your brother. And the more I sit here, the more ticked off at him I'm getting."

"Oh yeah? And why is that?" I asked, once again like I actually gave a shit.

Baxter frowned, and said, "Because, he never told me you were planning to pay me this little visit. And since I'm the one paying his damn legal fees, I think he should've said something."

My first reaction was to steal a glance at D.C., which I decided against. My second reaction was to ask why he was paying Marx's legal tab, which, although perfectly legit, was also perfectly strange. At any rate, I decided against that too. Instead, I simply grinned, and said, "Well, listen, considerateness isn't Ethan's forte." I let Baxter swim with that little dig a few seconds, before adding, "To tell you the truth, though, Gene, I never told Ethan I was coming to see you, so I doubt he knew."

Baxter marked his discontent with a long and tedious sigh, before saying, "You wanted to talk? So talk."

"Okay, I'll get right to it. What the hell does Marx do for you anyway?"

Baxter shrugged his round shoulders, his earlobes scraping his shoulder blades in the process, and said, "He's kind of a jack of all trades."

"Perhaps you can define jack of all trades." D.C. interjected.

Baxter let his chair fall forward (the chair groaning its discontent), and his hands fall into his lap, before responding, "Around here it means ordering liquor, bartending, helping out with parties... like that. And with the auto repair shops, he just sort of floats between locations."

"Doing what?" D.C. queried.

"Depends what's needed," Baxter replied. "Typically, we'll meet to go over things – employee problems, problems with a parts manufacturer, whatever. He has a good understanding how I run my business so he helps manage the day-to-day. And he can visit the stores I can't. I have several locations, you know."

"Yeah, that's nice," I said dismissively, followed by, "Where do you guys generally meet?"

"Usually here or at one of the stores. Sometimes at the house."

"And did I hear you say you live in Chestnut Hills?" D.C. asked.

"I do. Around the corner from Andrew's brother, in fact."

I pawed my forehead a few seconds, before letting my palm fall open. Then, "Any chance you and Marx ever meet at night?"

"Sure. If I know I'm gonna see him here, then we'll put off a meeting until later on."

"No, I meant at your house."

"Oh, yeah. I mean whenever my wife has him over for dinner we usually carve out a little time for business."

"And how often is that, if you had to guess?"

Baxter hemmed and hawed a few seconds, before replying, "We probably have him over… I don't know, twice a month on average."

"That often, eh?"

Baxter tossed up his hands, saying, "What do I know? My wife says invite him over, so I invite him over. She's fond of him. I am too."

"So then it's fair to say he was at your house in September and October?"

"I suppose."

"Would you happen to know the exact dates?"

Baxter peeled his eyes from mine and stared at D.C. for several moments, the room's uneasy silence broken only by the sound of his labored breathing. Finally, he turned his dubious focus back to me, and said, "Where you guys going with this, Andrew?"

Without elaborating too much, I explained to Baxter that we were following up on some leads in the Chestnut Hills rapes. For the most part he sat in his chair like an attentive blob of clay. But when I asked him again if he knew the exact dates, his mood quickly turned dour, as evidenced when he snarled, "Sonny Marx didn't rape anyone."

"That's his opinion," I said to D.C. on our drive back to the office. "But it still doesn't change the fact that Sonny Marx is a frequent visitor to Chestnut Hills."

"So you don't think we have to put him at Baxter's house the same nights the victims were raped?"

"That'd be great if we could," I said, glancing out the passenger window, "if only to tighten up our play. But by no means is it necessary. It's apparent he's been there so often, he's comfortably familiar with the area… if you know what I mean." A few seconds later I looked at D.C., who was busy navigating his way around a road construction detour, and added, "Obviously we just need enough evidence to get through the probable cause hearing so we can get him bound over for trial. Assuming we have that now, then with any luck we'll be able to nail down a few more things by the time we actually go to trial. But even if we can't, I still say we're in pretty good shape."

D.C. shot me a quick look. "Maybe I should pay a visit to Baxter's wife."

"Maybe you should," I concurred. "In fact," I added, after rolling the thought around a few more seconds, "make it a point."

"When does numb-nuts get out of the can anyhow?" D.C. asked.

"He got a week," I replied, promptly followed by, "watch that guy in front of you."

"That's it?" D.C. asked, before changing lanes.

"Yeah, why? What'd you expect for a first time probation violation?"

"Only reason I asked is because his arraignment on the assault charge is coming up in a few days. Would've been nice if he was still locked up while we're still poking around. No matter, if I get something relevant from Baxter's wife before then, maybe we can get charges filed, so he can also deal with two counts of rape in the arraignment. That way we won't have to go back for another one. What do you think?"

"I think we proceed with the charges now. Whatever we get here-on-out, we'll use at trial."

To say I expected my mother to show up unannounced would have been an out and out lie. To say I expected to hear, "Andrew, son, I've come bearing gifts," would have been a lie of epic proportions. And yet, I'm not back in my office ten minutes when my mother isn't walking toward my desk, garbed and bejeweled as though Queen Sheba, speaking those very words.

Rather than take hold of Evelyn's olive branch, however, knowing full well she never offered one up that didn't have thorns somewhere on it, I played the dumb card, and said, "What are you doing here, mother?"

"I got them at Neiman Marcus in case they don't fit," she said, putting the box on the corner of my desk, where it smothered a case file I was still working on.

"They're sweaters," she announced. She then peeled off her fur, and after resting it over the back of one chair, helped herself to the other, at which point, I said, "Have a seat."

"Cashmere. One's black, and one's blue. Larges, so they should fit," Evelyn continued, the waning light in her onetime glaring dark eyes sailing around my office before they finally settled on me. "It's been a long time since I've been here. I'd forgotten what it looked like."

"Seven years, mother."

"Seven years, what?" Evelyn returned.

"Seven years since you've been here," I replied.

"And you still don't have a family picture anywhere," she countered.

I sighed, and then said, "Thank you for the sweaters, mother. To what do I owe the generosity?"

Evelyn placed her perfectly manicured fingers into her perfectly postured lap, and said, "How about to good old motherly love."

"How about it?" I returned. I then pushed my chair back so I had enough room to put my feet on the desk, whereupon I stared at my weathered shoes, and listened to Evelyn say, "As long as I'm here, there is something I'd like to talk to you about though."

"And what would that be?" I asked, looking up at my mother just long enough to meet her faint smile with one of my own.

"The other night, of course."

"What other night?" I deadpanned.

"The other night in downtown Barrington. You were outside with that girlfriend of yours. It looked like the two of you had just left *Harper's Lobster House.*"

"I don't eat lobster, mother. Remember?"

"This is no time for games, Andrew."

I pulled my feet from the desk, and straightened up. "Okay fine, mother, no games," I said abruptly. "You saw me with *that* girlfriend of mine. Her name's Mickey, by the way. But hey, you've only met her a couple of times, so I can see how you'd forget."

"Yes, but this conversation isn't about her," Evelyn said without breaking stride. "It's about the other night. It's about me."

"Well that's something different," I remarked sarcastically.

"Shall I continue, or not?" Evelyn shot back, her contemptuous look revealing the subtle age lines she tried desperately to cover up.

"By all means," I said, an offer that lead my mother to tell me all about her plans for a new life. "A new beginning," she called it, which would start with the inevitable divorce of her old life.

# Chapter 12

Give a man a dollar, and he gives you fifty cents in return. That pretty much describes what bartering with my brother, Andrew, is like. Here, I feed him Gene Baxter a few weeks back, which magically evolves into the absurd arrest of my client, Sonny Marx, and, in return, he gives me the news my parents are divorcing.

Of course, I was more preoccupied with work than I was the sordid life and times of Evelyn and Arthur Rivers, so it wasn't something I had given much thought to. Besides, the dissolution of my parent's marriage had been a foregone conclusion for years. The fact my perceptively challenged little brother never wanted to acknowledge that little piece of reality was his problem, not mine.

My problem with the situation didn't arrive until dear old dad showed up at my office for a hastily scheduled meeting not twenty-four hours before I was due in court for Marx's probable cause hearing. I attempted to steer the meeting to another day for fear it would disrupt my preparation, and when that failed, I tried to convince the old man a simple phone call would suffice in the interim. That too, however, was greeted with an unwavering sense of urgency, so I finally relented.

My father was accompanied by his longtime friend, Stanley Robbins, who, like my father, had been with the law firm for some forty years, and, who, like my father, had been living off his reputation as a lawyer rather than furthering it along. As such, I was no more impressed with his WOW factor than I was convinced he still had the skills to play the role of a proficient divorce attorney. Too much to lose, too little to gain, and too ordinary and potentially careless a man to differentiate between the two. That being said, I was also convinced the quickest way to get on with the rest of my day was to sit back and get on with the conversation. "Have you talked to your mother?" my father asked, a question I found as awkward as the tone it was delivered in.

I waited until both men filled the chairs across my desk, before responding, "Not a word."

"Then I assume you haven't heard."

I sighed, saying, "Heard what?"

I suppose there was a time when my father was able to manufacture a look of strength, feign indignation (righteous or otherwise), and rouse dramatic flair whenever the situation called for it. But as time wore on… or out, as the case may be, his efforts in doing so became obvious embellishments. So much so, in fact, any attempt to square up his shoulders, convey a stern expression, or render a demanding tone was already trumped by the weary light in his tired eyes. As a result, when he leaned forward, pointed a cautionary finger in my direction, and grumbled, "She's not getting my life's work," all I could see was weakness, all I could hear was fatigue.

"Okay, so she's not getting your life's work," I returned, the words spilling out casually. "But why would you think she is?"

"She wants a full accounting, Ethan. Do you understand what that means?"

I nodded, saying, "Yes. I think I can figure it out." I then waited for my father to move beyond my shadow of sarcasm and respond. When all I got in return, however, was the prolonged gape of a solemn expression, I added, "She wants to add up a few numbers. So what? From what little I know about divorce law, that's standard fare."

"There's more to it, Ethan."

I fixed my sights on Stanley Robbins, a plain looking man whose one-time full head of hair had, over the years, receded to the point of comb-over, and whose one-time stocky frame had melted into a pair of narrow shoulders and a pot-belly gut, and replied, "I'm all ears, Stanley."

"Well," Stanley began, his accommodating expression quickly engulfed by his puffy cheeks, "we received a courtesy call from your mother's attorney."

"Nothing strange about that," I remarked.

"The call was expected, Ethan. The content was not."

"Well then perhaps you should tell me about the content."

"If you give me a second, I will," Stanley countered, his understated bulk lurching forward.

"Let the man speak, Ethan."

After neutralizing my father's reproach with an indignant glare, I extended an open palm toward Stanley, and said, "The floor is yours, Counselor."

"Okay, then. Here it is in a nutshell, Ethan: Your mother's divorce attorney, his name is Connor Banks. Anyway, he said your mother is willing to forego a large cash settlement, which, according to Mr. Banks, she'd be entitled to. Instead, she'd be willing to accept moderate alimony, the house, its contents, the condo in Palm Beach, and, are you ready? She wants one-half of your father's equity stake in the firm, which would theoretically include having a say in how things are run around here." Stanley arched a single eyebrow into the creases of his forehead, before asking, "What do you think of that?"

I glanced at my father, whose expression carried all the piss and vinegar of vanilla, before looking back at Stanley Robbins, who leaned back in his chair, rested his hands atop his stomach, and nodded his head. Finally, I said, "Maybe it's just a negotiating ploy, Stanley. But I think it stinks. Doesn't make a damn bit of sense either."

"Maybe not. But that's it in a nutshell."

"Any chance you misunderstood him?"

Stanley shrugged his shoulders, although movement was hardly discernible, and said, "There wasn't enough to misunderstand, Ethan."

I stroked my jawline a few seconds, before asking, "So how'd the conversation end?"

"With me hanging up... right after I told him to go to hell," Stanley replied.

I acknowledged Stanley's wry grin with one of my own, before announcing, "We need to find out everything we can on Connor Banks."

"What exactly do you mean, everything?" my father queried.

"It means we need to find out what we're up against. It also means looking for dirt, just in case we need some leverage."

"Whoa… slow down now, Ethan," my father cautioned. "I don't want this to turn into a mud-slinging contest. I think we just need to approach the situation with realistic, but hardline negotiations."

"I agree with your father," Stanley added. "The more mud we sling, the more mud we have to dodge. And once that type of train gets rolling, things can only get uglier, drag on longer, and cost more in the end."

After wading through a few moments of contemplative silence, I excused Stanley so my father and I could speak alone – a conversation that began with me looking squarely into my father's deadpan eyes, and asking, "What the hell is she up to, Dad?"

My father slumped back in his chair like an already beaten man, and muttered, "I wish I knew, Ethan."

"Well then take a fucking guess!" I snapped.

"Hey now, settle down," my father said, "and show some respect."

"Is it because of me?" I asked, ignoring the old man's feeble plea. "Does she want to retain some control over my life by having some control over the firm? Is it pure hatred for you? Her undisciplined rage acting out? Or is someone, or something else behind it? It's one of those things, or none of those things, Dad, but it is something. So don't," I said, while slamming my hand to the desk, "tell me you wish you knew, because you know plenty. And I'm not going to be minimized by you pretending otherwise."

"I honestly don't know what your mother is thinking," my father quietly responded, his expression aimlessly wandering between anguish and agitation. "In fact, in all our years together, I've rarely known. And when I did, it certainly didn't mean I understood. What I know today," he added, while straightening up in his chair, "is that I do not…correction… WE do not deserve to have her fingerprints all over a business that it's taken years to build."

"Which is why I want to get a pulse on her lawyer. I want to find out if this crap is coming from him, or her. Either way it needs to stop."

"I just don't want to see the situation digress is all."

"How could it digress anymore than it already has?" I asked.

"It could lead to places nobody wants to go to," my father warned. "Including your mother."

"You mean, especially my mother. Then again, Dad, you weren't a saint. But hey, you want realistic, hardline negotiations. Well here they are on a platter for you."

The last time I had a meaningful dialogue with Jack Francis was a couple weeks ago, right after he returned from Costa Rica. As Jack told me then, he did not have an easy time bouncing around the island streets looking for a long-haired American. Not because a long-haired American wasn't easy to spot, but, as Jack essentially explained, 'Jaco Beach is the land of the retired pirate. A place where people go to disappear from a dubious past. But they disappear as much into the obscurity of the setting as they do the shadows of each other. And that's the fortress that binds, as well as protects their anonymity.'

That's also why flashing a photograph while asking a stranger, "Does this person look familiar?" is not a practice suitable for the area, for there are no strangers living there. Just eyes, ears, and clandestine conversations, which, as Jack found out, can include the local police, for they apparently protect the local and expat alike, especially a well healed expat like Billy Maxwell.

As a result, Jack never located Billy. On the contrary, Jack was having a beer at a local bar when Billy Maxwell approached him from behind and said, "I understand you're looking for me."

Jack was obviously taken aback by the unexpected encounter, and yet, he instantly admired Billy for having, as he described, "The stones to do it."

"We have a mutual friend," Jack told him.

"I don't have any friends," Billy countered.

"Does the name, Ethan Rivers, ring a bell?"

Billy gave Jack a thorough once-over, before saying, "I hear you and your girlfriend are staying at the Villas Caletas. Is that true?"

"My compliments," Jack replied admirably. "And yes, we are. Ethan set it up for us."

Billy remained stoic. In fact, to hear Jack tell it, Billy didn't so much as blink during their entire exchange. He did, however, nod subtlety, when he said, "I own a deep sea fishing boat that I take out on charters. Why don't you and your girlfriend join me for a day of fishing tomorrow?"

"I'm sure Monica would like that," Jack responded. "Where and what time?"

"Daybreak, and Los Suenos Marina," Billy replied impassively. "Hermosa Beach."

"Where is Hermosa Beach?" Jack asked, just as Billy was turning to leave.

"You made it this far, Jack Francis. You shouldn't have any trouble finding Hermosa Beach."

It wasn't until they parted ways when Jack realized he never told Billy his last name, a clear but somewhat eerie affirmation that Billy Maxwell was in profound control of his environment.

"And what does that tell you?" I asked, after Jack relayed the story to me.

"That Frank Marino, or anybody else Anthony Ricci might send looking for him, will certainly have their hands full with the locals."

"Good. That's good to hear. And the boat ride, how was that?" I asked.

"Once we got into open waters, Billy spoke at leisure," Jack replied. "Not about anything in particular… just Costa Rican life in general, which, by the way, he says he owes all to you – a debt he can never repay."

"Does he live on the boat?" I asked.

"No," Jack replied. "He and his girlfriend, who also serves as his first mate, and, who, by the way, has magnificent legs, live up in the rainforest, surrounded by mountains and monkeys."

As I waited for Jack to arrive at my office, I kept replaying the story about Billy and his fishing boat, and for a few moments I found myself envious of his sun-drenched life. Maybe a day would come when I would be free to take my wife and children and start fresh. It wouldn't have to be on an island either. Just some place far enough away from the chains and drudgery that have kept hold of me all these many years.

Of course, my wife, Olivia, would laugh at the notion I wanted any such change. "You're addicted to your work," she'd say. "And you're addicted to the power, control, and lifestyle that comes with it." She'd be right, of course, to say such things, because they are, in fact, true.

Does that mean, however, I wouldn't like it if things were easier or quieter, or that I somehow felt less restricted? Does that mean I wouldn't like to slow down, and not so much smell the roses, as it were, but just slow down and accept the ease of the day? Does that mean I couldn't learn to live life an entirely new way, and, in essence, replace one kind of addiction with another? I closed my eyes and bathed in the possibilities until such time as my secretary's voice came through the intercom announcing Jack Francis' arrival, at which point my focus instinctively wrapped itself around the chains and drudgery of the present afternoon.

Jack, as usual, nodded to me on his way to my bar, where he helped himself to a shot of twelve-year-old Kentucky bourbon. "What's the emergency, Ethan?" he asked, doing his best to ease the cringe in his expression before turning my way.

"I want you to find out everything you can about a lawyer named, Connor Banks," I directed. "Is he a good guy, bad guy? I mean, what's his relevance?" Jack asked. He then reached for the bourbon and proceeded to pour himself a second shot.

"The relevance is he's representing my mother in her divorce from my father," I answered indifferently.

Jack put down the bottle, and said, "Hey, I'm sorry to hear that." He then moved over to my couch where he sat on one of the armrests, his shot of whiskey on the bar, still intact.

I waved off his words with a simple, "It happens," before adding, "I don't know much about him."

"Hell, I've never even heard of him," Jack added, as though he actually knew every wannabe player in town.

"Frankly, either have I, so I made a few calls to learn what I could." I then massaged my forehead a few seconds, before proceeding with, "Connor Banks is a self-professed top notch divorce attorney. He's known for generating large fees, and does so by generating spurious allegations, which obviously are meant to churn billable hours. He's young, say mid to late thirties, ambitious, and by all accounts, a well built, good looking guy, which, if he can string half a sentence together, means he probably makes a good appearance in court."

"What firm's he with?"

"None. He's a sole-practitioner."

"Well if he's that good," Jack asked, while folding his arms across his chest, "wouldn't every Tom, Dick, and Harry Law firm want him working for them?"

"Like I said, he's a self-professed top notch lawyer. The operative term being, self-professed."

"Gotcha," Jack said. Then, "So where's his office?"

"127 Baldwin Avenue. Right near the library in downtown Barrington. He probably rents out a single office suite, shares a secretary with a handful of other lawyers... you get the gist."

"Okay, I'll get on it," Jack stated.

"Couple things, Jack. I want all the dirt you can get, and I want it ASAP. Above all, I want you to keep it quiet."

As my afternoon continued to unfold, it had become clear that I was not going to be able to properly prepare for Sonny Marx's probable cause hearing. As such, once Jack left my office I contacted my brother and asked him to agree to a short postponement. Andrew, just as I surmised, did not want to grant any kind of extension because he figured, if I asked, he must have me on the ropes. When I explained, however, that I was suddenly thrust into the middle of our parent's chaotic situation, he quickly relented, even asking if there was anything he could do to help. I responded, by saying, "Yeah, stay the hell out of it."

With the probable cause hearing now put on hold for another ten days, I decided it was time to pay a visit to my mother, Evelyn. I didn't forewarn her of my plans, however, so the fact she wasn't home didn't come as any great surprise. Nevertheless, I let myself in the house, and after pouring a healthy glass of scotch, took a seat in the family room, where three gulps later I found myself sifting through our family's photo album. By the time I got mid-way through it, however, it occurred to me the book had been perfectly choreographed, for there wasn't a single picture – not of me, Andrew, or my parents, that didn't reflect a face far happier than I can recall any of us ever being. Granted, the photos of Andrew and I as young children, they might've been genuine. But as we got older, no amount of cajolery by my parents could actually hide the cloud of unhappiness we lived under. And yet, to look through the album was to grace one carefree smile after another.

The best part about the Brady Bunch Family Album, however, was reaching the end of it, discovering, in the process, a manila folder housing a variety of photographs I'd never seen before. Of course, having the inconspicuous distinction of being stuffed inside the back cover of a photo album as though a final resting place, I sensed they weren't pictures meant for public consumption. Nevertheless, there they were in all their weathered glory.

By all accounts, my maternal grandmother had been a beautiful woman. The photographs I now scanned, though cracked and yellowed, confirmed as much. Interestingly enough, all I really know about her is that she married my grandfather, gave birth to my mother, and died of an unspoken illness when my mother was four years old. In fairness to my mother though, I doubt there was much more a four-year-old memory could pass along. By contrast, my grandfather was not a particularly handsome man, and no photograph could paint him otherwise. Born in the Ohio Valley, where his own parents labored to build a successful wheat farm, only to lose it to drought, and to hear my grandfather tell it, stubbornness and stupidity, he moved to Michigan shortly after the Korean War to take a job at the Ford Motor Company. He began as a welder in the stamping plant, though quickly moved through the rank and file and within a five year span had been promoted to shop foreman. From there his work at Ford gets a tad sketchy. My grandfather always held to the story that he left on his own accord to start a business. My mother once told me, however, that my grandfather was actually fired after beating a labor union official senseless with a welding helmet. In fact, according to my mother, his firing was the only thing that kept the union official from pressing charges, and my grandfather from landing in jail. Either way, he did go on to build a successful business selling uniforms and rags to the manufacturing sector in the Tri-State area, only to lose it some years later to alcohol, and to hear my mother tell it, stubbornness and stupidity.

It was never made clear to me why my grandfather didn't come around more. Sure, there was the occasional Christmas and Easter, but given that he had no other family and never remarried, as a boy I found it strange. Later on I sensed his prolonged absences were simply a convenient way for my mother to escape being in the company of the only man to ever intimidate her; a notion my mother finally confessed to me as true after her father lost a short battle with liver cancer.

For a time, it was just the opposite with my father's parents. A reasonably affable and educated pair (he, an engineer who tirelessly boasted about helping build The Mackinaw Bridge, the gateway connecting Michigan's upper and lower peninsulas, and she, an elementary school teacher who professed an expertise in child rearing), they regularly visited on Sundays, after church services, sometimes staying an hour, other times staying for dinner. This routine came to an abrupt halt, however, when, during an impromptu midweek visit by my grandmother, she and my mother got into some sort of heated argument. One that ended with my brother Andrew, (who was probably five or six-years-old at the time), crying hysterically, and my mother announcing the moment my father came home from work, "Your mother is no longer welcome in my house!" Of course that surly declaration lead to another argument between my parents, one that began with muffled voices and ended with doors slamming. It was one of the rare times I remember me and my brother huddled together in my bedroom, the two of us frightened in our own, unspoken ways. Be that as it may, one thing remained certain... my grandmother never stepped inside our house again. Nor, for that matter, did my grandfather.

Given the cold and acerbic conversations my parents often had over the years, it's surprising their marriage lasted as long as it did. In fact, I can't begin to assess what brought them together in the first place. Granted, it's not a mystery that has sustained any relevance in my life. That honor falls on Andrew. Nevertheless, it is something I've occasionally thought about in years past. Was my father looking for, and did he find in my mother, an engaging, beautiful woman to accompany his rise to professional and social prominence? Was my mother, in turn, looking for, and did she find in my father, an ambitious man, strong enough to push for the finer things in life, yet weak enough to succumb to her control and manipulations? Maybe the answer lies somewhere between. Maybe not. Then again, the answer really has no bearing on me, or, for that matter, Andrew, for it was during their marriage, and not before, when darkness entered our lives, and traumatic blood was spilled – memories rekindled in the pages of the photo album – memories which bind me to a past I've sought to bury long ago – memories which I could not soothe with another glass of Scotch, prompting me, in turn, to leave before my mother returned home, though not without hastily scribbling a note.

*Evelyn,*
*I stopped by to have a chat. Obviously you weren't here. Will be in touch later.*
*P.S. Thanks for the drink.*

*Ethan.*

I spent the rest of the afternoon wandering the streets of downtown Barrington in a state of blur, and the rest of the evening wandering between my children's bedrooms, where, once asleep, their quiet faces radiated an innocence I doubt I ever possessed, and our library, where my wife, Olivia, sat content with her book until such time as she took my hand and led me upstairs.

Although it was my obvious hope Jack would obtain some useful information on Connor Banks, I did not anticipate he would do so in such short order. Yet, almost a week to the day of our last meeting, he strolled into my office, tossed his briefcase on my couch, and, after downing his typical shot of bourbon, said, "Your boy, Connor Banks, is quite the character."

It was a declaration that had me shift in my chair to find a comfort level (which, after a few moments, I still couldn't find), before replying, "I'm not sure I like the sounds of that."

"For starters," Jack began, while taking a seat on the couch, "he's all the things you said, Ethan. Mid-thirties, ambitious, speaks well, and cleans up well. But beyond that, he's not what you think."

I raised an eyebrow, so Jack continued, saying, "He opened his first office in Riverview, Michigan."

"Where the hell is Riverview, Michigan?" I asked.

"About an hour Southwest of here. Not far from Monroe."

"Never heard of it."

"No reason why you would," Jack responded. "It's small town, U.S.A."

"Why wouldn't he have set up shop in Monroe? At least it's a city of some magnitude."

Jack sighed, before saying, "Just hear me out, okay?"

I cupped my palms behind my head, leaned back in my chair, and replied, "I'm all ears."

Jack then proceeded to lay out the details of Connor Banks' first post law school scam, which he termed, *The Bandit Tow Truck Scam.* In essence, it played out like this: a tow truck driver would monitor privately owned parking lots in order to tow away cars whose owners were not patronizing businesses associated with that lot. In many instances, the tow truck driver ignored the fact that the car's owner had patronized a business associated with the particular lot before going to another business, yet leaving their car where it was. The tow truck driver would then swoop in, scoop up the car as quickly as possible, and make haste for a public road, where he now had a legal lien on the car. The car would then be towed to a predetermined secured lot, where it was kept until an exorbitant fee was paid. Connor Banks was the owner of one such bandit truck, which towed cars from business lots in Monroe and took them to a secured lot in Riverview, which he also owned.

"Was he even practicing law?" I asked.

"Nope. Just trading cars for cash. But," Jack was quick to add, "about two years into this thing there were so many complaints with the Better Business

Bureau, he closed up. Now the city owns the lot. They foreclosed on it for non payment of taxes."

"Sounds like a gem of a guy."

"That's not all, Ethan."

Jack then proceeded to describe Connor Banks' second post law school scam, dubbed, *The Magic Bus*. Simply put, a busload of vagrants would be picked up in the City of Detroit and transported to a handful of doctor's offices scattered throughout the suburbs. The vagrants would then be processed in as new patients before being transported back to the streets of Detroit, where another group of vagrants would be gathered up. This process would repeat itself up to three times a day. At any rate, the doctors would bill Medicare, Medicaid, or any other insurance company they could get their hands on, for a variety of x-rays and medical tests never actually conducted. The bus, of course, was owned by one, Connor Banks. And though the doctors were eventually arrested and prosecuted for insurance fraud, allegations that Connor Banks was paid one hundred dollars per delivered vagrant could not be substantiated, and therefore, no charges were ever brought against him.

"They obviously paid him in cash," I said.

"Obviously," Jack returned.

After spending the next few moments reflecting on the stories I had just heard, I peered at Jack, and said, "Tell me something..."

"What's that?"

"How the hell did you get this information, and get it so quickly?"

Jack dipped his head from side to side, as though debating which word should fall out of his mouth first, before turning his palms open, and then saying with a slight grin, "You pay me for the information, Ethan. Not how I get it."

I nodded, saying, "Fair enough."

"And besides," he promptly added, "you once told me never to divulge my methods because you wouldn't want to know if I broke the law."

"But I always assume you do," I quipped.

"There's more, Ethan," Jack cautioned, the abrupt sobriety in his tone snatching the life out of my poor attempt at levity.

"Okay, so there's more," I conceded, doing my best to ignore the dark shadow that suddenly occupied my office. "But first tell me something: does this guy even practice law?"

"Ah, but that's his latest scam, Ethan. I mean, don't get me wrong, he is an attorney," Jack quickly clarified, "it's just that he's only been doing divorce work a few years. And the word I got... straight from the horse's mouth, mind you... is that he shoots from the hip because he isn't that knowledgeable about it. His plan is to learn as he goes, rather than study up."

"What do you mean, straight from the horse's mouth?" I asked.

"Connor Banks talks when you buy him a drink. He talks a lot when you buy him four or five," Jack said. He then shrugged his shoulders, before adding, "Just lucky I happened to stumble into the same bar at the same time."

"So you're telling me, my mother, who's been surrounded by some very astute and experienced lawyers all her life, chose some scumbag who can barely get out of his own way to represent her?"

Jack responded by handing me an envelope he pulled from his briefcase. "Maybe this will help explain," he muttered.

Inside the envelope were a dozen photographs of my mother. Half of them showed her entering a townhouse at night. The other half showed her leaving that same townhouse the following morning.

"Notice the clothes," Jack pointed out.

Jack was right, of course, as the photos evidenced no change of clothes whatsoever.

"Naturally you're going to now tell me the townhouse belongs to Connor Banks?" I queried, my eyes still scanning the pictures.

"I'm sorry, Ethan," Jack replied solemnly.

I, too, was sorry. Sorry for my father, who was always too weak or too easily manipulated to fight off, or fight through his wife's iniquities – sorry for Andrew, who I somehow imagined cutting out large swaths of time in an attempt to try and understand something that will always be just out of his reach – sorry for my mother, Evelyn, who seems impervious to her own hedonistic depravity – and yes, sorry for me, for the simple reason, I carry her DNA.

Before Jack left my office, he left me with one final nugget – information he received straight from the drunk horse's mouth. Connor Banks has been involved in a handful of divorce cases, though the last two involved wealthy older women, who, after receiving their settlements, wined, dined, and bed him, for as long as he was willing to stick around. His plans were a little different for Evelyn Rivers, however. Apparently she was still attractive enough, and would certainly be wealthy enough, to keep around for the long haul. Therefore, Connor Banks' motive in having my mother seek half of my father's equity interest in the firm was not just an attempt to steadily milk her, but an attempt to steadily milk our firm.

Plainly stated, a probable cause hearing is a proceeding that occurs after a criminal complaint has been filed by the prosecutor. Its sole purpose is to determine whether there is enough evidence to require a trial. In so making this determination, the judge must find there is probable cause that a crime has been committed and that the defendant committed it.

Frankly, I always thought a probable cause hearing was a baseless procedure because if there was, allegedly speaking, enough evidence to put someone in jail when a criminal complaint is filed, and thereafter keep them in jail pending their criminal trial, then what purpose does a probable cause hearing serve? There is either enough evidence to proceed straight to trial, or not. Unfortunately, the founding fathers did not solicit my opinion on the matter, so I am forced to play along with this procedural charade.

With that said, when I first learned Judge Deborah Fletcher was assigned to the Sonny Marx case, I was far from thrilled. Mind you, Judge Fletcher was, by all accounts, a tough, but fair judge. Because she was female, however, she also had the reputation of being prone to go too far in proving her point. Either way, given that our courtroom history was steeped in contemptuous banter (the judge even calling me wildly arrogant because I once questioned her intellect before a packed courtroom), I knew I would not be given the benefit of any doubt. As such, I decided not to use my courtroom savvy to challenge the very facts my brother and his team relied upon in order to file a criminal complaint. Rather, I would use my skills to challenge Fletcher herself. She wouldn't like it, of course, but given that her clerk once confided to me the judge found my courtroom skills remarkable, I knew she also wasn't likely to dismiss me, or my case out of hand.

Nevertheless, to produce as level a playing field as possible for my client, I waited until Andrew entered the courtroom, whereupon I handed him the photographs Jack took, and whispered, "Your mother is having an affair with her divorce attorney."

In the short term, Andrew recovered well enough to preserve his courtroom demeanor, even delivering a bona fide opening statement regarding the alleged rapist, Sonny Marx. In the long term, however, the litany of thoughts and questions he no doubt entertained about our mother, bombarded his psyche to the point he ultimately lost focus, just as I had predicted he would.

The end result was this: Judge Fletcher ruled there was probable cause to believe that in addition to assaulting a police officer, Sonny Marx had also committed the rapes of Lauren Hill and Patricia Stevens. But given I made no real effort to challenge the evidentiary findings, knowing full well that dog would hunt far better in front of a jury, I expected as much. Until then, my only function was to see to it that Sonny Marx was released on bail, where he would remain free pending the outcome of his criminal trial.

Of course, Fletcher was initially steadfast in her refusal to grant such a request. Fortunately, however, Andrew had succumbed to the heat of his internal fire-pit, otherwise called, *Life With Mother,* and was, therefore, unable to mount a relevant counterattack to my arguments, or, for that matter, proffer any kind of worthy objection. Fortunately, too, I was able to persuade Judge Fletcher that given no reasonable objection was made by the prosecution, she really had no other choice but to set Sonny free, particularly if she didn't want me to file an appeal that afternoon seeking his immediate release. And just to make sure I drove my point home, I then brought up a couple of noteworthy statistics: one, the judge had ruled against defendant's seeking bail in 77% of her cases, and two, an alarming 58% of those rulings had been overturned on appeal, many with incidental admonishments from the appellate court.

"Stop grandstanding, Mr. Rivers. You have your bail," Judge Fletcher asserted. She then cracked her gavel against the woodblock (probably wishing it was my head), and dismissed the parties concerned.

Once outside the courtroom, it was virtually impossible to ignore my brother, so rather than try (my unabashed preference), I simply approached him, and said, "My first responsibility is to my client. End of story."

"That was a bullshit play, Ethan. Even for you," Andrew countered, his contemptuous glare giving me the once over.

"It's the difference between winning and losing, little brother. Nothing more. Nothing less."

"Not by my definition," Andrew returned sharply.

"You don't know the definition," I said, my tone simmering.

After a few moments of uneasy silence, our eyes locked in a turbulent embrace, I smirked, and said, "Have a nice rest of the day. And give my regards to that know-it-all-girlfriend of yours. In fact, let her know how well you did today. I'm sure she'll be impressed." I then turned to walk away, though when I did, Andrew grabbed hold of my arm, and muttered, "Fuck you, Ethan. And fuck your pictures."

"For the record," I said, staring at my brother's hand while it remained latched to my arm, "the pictures are real, the situation is real, and the next time you put your hands on me..." I then met my brother's contemptuous glare with one of my own, before adding, "my aggression with you will be real."

Andrew responded by removing his hand (ever so slowly, I might add), and saying, "Make a move anytime you want, Ethan. But first do me a favor. Go to hell."

After a moment's thought, I replied, "I've already been there and back." I then nodded my head, repeated my assertion, and walked away – the long and empty corridor echoing the adamant clacking of my shoes until I exited the building, where once outside, I inhaled the gray and arduous chill of winter's approach.

# Chapter 13

One of the first things I learned in law school was, never ask a question you don't already know the answer to. It's a great sentiment to be sure... so long as you're standing in front of a classroom teaching the ins and outs of practicing law in a perfect world. But litigation doesn't work that way, particularly in the practice of criminal law, where every other defendant is typically a natural born liar. Therefore, unless you're a mind reader, it's near impossible to predict how a defendant will answer a question because they'll say just about anything to stay out of harm's way.

Victims of crimes, on the other hand, have a tendency to float somewhere between fact and a fabricated version thereof. Put another way, there are times when the alleged victim is no less a party to a crime. Could be there's a grudge simmering between two contemptuous people that simply boils over when one cries foul before the other – could be an *injured party* is merely looking for a monetary windfall, which is a natural seduction for exaggerating what went down on Friday night, so to speak – or, could simply be the result of a convenient memory, which often occurs when something goes drastically wrong between otherwise innocent people.

The fact is, about the only time I've never challenged a person's veracity is when they're the victim of a heinous crime, like rape, and the physical and emotional toll is so great, and so obvious, they couldn't lie if they wanted to. Even in that scenario, however, a defense attorney will bombard a victim with question after question, pounding on the door until it's wide open and every nook and cranny of a victim's life is exposed, all in the hopes of making the accuser appear less the victim, and their client, in turn, less the assailant. To that end, I have to make certain I'm not caught flatfooted because the defense attorney knows something I don't. As such, I try to find out everything I can about the victim, the defendant, and the witnesses caught between.

If appearances count for anything, Lauren Hill was a loving wife, good mother, and kind neighbor; a description one might say is reminiscent of an obituary. And yet, since Lauren described her ordeal as, "The night part of her died," the portrayal is befitting nonetheless.

"I was just going to the drugstore," she said, the weight of her despondency swallowing the light in the room. "I wanted to get Peter some more cough medicine to help him sleep."

"I was down with the flu," her husband chimed in.

"Anyway, I was about halfway down the drive when I realized I'd left my purse in the kitchen. But rather than pull back into the garage, I got out of my car to walk in through the side door." Lauren dabbed her eyes with a tissue, before adding, "And that's when it happened. That's when this man… this monster…" Lauren's quivering voice then drifted into silence, where it remained until her husband gently pulled her from the sofa, and she quietly apologized, before leaving the room.

"We've already been through this with the police," Peter Hill said the instant his wife disappeared from view. "Is it really necessary again?" Without waiting for a reply, he then added, "I don't want Lauren to testify. She's not strong enough."

Rather than debate Peter on the importance of his wife's testimony, knowing full well Lauren Hill and her beleaguered state would play well before a judge and jury, I ignored his sentiment, and instead, made my way to the bookshelves that lined their expansive family room. "You read all these?" I asked. I then pulled Philip Roth's, *American Pastoral*, from the shelf and flashed it over my shoulder. "You read this?"

"Saw the movie," Peter acknowledged, and without turning his way I imagined his rigid frame standing in the corner – arms folded, expression wary, his wingtip shoe tapping the wood floor, as though waiting for my next play.

I returned the Roth book to its slot, before pulling Charles Dickens', *A Tale Of Two Cities*. "How about this?" I asked, flashing the book over my shoulder.

"What is this, library hour?"

"Just curious," I said calmly.

"No. Didn't see the movie either," came the abrupt reply. "And before you pull another book from the shelf, rest assure, I probably didn't read it. I'm not a big reader. Either is Lauren."

"Well they look good anyway," I offered, after putting the Dickens book away.

"I'm glad we have your approval," Peter countered, his refined presence riding the edge of acrimony.

"Look, Mr. Hill... Peter," I began, as I moved back to the center of the room, "I'm not your enemy." I then proceeded to explain that my focus was not to expose the intimacy of his wife's recent hell anymore than it was to subject his family to the shame or embarrassment he's afraid will follow. My focus was to see to it the scumbag who attacked his wife was put in jail for a very, very long time. I concluded, by saying, "I'm not here to hurt. I'm here to help. But I can't, if you don't let me."

After Peter hit me with an indignant look, I said, "You have to let me do my job, otherwise everyone loses, except the man who attacked your wife. If he walks, he wins. End of story."

Peter hemmed and hawed his way around the block a couple of times, before coming up with a rousing, "Let me think about it."

Okay, so it wasn't the definitive answer I was looking for, but his softened stance was encouraging enough that with a little more spit and polish, I could have him singing a different tune when the time was right. Until then, I had other fish to fry.

For the last fourteen years, Patricia Stevens lead an idyllic life. And then she got raped. At least that's how she began her story after making me promise I would not discuss the details with anyone, including her husband, Richard. Considering the fact I was sitting at her kitchen table for the sole purpose of discussing testimony she might soon be giving in open court, it was an unusual, albeit, strange request to be sure. But when she said, "What I'm about to tell you isn't just about the rape… it's something way more involved," my curiosity got the better of me. So, I settled back in the chair, and said, "I'm listening."

Married to a successful investment banker, and the mother of two girls, aged 8 and 10, Patricia Stevens slid through her Chestnut Hills life like every day was spring. "There's nothing my husband wouldn't give me, and there's nothing I wouldn't do for him," she said, the thought stirring the glint in her tepid brown eyes. "I have a beautiful house, two beautiful children, good friends, I'm active in the community…" Patricia suddenly paused, biting her bottom lip until a somber shadow enveloped the glint in her eyes, and she added, "And it's all a lie. My real name is Nancy Sudwell."

Born in Provo, Utah, to parents Jim and Lydia, Nancy was, according to her, just an average girl with an average upbringing. Average took on a new meaning, however, once Nancy entered high school and started hanging out with a group of kids that liked to get their little buzz on. So much so, smoking marijuana and drinking alcohol became a daily occurrence. Snorting cocaine would have as well, except it was too expensive for daily fare. As such, it was put aside for special occasions, although Nancy insists she was never a big fan, refusing to drift too far from smoking pot and swirling cocktails. Be that as it may, by the time Nancy turned seventeen she had been thrown out of her parent's house, and by the age of eighteen she had been busted for selling heroin to an undercover cop.

The story goes like this: on an *average* summer day Nancy drove her boyfriend to a pizza joint, but instead of picking up a pie, her boyfriend sold three dimes of heroin to some *average* looking guy hanging around out back. I'm not sure what three dimes of heroin actually consists of, having never prosecuted that type of crime, but apparently it's enough to piss off the local authorities, for at the end of the day she was charged with a felony offense. Her attorney, whom Nancy described as, "Some court appointed local cowboy who couldn't spell cat if you spotted him the C and the T," suggested she plead guilty since it was her first offense. "You'll get probation and a fine of a couple hundred dollars," she recalled him saying.

Yeah, well, her cowboy-attorney's advice notwithstanding, Nancy ended up with a ten-year spot in the Provo House of Corrections, where one of the guards not only raped her whenever the lighting was right, but also convinced her she'd die in prison should anyone ever find out. That's why when her older brother showed up for a visit eighteen months into her term, convincing Nancy to escape wasn't a difficult task.

"The difficulty was how," Nancy offered.

"So what'd you do?" I asked, in what was probably the dumbest question to ever fall out of my mouth.

"I was just getting to that," she replied.

Yeah, no shit, I thought to myself.

Anyway, Nancy's older brother didn't leave Provo for a couple of weeks. Instead, he spent each morning studying the prison activity, particularly around the fenced perimeter. Turns out, there wasn't any activity to speak of, so Nancy scaled a barbed wire fence one morning at daybreak, and then ran to a predetermined area where her brother was waiting in his pickup truck.

When I asked if she had any fears about breaking out of prison (confident it wasn't near as stupid a question as my previous one), Nancy replied, "You hear stories of people getting caught going over the fence, so I was nervous from that standpoint. Were the stories true, were they rumors? I didn't know what to expect. Would I get shot? Would I get beaten? Would I end up in solitary confinement?" Nancy then sighed, before saying, "I guess I was lucky."

"Real lucky," I muttered. I then flashed to my brother, Ethan, and thought, the son-of-a-bitch would've had me scale the fence, only to leave me high and dry on the other side.

Meanwhile, Nancy took the five-hundred-bucks her brother had given her, hopped on a bus for the East Coast, but then somewhere between Provo and Providence changed her tune to Michigan, where she assumed the name, Patricia Adams, a girl she had known from high school who'd unfortunately died of cancer. She worked odd jobs for cash, lived in cheap motel rooms (never staying in the same place for any longer than a two week stretch), and otherwise did her best to fly under the radar. "I had zero illusions," she said, her eyes scanning mine as though pleading for understanding. "I was hiding from the law, yes… but I was also in a place with new possibilities, and the chance to start over, so it was worth it."

She met her husband, Richard Stevens, in a coffee shop when she was 23 and he was 40, married him a year later in a small church service, popped out a couple of kids, and basically never looked back. Richard, it seems, was far more interested in Nancy's lovemaking talents than anything else, so she could pretty much sell him on anything, including her past. In fact, since he was already of the notion that his wife's parents died in a house fire years ago, and the older brother who was left to raise her, now lived the life of a nomad, questions about her previous life rarely surfaced – and even when they did, they were of the unobtrusive variety.

The reality was, however, Nancy had actually stayed in touch with her brother throughout the years, and when he told her of their mother's passing, Nancy hit, what she described as, "an emotional low point."

"I couldn't just tell Richard my mother had really been alive all that time, let alone go back to Utah for her funeral. I couldn't risk getting caught," Nancy said, before going on to explain that her mother's passing only further inflamed the inner turmoil she's wrestled with on and off since the day she changed her name and began leading a secret life. She then shrugged her shoulders, as though confounded by her own tale, before adding, "I can't tell you how many times I've kissed my children goodnight, wondering if they were going to wake up the following morning, only to find their mother being led away in handcuffs."

"And now you have the added burden of the rape case," I surmised, "and all the unwanted media attention it might bring your way."

Nancy and I studied each other for several moments before the unsettled conversation finally gave way to, "The rape… as much as I wouldn't wish something like that on my own worst enemy, might have been a blessing in disguise."

At that moment, I think the utterance, "Huh?" must've carved itself into my expression with neon lights, because I didn't say a word, and still, Nancy held up her forefinger, and said, "I'll explain," whereupon she promptly announced, "I know Lauren Hill."

"Lauren Hill, as in the rape victim?" I managed.

"Yes, Lauren Hill as in the rape victim."

"How well?"

"Well enough to know that she'll never testify in court," Nancy stated.

"Why do you say that?" I asked, figuring I was just going to hear Nancy echo Peter Hill's sentiments about his wife's weak state of mind. And I did. But I also heard that Lauren Hill once had a meltdown at her own kid's birthday party because there was too much noise and commotion – that her entire sense of balance gets thrown off if her weekly manicure is cancelled – that her mood changes as often as her outfits do, which neighborhood gossip pegs at multiple times per day – that her world is essentially made up of two components, the things she has, and the things she wants everyone to think she has – that she is stable only as long as the white picket fences in her world remain perfectly white. After Nancy concluded her little diatribe, by saying, "But the rape changed all that," I couldn't help myself, asking, "So I take it you guys aren't best friends?"

Nancy stared at me a couple of seconds, but her stoicism quickly turned into a smile, and the smile into a short burst of laughter (a much welcomed sound), which Nancy followed up, by saying, "All I'm trying to tell you is that you'd be lucky just to coax her out of her bathrobe, much less get her into a courtroom to testify. But you still have me," she added with a confident spin. "And you're obviously going to need me."

I could have deliberated my next question for the next ten years, and still, the only one that would have consistently remained at the top of the charts was, "Why did you refer to the rape as a blessing in disguise?"

Nancy spent a few moments putting her long dark hair into a long dark ponytail, and in the process, magnifying a thin and attractive face that also looked a bit pale and weary, compliments, I'm sure, of one or two sleepless nights. When she finished, she said, "I've been in two hells in my life," her words following the pensive gaze of a contemplative sigh. "The hell of jail, and the hell of rape. I can survive the rape. I'll never survive going back to jail. And that's where you come in. I want you to work out a deal with the prosecutors in Utah. I don't want to be a fugitive anymore. I want my freedom. In return, you'll have my testimony."

On the one hand, the 10-year prison sentence Nancy received was, in a word, ridiculous. In fact, she probably shouldn't have received five minutes behind bars. I mean, aside from accompanying her idiot boyfriend to a pizza joint, what the hell did she do wrong? The harder part of the equation is the prison escape. Obviously, getting raped by a guard points to extenuating circumstances, but jail breaks and extenuating circumstances don't really ride the same wave. So I don't know how far that would get me.

On the other hand, I could call Nancy's bluff, turn her into the authorities, and still take a shot at persuading her to testify in the rape trial. After all, she's still a victim, she has daughters, and it's her neighborhood where the madman is lurking. If I'm able to, great – if not, I turn my sights back to Lauren Hill, who I'm still not a-hundred-percent convinced won't step up.

Then again, could I really be that big of a schmuck?

# CHAPTER 14

After returning to my office, having spent all morning in court, I had hoped for a little quiet time so I could, one, take a well-deserved nap on my couch, before two, confronting my mother and her perverse, misguided approach in divorcing my father. Twice postponed, meeting with my mother had, in no small measure, become a pressing matter, for with each passing day it was becoming more and more apparent that Connor Banks was gaining a stronger foothold into her life; an observation which stemmed from her indifferent, if not altogether callous attitude regarding the odious trespasses she left behind.

Unfortunately for me, a nap was not to be had. In fact, no sooner did I toss my suit coat into the lap of an empty chair when the voice of my secretary breached the intercom, saying, "Ethan, there's a man in the lobby waiting to see you."

"Do I have an appointment I somehow forgot about?" I asked, after a moment of deliberation.

"There's nothing on the books."

"Fine," I grumbled, before instructing Barbra to go see who it was, a move designed to put the discretionary burden on my dutiful secretary rather than the firm's receptionist, who, although soft on the eyes and quite spirited, was essentially void of brain matter.

A few minutes later Barbra's deliberate tone returned, saying, "His name is Albert Ness."

I chewed on the name a few seconds, before replying, "I don't know any Albert Ness. What's he want to see me about?"

"I don't know. All he would tell me is that he's an agent with the Treasury Department."

"Treasury? Why would... you sure about that?" I queried.

"He showed me credentials," Barbra offered.

"What, a note from his grandfather, Elliot?" I returned, my caustic manner quickly regaining it's form. When Barbra replied with silence, I added, "Okay, give me five minutes. Then bring him and his credentials to conference room #3."

"He did say you could contact the regional office downtown if you have any questions," Barbra added.

"That's alright, my curiosity is sufficiently piqued," I said. I then reached for my suit coat before deciding against it. Instead, I loosened my tie and rolled up my sleeves in an effort to portray a lawyer too busy to be interrupted for any length of time.

Minutes later a balding, bespectacled man pulled his tall, sinewy frame from the conference room chair, extended his hand, and announced, "Mr. Rivers, my name is Albert Ness. I'm an agent with the Treasury Department."

Given my druthers, I would avoid shaking hands whenever possible. Unfortunately, mine is a profession where pressing the chapped and clammy palms of another is the rule, not the exception. That said, every once in a rare while one can discern something from this customary business dance. Meaning, Albert Ness had the weathered skin of a rough-carpenter, not the velvety texture one might expect from a well dressed, pencil-pushing treasury agent. "Can I get you something, Agent Ness – coffee, water?" I offered.

"No, I'm fine, thank you."

"I nodded, saying, "Then what can I do for you?"

"May I?" Ness asked, while motioning to his vacated chair.

"Of course," I replied. I then watched my uninvited guest fill his seat before taking my own on the opposite side of the conference table.

"I'm here to discuss an old client of yours, Mr. Rivers."

I stared at Albert Ness a few moments, his expression as stoic as his inflection, before offering a faint smile, and saying, "Any information regarding my clients is privileged, Agent Ness. But then, you probably already know that."

"This isn't someone you continue to represent, Mr. Rivers."

"It doesn't matter, Agent Ness. I make it a habit of never discussing my clients, past or present."

Albert Ness tipped his head to the side, and then offered up a deliberate, if not dramatic sigh, before saying, "Perhaps we can find some common ground."

"I sincerely doubt it," I replied.

"How can you be so sure when you haven't even heard me out?"

"Call it an educated guess."

Ness reclined in his chair. "Aren't you even curious who it is I want to discuss?" he posed.

"Frankly, Agent Ness, I couldn't care less."

An uncomfortable silence quickly descended and for the next several seconds we stared at one another, Ness no doubt searching for any sign of weakness or contradiction on my part, and me, calmly waiting out his palpable efforts. Finally, he frowned, the shallow creases across his forehead embracing over the bridge of his nose, shook his head, and said, "I don't believe that for a second."

"Agent Ness," I began, my words trailing my own deliberate, if not dramatic sigh, "this conversation is pointless. Now if you'll excuse me, I have a busy afternoon."

"I know you have the money," Ness countered, just as I was lifting myself from the chair.

"Excuse me?" I returned, my body suddenly void of further movement.

"You heard me, Counselor. I know you have the money," Ness replied. He then smirked, and added, "Please... sit, Mr. Rivers. Let's see if we can't find that common ground after all."

Fortunately, years of litigation taught me not to overreact to the unexpected for fear an abrupt change in expression would paint an adverse portrait to a jury. As a result, by the time I settled back in my seat, I managed to forge a subtle, yet cynical grin, and say, "Lucky for you, Agent Ness, my curiosity is driven by an overwhelming sense of perversion."

Ness glanced at his watch, before saying, "Well then, in the interests of your perversion, I'll do my best to keep it short and sweet."

"How thoughtful," I responded.

Albert Ness then proceeded to tell me his office had Judge Richard Beckett under surveillance several months prior to his death. Apparently Ness was made aware of some questionable situations the judge was involved in, not the least of which was a rather large payoff. He then made it a point of outlining the exact dates and times I met with the judge, and though Ness wouldn't confirm as much, it meant I too had likely been followed on occasion. Either way, once Judge Beckett was found dead, surveillance at his house continued. The long and short of it, Ness produced photographs of me entering Beckett's house empty-handed, only to come out thirty minutes later with a briefcase in each hand.

After Ness concluded his little narrative by saying, "We assume the briefcases were full of Beckett's payoff money," I calmly shrugged my shoulders, and replied, "Since your assumptions are absolutely meaningless, what's your point?"

"Have a little patience, Mr. Rivers. I haven't gotten there yet," Ness said, his words basking in the glow of his understated arrogance. He then jutted his chin forward, toyed with his perfectly straight tie, and launched into another story, the gist being that Ness has also been keeping a close eye on Connor Banks. Not because Banks had engaged in criminal activity worthy of Ness' involvement, (frankly, Banks was, according to Albert Ness, 'a ham and egger of a crook'). Rather, it was because Banks was involved with my mother. And when I questioned why that situation was relevant, Ness went on to explain that in addition to examining all of the documents filed with the court regarding my parents pending divorce, he had it on good authority that Connor Banks was behind my mother's quest for control of the law firm.

Ness then fidgeted in his chair until he was sitting posture-perfect, folded his hands neatly in front of him, and concluded with, "It's all about money. It always is."

After proffering a look of indifference, I promptly said, "So that's your point?"

"C'mon Mr. Rivers, you know better than that," Ness suggested.

"Actually, if that's all you have, then I'm afraid you've lost me altogether."

Ness grinned, saying, "Then let me make it plain for you." And with that, Albert Ness went on to explain that the Treasury Department was prepared to forget all about Judge Beckett's payoff money. Lose the file, is how he put it. Then again, if I forced Ness to press on, it wouldn't matter if his office could prove the briefcases I took were stuffed with cash anyway. Between Treasury and the IRS, he could make my life a living hell for years to come. Ness then explained, in no uncertain terms, that he could also make Connor Banks magically disappear from my mother's life. "You'd have your law firm, Ethan. Something you've worked your entire life for."

I snickered at Ness' unexpected conciliatory tone, before saying, "And all I have to do in return is…?"

Ness leaned into the conference table, resting his weight on his forearms, and said, "Give me the whereabouts of Billy Maxwell."

Once again an uncomfortable silence quickly descended, and for the next several seconds we stared at one another – Ness ardently waiting for my response, and me trying to determine the best way to deliver it. Finally, I glanced at Ness' watch, and said, "Nice Piaget."

"What?"

"Your watch, it's a Piaget."

"So what?"

"The Treasury Department must pay pretty well these days."

"It was a gift," Ness returned, his eyes burrowing into mine.

"I'm quite sure it was," I remarked. "Was the Armani suit a gift as well, or just the money to buy it?"

"What are you driving at?"

I sneered at Ness. Then, "Obviously you're here at the behest of Anthony Ricci."

"That's correct," Ness returned, his expression once again as stoic as his inflection. He then nodded his head, and added, "And obviously you now have a decision to make."

# CHAPTER 15

One thing I've always thought about D.C. – he doesn't lack for enthusiasm. Mickey says he has a tendency to get carried away, and who knows, she could be right. I just think some of the daily bullshit he runs into catches him completely off guard, such, that when he regurgitates the situation to someone, he's still in disbelief-mode.

Either way, when he found me tucked away in a secluded corner of the circuit court law library, he eagerly called out, "Drew, you're not gonna believe it," much to the chagrin of every other lawyer and paralegal quietly scanning computer screens or thumbing the pages of books.

I chuckled to myself, watching as Danny Cranston, former police officer and current assistant prosecutor, bound toward me in a dress-shirt too tight, a necktie too loose, and a jacket and slacks color combo a bit too questionable – topped off, of course, by a nice pair of worn out brown shoes.

"What's up?" I asked, when he finally reached my table.

D.C. tossed his briefcase on one chair, before pulling out another to sit down. He then smiled, sending ripples across his puffy cheeks, and repeated, "Drew, you're not gonna believe it."

"Not going to believe what?" I calmly returned, careful to keep my volume in check.

"You remember a guy by the name of Rudy Stamkos? He came on board my last year in the department. Nice kid. Good looking kid. I think I mentioned him a time, or two. Anyway, does the name strike a chord?"

I once again chuckled to myself, although I couldn't keep a subtle grin from spilling over, when I replied, "Not really," which seemed to disappoint D.C., so I quickly added, "Yeah, maybe. I dunno… why, what about him?"

"He partners with Wally Clemens, who was also my first partner on the force. Surely you remember Wally?"

I simply nodded my head, all the while thinking D.C. must send out a helluva lot of Christmas cards. Meanwhile, it prompted D.C. to lean his stuffed frame forward, rest his arms atop the table (which placed them on a couple of legal pads of mine), and say in as muffled a tone as he could probably muster up, "You're not gonna believe who he used to sleep with."

"Who?" I asked, my subtle grin no longer subtle.

"Carol Baxter," D.C. replied, while sporting his own unsubtle grin.

"Carol Baxter, as in Gene Baxter's wife?"

"Yep. One and the same."

"While they were married?"

"Yep."

"Does Gene know?"

"Not sure. All I know is Rudy isn't the only one," D.C. replied, his grin in tow.

"No shit," I mused, which D.C. used as the impetus to repeat, "No shit," before moving on with the particulars.

Rudy Stamkos and Sonny Marx, it seems, met in a local bar when happy hour began at four and ended at six, and they both showed up at three and left at eight. In between, however, their hours long conversation drifted from one braggadocios rant to the next, until they finally landed on a topic both actually knew something about: sleeping with a married woman… as in, the same married woman…as in, Carol Baxter.

"Are you telling me Sonny Marx is doing Gene Baxter's wife?" I asked.

"According to Rudy, he is. Or, at least he was a couple of months ago. But that's about the time Rudy stopped seeing her, so Marx could still be at it."

"Back the fuck up, I'm not following," I grumbled. "How in the hell does your friend Rudy suddenly bring up the very guy we just brought rape charges against?"

"That's the funny thing," D.C. replied, "Rudy didn't realize it was the same guy until last night's card game. We were playing poker over at Wally's when one of the guys asked him if he had any good stories to tell. He's the only bachelor in the bunch so the boys live vicariously through him." D.C. then proffered a dubious look, and said, "Actually, that's not true. Charley Deaver's not married. But he's been engaged for over two years now, so it's pretty much the same thing. I don't think you know him."

"I don't," I said, on the backend of an eye-roll.

"Anyway," D.C. continued, "Rudy tells us about a couple of dates which weren't all that exciting, when he suddenly goes, "Oh, I got a good story for you guys. He then proceeds to describe how he walks into a bar, plops his ass down on a barstool, and starts talking to the guy next to him like they're old friends. A few beers later the superficial conversation becomes the drunk conversation, and the next thing you know, bam!" D.C. exclaimed, his hand crashing to the table, sending another shockwave through the library. "They go from comparing notes about some of their conquests to comparing notes about Carol Baxter... if you know what I mean."

"I think I get the gist, D.C."

"Pretty crazy, eh?"

"No doubt."

"Well it gets crazier, Drew."

"Why am I not surprised?" I muttered, on the backend of another eye-roll.

"Oh, believe me, you ain't heard nothin' yet," D.C. declared. He then leaned his stuffed frame forward again, and said, "Apparently when these two guys were comparing women, they were also comparing what some of the women liked. But Marx took it a step further, telling Rudy what he likes to do to women. And then he tells him he works in a bar that hosts sex parties – says they have a dungeon with whips, chains, and every sex toy and apparatus imaginable – says the women who show up are pretty much game for anything, so he's always pushing the envelope – says the place is in downtown Springdale..."

"And it's called, *The Knight Owl Bar & Grill*," I interjected. "And it just so happens to be owned by the one, and only, Gene Baxter."

"Yep," D.C. spouted. "And those must be the parties Baxter was referring to when he was giving us Marx's job description."

"Yep," I returned in like fashion, "and now it makes me wonder why my brother told me to go there in the first place?"

"I always figured he was just tossing you a bone because he didn't think it was that big a deal," D.C. said. He then slumped back in his chair, before adding, "But now you've got me wonderin' too."

"All I know is, Ethan doesn't do anything for anybody unless there's something in it for him."

"So, where you think he's going with this?" D.C. queried, his expression the equivalent of a jigsaw puzzle.

"No clue," I replied. "He could have a trick up his sleeve, which is gonna have to play out sooner or later. Or, in typical Ethan fashion, it could be as simple as trying to embarrass me because he knew something I didn't. He gets off on crap like that. Either way, though, we now have something he never saw coming."

"What's that?" D.C. cautiously returned.

"We have Rudy to testify about his conversation with Marx – about his job at the bar and all. That kind of slimy shit goes right to Marx's character. It'll play well in front of a jury, don't you think?"

When D.C. met my question with silence (his head cocked to the side, his meditative gaze stuck in neutral), I repeated myself, whereupon he finally replied, "This case is getting interesting."

After D.C. left the library, I continued to ponder my brother's intent. Had he really wanted me to find Baxter's dungeon? Was Ethan hoping to derail my focus, thinking I'd somehow feel obligated to investigate the legality of a bar hosting sex parties? And if so, was he then hoping I'd make a big stink of its existence, thereby taking some of the focus off his client and resting it squarely on the shoulders of some piece of shit building and the whacked out people who frequent it? Or, was he hoping I took the opposite approach and said nothing so as not to interfere with the progress of the rape case – but in doing so, give Ethan something to hold over my head? On the other hand, was the entire situation just a tit for tat scenario? Did my brother really think by tossing me a bone on this case, I would've actually tossed him something back for Judge Beckett? Then again, was it nothing more than what I said to D.C. at the outset – that Ethan was just fucking with me – that he was trying to get me to overthink a situation merely because he could, and, in return, have a good laugh at my expense?

Yeah, well, I suppose I could go on and on, but at the end of the day the only thing that'll remain clear is this: when Ethan muddies something up, he muddies it up for a reason. Figuring out why, now that's a different story. One I've already spent way too much of my life trying to understand.

*Henry Flannigan's Brasserie,* a Detroit landmark, popular for its leather high-backs, single malt scotch, and certified Wagyu Kobe beef, was also my father's favorite restaurant. I would've preferred taking Mickey to dinner, particularly since I'd only seen flashes of her the last couple of days, but the old man invited me a week ago, so what the hell choice did I have? Besides, after meeting with Patricia Stevens (aka, Nancy Sudwell), I was at a loss on what to do, and hoped to pick my father's brain. Could I have talked to Mickey about the situation? You bet. I just didn't want her to risk going out on a limb because I was contemplating it. By the same token, I didn't want to be pulled off the case because I was contemplating it. Could I have mentioned it to D.C.? I suppose, although D.C.'s first impulse always comes from his gut, and the issue at hand called for something a bit more cerebral. That meant I could either talk to another attorney in my office, none of whom I trusted to hold a glass of water, much less a secret, or dear old dad. The choice was easy. That being said, was it dangerous bringing it up to him, knowing he's law partners with my brother? Absolutely. But that's why I planned to keep the particulars to myself – feed him only enough to get a sense of what he might do if standing in my shoes. Sure, he was mentally and emotionally void for much of my childhood, and therefore, not someone I ever sought out as though a great sage for advice. Nevertheless, I always believed he possessed a keen understanding of the law, as well as the moral compass to represent it; components essential for weighing the pros and cons of what I could be headed for.

By the time the Maître' d showed me to the table, my father had his familiar Dewar's in hand, which he promptly set down, and said, "Andrew, son. Good to see you." He then stood up and gave me one of those stiff hugs that only a stiff relationship can produce.

Be that as it may, our dinner, as well as the incidental conversation throughout, progressed without incident or fanfare. In fact, the evening had been downright easy going, if not altogether pleasant… right up until my father abruptly pushed his desert plate away, and then launched a series of verbal assaults aimed at my mother – reigning it in only when he realized the nearby patrons were gawking at him.

"Yeah, hey Dad," I said, once his forefinger stopped stabbing the table for good, "I'm really sorry about all the shit you're going through right now."

"Drew," my father began, his tone once again basking in the glow of restraint, "the only one who should apologize at this table is me," for what he then termed was his, "unacceptable behavior as a father."

If Mickey had told me when I woke up this morning that my father was going to apologize to me at dinner, I would've thought her nuts, a sense only heightened when he cupped his hand over mine, and added, "Your mother has some issues, Andrew. Issues I didn't know about until after Ethan was born. Issues I doubt you're aware of. And rather than deal with them, as I should have when you were growing up, I buried myself in my work, hoping they'd disappear on their own. But they didn't, and because they didn't, you suffered every day. In fact, we all suffered every day."

Unsure how to respond (hell, I didn't even know what to think, much less what to say), I remained silent until my father once again apologized, this time for what he termed, "being a terrible mentor," at which point I managed, "C'mon Dad, it wasn't that bad."

"You don't have to say that, son," my father countered. "But thank you just the same. I appreciate it." He then manufactured a sheepish smile, though it wasn't enough to mask the pain on his face.

"Alright, so how about you be a mentor now?" I suddenly posed, the pop in my tone taking a swipe at his despondency. I then proceeded to explain the Patricia Stevens dilemma, disguising the particulars, and their relevance, as a hypothetical. Once finished, my father settled back in his chair, folded his arms, and said, "Many years ago I had a client... went by the name of Bernie Singer."

He went by the name of Bernie Singer, unless, as my father was quick to point out, he traveled to Huntsman, Indiana, where he was known as, Gordon Block.

An avid reader, sportsman, and friend to the arts, Bernie Singer made his fortune building roads and bridges throughout Michigan and the upper Midwest. He met his first wife, Joan, soon after graduating from Foster College, where he received degrees in both engineering and accounting. Four years, and two kids later, they were living in a stylish ranch with a walkout and swimming pool. But that only lasted until Bernie could piece together the money for a five-bedroom, six-bath house on the shores of Lake Claret in the fashionable confines of Glacier Pointe, an exclusive, blue-blooded community twenty minutes north, yet a lifetime away, from Detroit Proper. And from there, Bernie never looked back. But as his children grew and his home life blossomed, so too did his need for something else.

"Further expansion?" my father had asked him at the time. No, Bernie's company had already become a regional powerhouse, and that was big enough to suit him. Besides, he was traveling two weeks a month on business as it was. Any more would be too hard on his family.

"Real Estate?" No, Bernie had invested in enough apartment complexes.

"Something with the Arts?" No, apparently Bernie's annual donations were as close as he wanted to get to artists.

"A restaurant, or a chain of restaurants, perhaps?" Perhaps, if it was the only type of business left on earth.

"Then what? Surely there's something out there that interests you?"

What interested Bernie Singer, it turns out, was located in Huntsman, Indiana, a small town that separated Bernie from his home in Michigan and his annual Grouse hunting trip in Spokane, Illinois.

Her name was Helen Tilson and she ran the very gas station Bernie pulled into after his chartered flight was forced to make an emergency landing some 40 minutes after takeoff, leaving Bernie with a simple choice: return to Michigan, or rent a car and drive the rest of the way to Spokane. Bernie decided on the latter, a choice reaffirmed the instant he saw Helen behind the gas station counter. Twelve years younger than his wife, Joan, and 250 miles newer, Bernie sensed she was also refreshingly gullible, having convinced her in no time that his name was Gordon Block, he was an auditor for British Petroleum (traveling two weeks a month on average), and she was singlehandedly the most beautiful woman he had ever laid eyes on, a compliment which served as the first step to a brand new family.

Fast forward ten years, and Bernie, i.e., Gordon, died in his sleep while at home in Huntsman, Indiana, leaving behind his wife, Helen, and their two young children. As instructed by her husband years earlier, Helen contacted Gordon's attorney, one, Arthur Rivers, who promptly requested further identification since he didn't know what to make of the situation. Any confusion dissipated, however, once Helen sent him an 8x10 glossy of her late husband. The long and short of it, my father had the unenviable task of notifying Joan Singer her husband had died. And by the way, he left behind another family because he was leading a double life.

My father's unenviable task didn't end there, however, as dear old dad was also charged with administering Bernie's estate, since Bernie never changed the will dad's firm originally drafted. And therein was the dilemma. Arthur Rivers, as executor, had the discretion to include beneficiaries if he reasonably concluded they were entitled to a share of Bernie's assets. On the other hand, he could follow Bernie's last will and testament to the letter and only include those beneficiaries specifically identified.

Dad's initial reaction was to include Helen and her two kids because Bernie never gifted them any money to speak of, and Joan and her children already had more than they could spend in a lifetime. But Joan, and her eldest son in particular, vehemently objected to the notion, and since Bernie's company was still a valued client of the old man's firm, the old man quickly acquiesced to their wishes.

"It's a decision I've regretted ever since," my father concluded. "I let greed get the best of me all because the Singer family let greed get the best of them."

"Or anger," I tossed in.

"Or anger," he conceded. "The point is, though, I should've followed my instincts."

"So is that the moral of the story?" I queried.

"In a word, yes."

"That's a long way to go just to tell me to follow my instincts," I joked.

My father laughed, before responding, "I know, but in the grand scheme of things, it's the truth, son. Because good instincts, like you have... they won't let you down."

Before we parted company for the night, my dad left me with a wink, and the words, "And don't worry, I won't tell Ethan about this Patricia Stevens woman of yours," a statement which brought home another moral to the story. I guess I could confide in the old man after all.

# CHAPTER 16

M y mother opened the front door, her haughty glare promptly refueling my angst in meeting her, and then abruptly turned and walked away, skimming over marble floors as though Lady Tremaine shimmering through the halls of her castle, before disappearing around the corner, where I begrudgingly followed after her until we landed in the kitchen.

"Sit," she said, her tone befitting a mother scolding a five-year-old.

"That's okay, I'm not going to be here that long."

"What does that mean?" Evelyn asked, the light in her eyes muted under the weight of the dimly lit room.

"It means, I'm not going to be here that long."

Evelyn smirked, saying, "No one likes a smart-ass."

"Is it possible to have at least the pretense of a civil conversation?" I asked, my words couched in the embrace of a beleaguered sigh.

"I suppose that depends on you," Evelyn returned, along with her own beleaguered sigh.

The two of us then stared at one another for several long and restless moments – my Mother in all of her overbearing glory, and me, the unfortunate overborne, before I finally said, "What you're doing is just plain wrong."

"And what is it you think I'm doing?" Evelyn promptly countered.

"Where would you like me to begin?" I asked. I then tossed my palms upward, and added, "The divorce, Dad, the law firm, your new boy-toy? Pick a spot, Mother, and I'll dig in."

"I've got a better idea," Evelyn snapped. "How about if you just mind your own damn business!"

"News flash, Mother," I shot back, abruptly pulling a stool out of the way so I could lean against the kitchen island, "it is my damn business… literally. I worked long and hard for it, and I'll be goddamned if you're going to take away what I've made." I then flashed a cautionary finger, and added, "It's not going to happen."

Evelyn sneered, saying, "Get off your high horse, Ethan. You didn't make anything. Your father's firm… that's right, your father's firm… it existed long before you. And I helped him make the place prosper. And now I want my due."

"Yes, it started as my father's firm, but face facts, mother," I said, tapping my finger against the island countertop, "I made the firm a juggernaut. Was it successful before me? Sure, but it wasn't a player until I got there. I turned it into a beast, and I became the face of that beast… like it, or not."

"Oh you poor, poor, thing," Evelyn said, her smugness giving way to a sardonic grin. "Baby boy's not going to get his way, and he can't stand the thought."

"Spare me the bullshit, Mother."

"I'll do nothing of the kind," Evelyn returned, and just like that, the sardonic grin disappeared behind her clouds of darkness – first, the menacing glow of disapproval, followed by the obstinate scorn of ridicule, until finally, the cryptic glare of punishment. From the time I was a boy, my mother would throw each one at me in succession, letting them hover over me until I was overwhelmed by immense sadness and guilt, causing me, in turn, to acquiesce to whatever demands she had at the time.

That was a long time ago, however. Now the thought of being shamed or browbeaten by Evelyn, although morbidly profound, was a distant memory. As such, I nonchalantly shrugged my shoulders at the thought, and said, "Think what you want, do what you want, I don't care. You're not getting control of the firm."

"You know, you surprise me, Ethan," Evelyn said, her rigid tone having softened. "I mean, you were always such a self-absorbed child. I guess I just never realized how much you still are. Then again, maybe that's why you're so driven. And maybe it's that drive that has you so convinced the law firm is yours, and yours alone."

"Listen," I began, "I don't deny the fact you've earned the right to collect money from dad as a result of your many years of marriage. But shares in the firm? Control of my livelihood? That's just plain crazy."

"I see. So you think your business, your livelihood, is more important than my happiness. Is that what I'm to believe?"

"Happiness is one thing, Mother. Letting some used car salesman of an attorney talk you into making a play for something that isn't yours to grab, is quite another."

Evelyn remained poised in her demeanor. In fact, after she cupped her hands together and gazed upon the kitchen window, her body appeared to harden, and for a moment she radiated the well-appointed elegance of a Saks Fifth Avenue showcase mannequin. It was only when she opened her mouth, and spewed, "Did your father put you up to this?" that the elegance disappeared.

"What the hell are you talking about?"

"It's not beneath him, you know," Evelyn said, her gaze still fixed upon the window. "I expected this type of behavior from him all along. I just didn't think you, of all people, would go along with it. Your brother, maybe. But you? Never."

"Go along with what?" I asked, shrugging my shoulders.

Evelyn turned my way. "Try not to look so aggravated, Ethan. It's unbecoming. And don't play dumb either," she advised. "It doesn't suit you. Your father, the kind and caring, Arthur Rivers, is going to pit his sons against their mother, all in an effort to get me to give in to his unreasonable demands. Now do you think that's right, pitting sons against a mother? Pitting you against me?"

After asking my mother where on earth she came up with such a misguided scenario, I was not surprised to hear the name, Connor Banks, take front and center. He was, to hear her tell it, a successful lawyer and businessman (notwithstanding the exact opposite to be true), a charitable soul (even though he didn't have two nickels to donate), a wonderful communicator (which simply meant he was smart enough to tell my mother whatever she wanted to hear), and an otherwise kindred spirit who had brought excitement back into her life (and embarrassment into mine).

"If anything is beneath anyone, Evelyn, it's you believing that Connor Banks is actually interested in something besides your money, or the power and prestige that go along with it."

"You don't know anything about it," Evelyn bristled, her hand shooing away my words as if they had wings. "And you don't know anything about him either. For your information, though, he makes me very happy, whether you like it, or not. And that goes for your brother and father too."

"Yeah, I'll make sure to tell them," I deadpanned.

"What you do is your concern, Ethan. And what I do is mine."

"Give me a break," I said. Then dipping my head to massage the bridge of my nose, I added, "Don't be surprised if your boyfriend just up and disappears."

"What did you just say?"

I slowly looked up and then repeated myself, to which my mother responded, "Is that some sort of threat?"

"You're getting a bit melodramatic, Mother."

"Yes, but I know you, Ethan, and that sounded like a threat."

"What I meant, Mother," I began, after rolling my eyes, "is that he, Connor Banks, will take from you whatever he can get. And when he can't get anymore, he'll leave." Then snapping my fingers, I added, "Poof! Just like that."

My mother suddenly tilted her head to the side, and smiled at me, warmly, wistfully. "We used to be so close, you and I," she mused.

"I know Mother," I said, my eyes finding their way to the kitchen floor. "But things change. I have my own family now."

"Two beautiful children, I might add," Evelyn said.

I glanced up, saying, "Not to mention a beautiful wife."

"Any woman with any sense would be jealous," Evelyn promptly noted.

"She takes good care of me and the kids, Mother."

Evelyn gazed at me for several seconds, though her face remained void of expression, so I finally said, "What's up, Mother? Where are you?"

"God, I remember the first time I held you in my arms," she replied, her voice barely above a whisper. "I knew right then you were going to be something special. And now look at you... my beautiful boy turned into a beautiful man."

I nodded, saying, "Thank you Mother, but let's not take a trip down memory lane."

"It wasn't like that with your brother. With Andrew, I don't know, I guess I'd just always get my fill of him rather quickly. But not you. You were the one everyone else wanted to be around. From the time you were a boy other kids gravitated to you. I did too. You were always very special." Evelyn then offered me a sheepish grin, before saying, "You still are."

"Thanks, that's kind of you to say," I replied, after a long and arduous sigh. "But really, I think we're getting off track here."

Evelyn moved to my side of the kitchen island, where she stood with outstretched arms and open palms, an obvious invitation for me to take her hands. When I made no effort to accommodate her, however, she said, "So now my son won't even take hold of my hands? Is this where we're headed, Ethan?"

I said nothing, yet inched my way closer where, once within reach, I took her palms in mine.

"Can you at least look at me?" Evelyn asked.

"Of course," I said, as I peeled my eyes away from the wall and placed them squarely on hers.

"Now then, you mustn't let this divorce get between us, son," Evelyn said, the look in her eyes as conciliatory as the tone of her voice.

"I understand," I said, as my eyes drifted back to the wall, before landing on the floor. Seconds later I looked up to add, "But there are consequences to what you're doing, Mother."

"My sweet boy, I'm not asking you to agree with what I'm doing, or to even understand it. All I'm asking is that you give me the benefit of the doubt. Just like you used to."

I suddenly jerked my hands away. "This is just another one of your ill-conceived charades," I said, and as the words left my mouth, the contempt in my tone, not to mention my expression, was obvious. "Now whether you know it or not... whether you even give a shit, or not, I've been giving your mindless charades the benefit of the doubt my entire life. But I can't do that anymore. I won't do it anymore. I've got too much at stake."

Evelyn's eyes suddenly narrowed, her jawbone grew taut, and her expression dark, as though a shadow had come to rest upon it. "You have no idea what's at stake if you take your father's side against mine," she cautioned. "No idea whatsoever."

Minutes later I was back in my Mercedes, uncertain what she meant, uncertain where I was headed.

# Chapter 17

*There are seasons in a man's life that both pass and never pass, for they end at the same moment in time.*

I once read that sentence somewhere, but I no more remember the author who wrote it, than I do the book it was in. The truth is, I never even understood what it meant. And then my father suddenly passed away, and it's meaning became both poignant and crystal clear, for the season that took his life is the very memory that will continue in mine.

Although it's fair to say there is no good time to be given news about a loved one's death, receiving word about my father on the heels of our recent dinner seemed particularly harsh. I was in the circuit court cafeteria, which is little more than a brightly lit basement with bad food and cheap furniture to sit at while eating it, when my secretary came looking for me. She didn't know why, saying only that, "Mickey asked me to come find you. She needs to see you in her office."

I assumed Mickey's request was work related, and even thought it may've had something to do with Patricia Stevens, as I had recently reached out to the lead prosecutor in Provo, Utah. Unfortunately, I was wrong on both accounts, because after I closed Mickey's office door, she peered at me, her expression all but abandoned, save for the somber look in her eyes, and said, "I'm sorry to have to tell you this, honey, but your father... something's happened. He's umm... he's passed away."

117

I don't remember my immediate reaction after hearing those words – not how I looked, how I responded, or how long I stood in stunned silence. The truth is, it was only when Mickey and I embraced and I could feel her fingers burrow into my back as I wrestled to keep from sobbing, that I managed to whisper, "What happened?"

After Mickey sat me down, she kneeled in front of me (our eyes and fingers locked together), and quietly said, "Arthur collapsed in his office. He had a heart attack. They tried to reach you on your cell. When they couldn't, they called the office. Whoever called was apparently frantic because they couldn't find you. So I took the call, not knowing what it was about."

"I left my phone in my office," I muttered.

Mickey squeezed my hands, saying, "He loved you. You know that, right?"

"Where is he?" I asked, the words stumbling over the catch in my throat.

"EMS took him to Detroit Kettering Hospital."

"I've got to go," I said, though I made no effort to move until Mickey squeezed my hands again, triggering a beleaguered sigh, at which point I slowly stood.

"Do you want me to go with you?" Mickey asked, as she moved away from the chair.

I simply shook my head and then pushed myself toward the door, my eyes welling with tears, when she repeated, "He loved you, Drew. You know that, right?"

After arriving at the hospital, an attendant led me to a curtained triage section in the emergency room. "This is Mr. Rivers' son," he said to the nurse stationed outside the curtain.

"I'm very sorry for your loss," the nurse offered, her demeanor sincere, though robotic.

"Is he...?" I asked, tipping my head toward the curtain.

"Yes. Take all the time you need," she replied, pulling the curtain open and then stepping aside so I might enter.

And there Arthur Rivers slept: well-known lawyer, community leader, friend to many, enemy to so very few, and my father... now so very gone. I felt an onslaught of emotions, a barrage of thoughts, and not a single clue how to express any of them adequately. So I simply cupped my hand over his, and said, "I just wish we'd had more time, Dad," whereupon I quietly wept, my tears falling like silent raindrops.

I can't pinpoint when Ethan showed up exactly – it could've been five minutes later, it could've been fifty. Either way, I was standing beside my father's lifeless body when the curtain was pulled to the side and my brother walked in, his unsettled appearance a rare sight.

"Hey," he offered.

"Hey," I returned, my voice, like Ethan's, just north of a whisper. We then shared an obligatory hug before I stepped outside the room to give Ethan some time alone with our father.

A short time later, he emerged, instantly scanning the surrounding area, which lead me to say, "She's not here."

Ethan looked my way. "You okay?"

I shrugged, and said, "As good as I can be. You?"

Ethan nodded. Then, "You think she'll show?"

"You know her far better than I do," I returned.

Ethan sighed, before saying, "C'mon, let's get out of here. We'll leave the paperwork to her." When I appeared hesitant, Ethan added, "She put him here, Andrew. The least she can do is get him out." He then turned and headed down the corridor, a lonely figure.

After taking one last look at the curtained space that held my father's body, I followed suit, and it wasn't long before my lonely figure was walking step for step with my brother's.

When we reached the outside we were met by a dreary gray sky and a penetrating December chill – a barren setting somehow appropriate for our silence, not to mention the day's ugliness. "We'll talk about funeral arrangements later," Ethan said, once his Mercedes came into view. "Right now, I've got a few things to take care of."

I grasped Ethan's arm and stopped walking. When he turned and faced me, I said, "She's gonna get what she wants now, Ethan. Just like if they never divorced. Something about that doesn't seem right."

Ethan scanned the cars separating him from his own. A few moments later his eyes settled back on mine, and he said, "You leave Evelyn to me. I'll make sure justice is served."

"What does that mean?" I asked, hunching up my shoulders as the wind kicked up.

"People often change their estate plans when divorce is contemplated," Ethan replied. He then looked away, as though lost between today and tomorrow. But I knew better.

Ethan wasn't lost. Ethan was scheming.

# Chapter 18

I did not become visibly shaken until I told my wife, Olivia, about my father's untimely passing. Perhaps it was hearing her cry on the other end of the phone – perhaps it was the thought of Olivia explaining to our children their grandfather had died – perhaps it was nothing more than the sudden realization I would never see the man, I called my father, again. Whatever the reason, as soon as our conversation ended, I pulled my car to the side of the road and took several deep breaths in an effort to quell my anxiety.

My original intent had been to leave the hospital and head directly back to the office so I could announce the death of my father. The thought of some disenfranchised paralegal or secretary passing along the news did not seem sufficiently dignified for a man of Arthur Rivers' stature. With my sudden and unforeseen ability to speak, however, much less make a fitting announcement, I spent close to an hour processing the somber state of events and the gnawing void it had left in the pit of my stomach. As a result, by the time I pulled my car into the office parking lot, I was certain the tragic news had already spread like wild fire.

Less certain was whether my mother had been notified, and if so, her reaction. I suppose I was going to have to speak with her at some point, but after our last conversation I was in no hurry to pick up the telephone, regardless of the circumstances. Besides, my instincts told me that if she hadn't already been contacted, she would be in the foreseeable future. That would mean, in turn, that she would soon be advised by her ill-advised attorney, and boyfriend, Connor Banks, that she will get from my father's estate what she has been seeking all along, assuming, of course, I allow the unconscionable to actually occur.

After making my way through the solemn hallways of the law firm, dutifully nodding my head to anyone who offered me a word, I entered the confines of my office, whereupon I promptly closed the door, threw my suit coat on the nearest piece of furniture, loosened my tie, and then poured myself a scotch, suddenly wondering where Andrew had gone after I left him standing in the hospital parking lot.

Some twenty minutes later I found out, when my secretary's voice broke over the intercom, "Ethan, your brother is on the phone."

I steadied myself with a deep breath, before picking up the receiver. "Hey," I said quietly.

"I tried your cell," Andrew returned. "Couldn't get through."

I nodded, and said, "I figured people would start calling nonstop, which would've driven me nuts. So I turned the damn thing off."

After a moment or two of silence, Andrew said, "Olivia called to invite me over tonight. I appreciate it, I really do. But if you don't mind, I think I'm gonna pass, big brother. Think I'm gonna stick around here, have another drink or two, and then head back home."

"Where are you?"

"The Towne Pub."

"You okay?"

"Yeah, I'm fine. Just not feeling very sociable."

"I understand," I said. Then, "Are you going to see your girlfriend?"

"Maybe... no... I don't know," Andrew replied. "At the moment, all I keep thinking about is Eugene O'Neal."

"The playwright?" I asked.

"Long Day's Journey Into Night," Andrew said, his voice weary. "A perfect description for today."

I promptly swallowed some scotch, the raw blend of smoke and honey easing the sudden lump in my throat. Yet, I remained silent.

"You still there, Ethan?"

"You going to be okay getting home?"

"As long as I can walk, I'll be fine," Andrew said. He then abruptly laughed, before adding, "really, it's fine. I'll be fine."

I nodded my head, and said, "Okay, I'll tell Olivia. But if you change your mind, just head on over. I'm sure the kids would like to see you."

"Yeah, okay. Thanks," Andrew said, his voice quickly tailing off.

My father's funeral took place in the warm embrace of the White Chapel Cemetery, a small but elegant building otherwise surrounded by the bleak, yet somehow fitting gray of December's wintry grasp. The attending crowd was also small, what with only immediate family (sans my mother), and my father's closest friends and the firm's partners invited.

A much larger gathering filled the Barrington Hotel Banquet Room, as a luncheon was held in honor of my father later that afternoon. And though incessant palm pressing and nonsensical small talk with attorneys, local politicians, business dignitaries, clients (past and present), the firm's employees, as well as a bevy of family and friends, proved to be a surreal haze of commotion, it was only when I saw my mother and Connor Banks walking toward me that my clarity was restored.

"What's he doing here?" I asked, my eyes firmly entrenched on my mother.

"He's my guest," Evelyn declared.

"You weren't invited with a guest, Mother."

"I've come to pay my respects," Connor Banks interjected.

"You'll be lucky if they don't carry you out on a gurney," I replied, though my ardent glare never left my mother's side.

"Now is not the time for that kind of attitude," Evelyn remarked.

"What's going on?" Andrew said, as he came up behind me. "What's he doing here, Mother? And why are you here with him?"

"He's my guest, Andrew, and that's that."

I could feel Andrew glance my way, so I subtly nodded my head, and said, "Ya know what? It's okay, Andrew. Let Mother and her joke of a boyfriend parade themselves around. She's earned it."

Evelyn scowled. "And just what the hell does that mean?"

I smiled, before replying, "It means, quite frankly, that no matter what else, Mother, you always had me convinced you were a sophisticated lady. Now I realize just how full of shit you always were."

"Hey, hey, go easy partner."

Andrew glared at Connor Banks, and said, "Or what?"

The question was not met with a reply. In fact, Connor Banks promptly took my mother by the arm and lead her away, where they quickly disappeared inside the extensive crowd, leaving Andrew and I to share a drink we probably should've had after leaving the hospital a few days before.

It was approximately 7:30 at night by the time me, Olivia, and the kids returned home. Fortunately, the kids were tired to the point all Olivia had to do was tell them to head upstairs, leaving the two of us in the cradle of our own thoughts and emotions.

"Can I get you anything?" Olivia asked, after I dropped my body onto the sofa.

"No, I'm good," I said. "But thanks." Then just as Olivia turned her statuesque frame to walk out of the room, I said, "Tell me something."

"What's that?" she said, while turning back toward me, her radiant blue eyes literally jumping under the glare of the living-room lights. "How was it for you when your father died?"

Olivia pondered the question a few moments, before responding, "It was hard, honey. For sure it was hard. But don't forget, my parents divorced when I was ten, so I didn't see my father but a few times a year after that. And even then, it seemed like it was more by requirement than design. It was much harder when my mother passed away," she concluded.

"How so?"

Olivia secured her long, dark hair behind her ears, and then smiled wistfully, saying, "I just felt alone and vulnerable. And not that you feel vulnerable, but I think you're beginning to understand the emptiness that goes along with the loss. It's a terrible feeling."

I stared at my wife in silence, and though lost in her words, I could still comprehend the measure of her beauty. Finally, I said, "I get it," at which point she turned and walked out of the room.

A few minutes later, she returned, however, saying, "Ethan, have you noticed a black limousine parked in front of the house? This is the third night in a row that I've seen it."

I shook my head, and replied, "Frankly, with all that's been going on, I haven't noticed who's parked on the street. Is it out there right now?"

Olivia nodded, prompting me, in turn, to go see what she was talking about. And sure enough, in the obscurity of nightfall I could see a limousine parked at the end of our long, circular drive.

"Who do you think it is?" Olivia asked.

"Not quite sure," I replied, still looking through the window. "Though I have a feeling it has something to do with an old client of mine."

"Should I call the police?" Olivia queried.

"No. In fact, I'm going to walk down there now and see what's going on." Then, over the concerned objections of my wife, I opened the front door and began my march down the driveway. When I was close enough to spit on the window, however, the limousine's headlights suddenly came on, and the car sped way, though not before I was able to make out the grimy face of Frank Marino, which meant Anthony Ricci was probably watching me from the backseat.

# CHAPTER 19

Ever since my father's death, two things became abundantly clear. Ethan would not give an inch to my mother regarding her purported interest in my late father's estate (and in particular his equity stake in the law firm), and my mother was not going to take it lying down. As such, once Ethan produced copies of my father's will and trust, which, on their face, excluded Evelyn Rivers from anything beyond the marital home, my mother filed a lawsuit against the estate, and the estate's executor (my brother), alleging, among other indiscretions, fraud and misrepresentation. Suffice it to say, an all out probate battle was in the works.

On another front, a trial date had finally been set in the Chestnut Hills rape case. As a result, I would be aligned with my brother on the one hand, but adversaries with him on the other – strange circumstances on a good day, a little too strange on a bad. The situation didn't go unnoticed as far as Mickey was concerned either. That's because her ass was on the line anytime the county prosecutors were involved in even the appearance of impropriety. And since I was playing on both sides of the fence, so to speak, Mickey had no choice but to decide whether to replace me on the Chestnut Hills case. Of course, she wouldn't do so without discussing it with me first, so when she said, "How 'bout I buy you dinner tonight?" I had a hunch where our conversation might be headed. Then again, since it was probably time to bring Mickey in on the Patricia Stevens, Utah connection, the conversation was likely going to spin off in that direction as well.

Either way, I hadn't had a night out since my father's funeral, so the thought of dinner was a welcomed idea, prompting me to respond, "How about 7:30 at *Max's Prime*? On me."

"What's the occasion?" Mickey asked with a smile.

"I dunno… guess I'm just in the mood for a steak and a bottle of red. Sound good?"

"Sounds perfect," Mickey replied, followed by, "but I'm gonna have to meet you there, and I might be a couple minutes late. I have that fundraiser I have to make an appearance at first."

"Not a problem," I returned. "I'll see you at the bar."

What were the odds I'd get home at 6:00 p.m., ride the elevator up to the fifth floor, take a shower, change clothes, toss back a quick beer, and head back out by 7:00, only to find the elevator suddenly out of service? And if that wasn't bad enough, what were the odds I'd make it all the way down to the second floor landing when the lights momentarily flickered, before dying out for good, sending the stairwell into complete darkness? Needless to say, that's exactly what happened, prompting me to reach for my cell phone… which I then dropped, upon hearing, "Hi there, lawyer-boy."

I turned and scanned the stairs behind me, but couldn't see a damn thing, when another voice from the steps below, grumbled, "What's the matter, cat got your tongue, lawyer-boy?"

The last time that question was hurled at me was in high school. Tom Brewster, a two-time senior, who looked upon himself as the toughest kid in school, was also of the mind that you couldn't approach his girlfriend without first getting his permission. Therefore, when she dropped her books in the hallway one day, apparently I wasn't supposed to help her pick them up without Brewster signing off on the deal, let alone engage her in friendly conversation. It also didn't help when he walked up behind me, asked what the hell I was doing, and I ignored him.

Now here's the thing: I don't recall Brewster being particularly bright (ergo his recurring status as a senior). What I do recall is that he liked to brag about his tough upbringing, his history of fighting, his boxing and karate skills… anything to make someone else think twice about standing up to him.

But here's the other thing: I grew up playing organized hockey, and was still playing in high school, so I had tangled with lots of self-proclaimed tough guys. And the tougher they acted, the more chicken-shit, it turned out, they were. As such, when Brewster spun me around because I hadn't replied, only to say, "What's the matter, cat got your tongue?" I drilled him chin high, dropping him in the hallway like a bad habit.

Unfortunately, I wasn't back in high school and Tom Brewster wasn't challenging me. No sir, I was standing in the blacked-out stairwell of my apartment complex, when a raspy tone cut through the darkness, and said, "Apparently lawyer-boy's got nothin' to say."

Boy, was he ever right. In fact, beyond getting the hell out of there, I wasn't thinking at all. Rather, I went into head-down/ass-up mode and charged forward, burying my shoulder into the guy below until we both tumbled down one too many concrete steps. As luck would have it, though, I had the misfortune of landing at the feet of a third accomplice, who promptly said, "Hi there, lawyer-boy," before kissing me with, what turned out to be, a 2x4.

The next thing I know I'm lying in a hospital bed, a bruised and battered mess, with Mickey sitting beside me, feeding me a mix of shaved ice and tidbits of my night out. Apparently I had made it into the parking garage where a fellow tenant found me lying flat on my back talking nonsense and spitting blood. Turns out, the elevator had not been out of service after all, which would indicate it was merely a ploy to get me into the stairwell. The question is why, and by whom? Was it someone from my past… someone I had prosecuted? Maybe someone from a case I was presently working on… someone associated with Sonny Marx. Maybe someone was using me to get to Mickey… someone who didn't like her politics. Better yet, maybe her soon to be ex-husband hired some goons to send me a message… as in, *stay away from my wife.* By the same token, maybe someone was lashing out at me because of something Ethan did, or even my father. Maybe it had something to do with my mother, and that crooked lawyer of hers, Connor Banks. Lord knows that scumbag's not beyond reproach, especially since he knows I'm on Ethan's side in the probate fiasco.

Then again, maybe it was a general assault on all the county prosecutors, and I was just made the first example – the gist being, no one in our office is safe. At least that scenario had some history to it. In fact, it was just a few years ago when three of our prosecutors were attacked in separate incidences, yet all at the behest of one, Redbone Rick.

Richard Ellis Harrison, better known as Redbone Rick, was half white, half Native American, and one-hundred-percent responsible for operating the largest drug ring in the Midwest, with his principle place of business falling within the jurisdiction of Miles County... my county. He began selling drugs at the ripe old age of fourteen, but as he got older, his body grew to an intimidating size, and his balls, and reckless abandon, followed suit. As a result, Redbone never flew under the radar. Redbone never even tried to fly under the radar, content, instead, to squash whatever stood between him and what he was after. In most cases it was the almighty dollar. In other cases, however, it was either retribution or intimidation, which is where my office personnel come into play.

No one thought much of the first attack, or even the second attack, for that matter, beyond, of course, feeling bad the two people were harmed at all. It was the third attack when the proverbial light bulb went on, so to speak, and the realization set in that Redbone was sending a message our way – that being, 'Don't prosecute me, and I won't come after you. Fuck with me, however, and spend the rest of your life looking over your collective shoulders. You may not see me on Monday, you may not see me on Tuesday, but one day, sooner or later, I'll be there, and you won't like what you see.'

The message certainly wasn't taken lightly, and yet, the matter never escalated further, as Redbone Rick was found dead a short time later in some backstreet alley of Detroit.

Yeah, well, Redbone Rick notwithstanding, I still had to digest the fact that whoever was behind my attack knew I was a lawyer, knew where to find me, and knew how to inflict just enough of a beating to get my attention, but not enough to cause serious injury.

In fact, beyond a handful of facial lacerations, which required a handful of medical glue to close up, some badly bruised ribs, which would explain the uncomfortable compression in my bandaged midsection, and, what doctors deemed a slight concussion, which would explain the dull pounding in my head, I was okay.

Still, when the nurse walked in the room to let me know I was being discharged, but first asked how I was feeling, I couldn't help but say, "Like someone took a 2x4 to my head."

"That's not funny," Mickey responded. She then squeezed my hand, before saying to the nurse, "Believe me, he's fine."

I spent the following week in Mickey's bed, which, beyond convalescing, wasn't all that unusual, given that we slept together most nights. In an effort to help with my recovery, Mickey took the time off from work as well, and though I certainly welcomed her company, she seemed curiously pensive – by week's end, even somewhat subdued.

So finally I just asked, "Is everything okay, babe? You seem preoccupied in thought."

Mickey didn't respond right away, and instead, settled her eyes on the second story window, likely gazing at everything and nothing simultaneously. Several moments passed before she turned back my way, and said, the timidity in her voice a reflection of the look in her eyes, "I need to find my husband."

"What... what are you talking about?" I asked warily. I then sat up in the recliner, and for the first time in days, winced instead of grunted.

"I need to find my husband," Mickey repeated, her tone a bit more resolute. "So I can finally divorce him."

I started to take a deep breath, but a sharp pinch in my ribs convinced me otherwise, so I simply shrugged my shoulders, and asked, "Don't take this the wrong way, but why all of the sudden now?"

Mickey stammered nervously, looking at me, then the floor... me, then the floor... me, then the floor.

"Babe?"

Mickey looked at me. "Because, seeing you in the hospital... seeing you hurt... I just want to marry you, okay?"

My immediate reaction was one of utter surprise, but there was no way Mickey could tell given that I stared at her in stoic silence. In fact, it wasn't until she put her hands on her hips, and urged me to, "Say something, damn-it," that I managed, "Wow, okay."

Mickey hunched up her slender shoulders, and scowled. "That's what you have to say... wow, okay?"

"No... god no," I countered, as though jolted back to the moment. "That was about the last thing I expected to hear from you. So it took me by surprise, that's all." I then waited for Mickey's expression to soften to the warmth I had come to expect whenever I looked into her eyes, at which point, I added, "Babe, if you would have been divorced in our first week of going out, then I would've married you in our second. Does that about cover it?"

Yep, that about covered it, because after another word here, and a tear or two there, Mickey was on the phone with Russ Gary, one of the private investigators our office employs in cases involving missing persons. The call ended with, "Just find him as soon as you can," whereupon Mickey looked at me, and said, "I guess I can do a little research on divorces in absentia. What do you think?"

I nodded my head a few seconds, and then replied, "I think I want to get married by Elvis."

# CHAPTER 20

When Treasury Department Agent, Albert Ness, showed up unannounced at my office a few weeks back, and then proceeded to inform me that photographs were taken of me leaving Judge Beckett's house with a briefcase in each hand (presumably full of Anthony Ricci's payoff money), I brushed it off as just another cheap threat made on behalf of Ricci himself. When I saw Ricci's limousine parked at the bottom of my driveway, however, where, according to my wife, it had made a pit stop for three consecutive nights, the tarnish of a cheap threat had immediately worn off. As a result, I decided it was time to meet with Ricci head-on. Therefore, I placed a call to Albert Ness.

"Counselor, what can I do for you?" Ness asked, after keeping me on hold for a couple of minutes, no doubt by design.

"You free to talk on the phone? Or would you prefer we talk in person?" I queried.

"What's the difference?"

"No difference to me," I said. "I just don't know if you're comfortable discussing certain issues on the telephone."

"What kind of issues would those be, Counselor?"

"C'mon Ness, don't play me. You know exactly what I'm talking about," I responded.

"Hmm, do I?" Ness mused. "Yeah, I suppose I do," he continued, his bloated ego spilling like blood. "You're calling to discuss our mutual acquaintance. How's that for a guess?"

"Bingo." I returned.

"So, what's the problem?" Ness asked.

"I didn't say there was a problem – at least not on my end. I'm just not sure if there's one on yours. After all, you're probably in a small office, maybe even a cubicle, surrounded by more people than you know what to do with. And all the commotion probably makes it difficult to have a sensitive conversation."

"Okay, for your information, I'm not in a small office. That's number one," Ness crowed. "Number two, I have a staff that reports to me, which means, number three, I can talk whenever, and wherever, I damn well please."

"Fine. Then here's the deal. I want you to set a meeting with me, and as you said, our mutual acquaintance."

"He's going to want to know particulars," Ness responded.

"Particulars about what?"

"He's a methodical man," Ness replied. "I've done this sort of thing with him several times in the past. He's going to ask me what the agenda is. That means, I'm going to need some particulars before any meeting is set."

"Methodical man, my ass. This is all about you and your giant ego keeping a foot in the door. But hey, you want to stick your crooked dick in, Ness, then fine. Tell our mutual acquaintance it's about his method of doing business, as in payoffs and threats. Tell him it's about me giving up the location of an old client of mine, or else. Tell him it's about you coming to see me with a bribe. Tell him it's about Judge Beckett found hanging from a rope. Is that enough for you, Ness? If not, then don't set the meeting. And the next time our mutual acquaintance pays me a visit, I'll be sure to tell him, I asked, and you refused."

After a few moments of listening to Ness' staggered breathing, he finally responded with, "Who said I refused?"

"Good. Then set it up for anytime in the next two days. After that, my schedule gets dicey. Got it?"

"I'm listening."

"Make it in a restaurant," I stated. "Any place but Italian. Make it in the middle of the day, close to my office… two, three miles tops. Once set, leave a message with my secretary, Barbra, as to where and when."

"Gee, is that it?" came Ness' caustic reply.

"No, there's actually one more thing. Tell your Mafia boss not to bring his Neanderthal henchman, Frank Marino." I then promptly concluded our conversation by saying, "And now the next sound you hear is…"

After dropping the receiver in its cradle, I removed the digital memory card from my telephone recorder and locked it in my office wall-safe, where it would remain unless I needed to produce evidence of a criminal conspiracy between Treasury Agent, Albert Ness, and reputed mob boss, Anthony Ricci.

Two days later, at precisely 1 p.m., I walked into the *Maple Grille*, a wannabe upscale restaurant dressed in an array of glass, granite, steel and wood, all under an exposed ceiling offering bright, pendulous lights.

Anthony Ricci was seated, as I might've guessed, at a corner table with his back to the wall and a drink in front of him. He didn't stand when I approached. Instead, he gestured his hand toward the other three empty chairs, and directed me to, "Sit."

After peeling off my coat and resting it over the back of one of the empties, I turned and caught the attention of a server, and said, "Glenlevit, rocks. And another for the gentleman."

"I'm fine," Ricci said, waving off my order.

"Another for the gentleman," I repeated, waiting until the server nodded his head, before turning to face Ricci.

"You have a habit of taking liberties, don't you?" Ricci asked, the anger in his dark eyes palpable, notwithstanding his poised demeanor.

Once seated, I replied, "No more than anyone else playing high stakes poker."

Ricci fashioned a wry grin, and then said, "I'm not sure you know what high stakes poker is."

"Different livelihoods, different game," I countered. "But trust me, it's still a game."

Ricci's wry grin promptly disappeared behind a veil of austerity. "You apparently have an answer for everything too," he said. He then picked up his drink, and muttered, "Salute."

"It comes naturally," I replied.

After Ricci drained his glass, he set it on the table, took a deep breath, his tapered shoulders moving up and down slowly, deliberately, and said, "You know why I chose this place to meet?"

Shaking my head, I proffered, "Don't know. Don't really care."

"Because it's trendy," he said. "Figured you had something in common with trendy."

"How enlightening."

"Funny thing about trends, though."

"Yeah? What's that?" I asked.

"They come and they go," Ricci replied.

I ignored the obvious threat, figuring that would bother Ricci more than not, and said, "You know, I underestimated you, Mr. Ricci."

"Yeah? And how is that... Mr. Rivers?"

"Sending Ness to see me. I never saw that one coming."

Ricci tipped his head to the side, and then shrugging his shoulders, said, "Sometimes things come at you when you least expect them."

"You have more like him stashed away?"

Ricci smirked, before saying, "Discussing men like Ness is not why we're here. So why don't we just get to it, eh?"

"I beg to differ," I said.

"What the hell does that mean?" Ricci asked, his cold glare studying my face.

"It means I have a taped conversation between me and Ness." Anthony Ricci didn't so much as blink, so I added, "It'll go a long way in proving the complicity between you and Ness, something I think the United States government would be quite interested in."

For the next few moments silence engulfed the table as our server approached with the drinks I had ordered. After he set them on the table and walked away, Ricci took hold of his, twirled the ice a couple of times, and then asked, "How do I know you're not wired now?"

I took a sip of my drink, before responding, "Because I don't need to be. I've already got Ness. And while it may not be perfect, it's certainly more than enough to cause you plenty of discomfort. And by the way," I added, after tipping my glass toward Ricci, "Salute."

Ricci pushed aside his drink and leaned forward. "You really want to go to war with me?"

I too leaned forward, and replied, "You really want to go to war with the United States government?"

Ricci dropped his gaze on the table and shook his head. Seconds later, he looked up, his eyes narrowing, his jawline tightening, and said, "All I've ever wanted was information leading to the whereabouts of the scumbag who murdered my son."

"Why? It won't bring him back," I offered.

"Because," Ricci declared, as his palm dropped to the table, "He was my son, and it'll bring me closure."

"That may be, Mr. Ricci, but as I've already told you, I don't know his whereabouts."

"I'm not sure I believe that," Ricci said, the words following an impatient sigh. "But even if that was true, I do believe you could find out. And that's what Ness came to see you about. That, and to discuss that little bit of money you took from the judge's house. My money, which I'm willing to gift to you in return for the information."

"I see," I responded, my expression, like my tone, without distinction. "Then why show up at my house with Marino? What was that, a ploy to intimidate me?"

"I don't do ploys, Counselor. I never do ploys," Ricci returned.

"You just make good on your threats, is that it?"

"Recording the conversation was a bad choice on your part," Ricci said, after a few moments of foreboding silence. "It paints me into a corner, where, as you can probably guess, I don't like to be."

"I'm not painting anyone into any corner. I'm simply hedging my bets. But rest assured, if anything happens to me, or my family, that taped conversation will be all the rage."

Anthony Ricci slowly stood, brushed at his lapel as though it had been collecting dust, then glared at me, and said, "Maybe you're bluffing about this tape of yours. Maybe not. Either way, there are a couple, three things you should know. One, I don't back down, regardless of the situation I'm in. Two, I'm not a patient man. And three, what little patience I do have, you've just about used up." Ricci then pointed a finger-gun at me, pulled the imaginary trigger, and whispered, "Poof," at which point, he turned and walked away.

When I returned to my office, the angst from meeting Anthony Ricci still swelling inside me, I had planned to spend the remainder of the afternoon preparing my answers to the various charges my mother filed against me in the wake of my father's passing. And yet, the more I reviewed the allegations, the angrier I turned, for the notion that Evelyn would allow herself to be so unduly influenced by her lawyer, all for the sake of keeping her young boyfriend happy, so he, in turn, would stick around, was, at best, a pathetic display of self-indulgence. So much so, in fact, I felt it necessary to abandon the promise I made to myself, and gave her a call. "Mother, we need to talk," I said, after she picked up the phone.

"I'm not supposed to talk to you. Connor has advised me against it."

"Connor doesn't know a goddamned thing," I stated.

"He knows a lot more than you think," Evelyn returned. "The fact that you refuse to acknowledge it is your problem."

"Mother, listen to me closely," I said, balling my hand into a fist, "because I'm only going to tell you once. You're with a conman. Not a lawyer, not a businessman, just a simple conman."

"We've already had this discussion, Ethan. I'm not having it again."

"Well here's something we haven't discussed. You're an embarrassment, Mother – to yourself and your family. And everyone you know is laughing at you."

"The only one who should feel embarrassed, Ethan, is you, for the way you're trying to cheat me out of your father's estate."

"That's Connor Banks talking."

"No, that's me talking. And no matter what else you say, Ethan, understand this: I'm going to get what I deserve."

I nodded my head, and muttered, "You're going to get what you deserve, alright."

"Be careful who you threaten, Ethan," she remarked tersely. "Don't forget, I know you best."

"Yeah, so what does that mean?" I countered.

At that juncture I could hear my mother's breathing hasten, which also meant the look on her face was simmering with anger. "It means, if you're not careful," she replied, as if pushing the words through clenched teeth, "I just might decide to reveal the indiscretions of your past."

# Chapter 21

"Where the hell have you been? I must've called you three times last week," Ethan barked into the receiver.

"Probably a personal record for you too," I responded.

"Very funny," Ethan said. "So why didn't you return my calls?"

"Because I didn't get your messages. They're likely floating around in cyberspace."

"What are you talking about?"

"I dropped my cellphone last week. It broke, and I haven't had time to replace it. Was hoping to do so in the next couple of days."

"You should've replaced it by now. People, besides me, might want to talk to you."

"Yeah, well, they can call me at work during normal business hours, like you just did. What was the big urgency anyway?"

"I wanted you to sign an affidavit for a motion I'm planning to file against mommy dearest."

"What kind of motion?"

"Just a discovery motion. Her and that jackass lawyer of hers apparently don't think evidentiary rules apply to them. You'll read it before you sign the affidavit. But I want to get the thing filed already, so it'd be nice if you'd move on it."

"Hey, you could've got it to me last week," I asserted. "All you had to do was call my office. They would've told you I was laid up, and to try me at Mickey's. For that matter, you could've sent me an email."

"I could have," Ethan returned, "but I wanted to discuss a couple of things with you anyway."

"Discuss away, I'm listening."

"Wait, why were you laid up?" Ethan asked, as though my assertion finally reached his ears.

"I got jumped by three guys at my apartment complex."

"You're kidding. They rip you off?"

"Nope, not kidding, and nope, they didn't rip me off. It wasn't a random thing. It was planned."

"How do you know?"

After regurgitating the details of that lovely evening for my brother, I concluded with, "But to tell you the truth, I think they could've hurt me a lot more than they did. It seems like they knew where, and just how hard to hit me."

"What makes you think that?"

"Well, considering they could've easily split my head open with a 2x4, and didn't. It just stands to reason."

"Okay, so let's assume that to be the case. Do you know anyone with a motive? Do you or that brain thrust over there have any leads?"

I rolled my brother's questions around for about as long as it took me to roll my eyes, before responding, "So how you feeling, Andrew? Is there anything I can get you, anything I can do for you?" Then, "Why no, Ethan, I'm fine. Don't you worry about me one little iota. But hey, thanks for asking."

"Oh, I see, Mr. Manners wants to play the *oh-woe-is-me* card, is that it?"

"Christ, you could at least ask, Ethan."

"You want me to ask? Fine, I'll ask," Ethan quipped. "So how you feeling, Andrew? Is there anything I can get you, anything I can do for you?"

"You're such an asshole," I said, before covering the receiver so he wouldn't hear me laugh.

"That's certainly the rumor," Ethan returned. "Meanwhile, you didn't answer. Anyone with a motive? Any leads?"

"Nary a one. Truth is, beyond the sound of one of the guy's voices, I've got nothin' to go on."

"Strange was it?"

"Not so much strange. Just deep and raspy... almost smoky-like. I'll remember it if I hear it again."

One thing about Ethan: whenever he shuts down in the middle of a conversation, it's only because something was said to set his wheels in motion. That's been the case for longer than I can remember. The other side of the equation, however, is his propensity to reignite the conversation in an unexpected direction. The instant situation was a prime example, for just as he piped down to sit with his thoughts, he piped back up with the name, "Frank Marino."

"Excuse me?"

"Frank Marino," Ethan repeated.

"Yeah, so, what about him?" I queried.

"The guy with the raspy voice... it was Frank Marino. You've heard of him, haven't you?"

"Of course I've heard of him," I countered.

"So what do you know about him?"

"No, no, no. We're not playing it that way," I stated. "You tell me why you think it was Marino, and we'll go from there."

"I don't think it was Marino," Ethan asserted. "I know it was Marino."

"Okay, and why are you so sure Frank Marino and a couple of his guys singled me out for a little slap dance? What the fuck did I do to deserve his attention in such a way? Or, should I say, what the fuck did you do, Ethan, to make him come at me?"

Once again Ethan disappeared from the conversation, returning seconds later with, "This is something we should discuss in person."

"Why, you think my phone lines are bugged?"

Ethan ignored my sarcasm, and replied, "We do it in person, or not at all."

"Okay, fine. Where and when?"

*Johnny Rogers* was about the last place I would've ever expected to meet my brother. A greasy diner that doubled as a greasy bar, J-R's, as it was otherwise known, was, as far as I knew, far more popular with the breakfast crowd than it was the happy hour crowd.

Whatever. When sundown approached, so did I, finding my brother sitting at the end of the bar, as out of place as an expensive Italian suit on a sales rack in a discount store.

"Great choice," I said, as I pulled out a stool. "You bring the motion and affidavit?"

"They're in the car," Ethan replied. "I'll give them to you when we leave. And for the record, I picked this place because I figured you'd be comfortable here."

I scanned our surroundings before looking back at my brother, and saying, "Bullshit, you picked it because you thought it would be crowded and noisy. You're getting paranoid in your old age."

Ethan gave my face the quick once over. "So, did you have any stitches?" he posed.

"None. They used medical glue… skin glue, whatever, to close me up."

"I don't know, you don't look too much worse for wear."

"Believe me, it was a lot uglier last week. But yeah, for the most part, everything's been healing up pretty well."

"Must be all that good DNA you have."

After I flagged down the bartender and ordered a beer to go with my brother's martini (which, unless Ethan orders another, will likely be the only martini the bar serves the entire day), I said, "As long as I have mother's DNA floating around, there's nothing good about it."

"You have no idea," Ethan muttered, and for a few bleak moments, despair hovered over him like a rain cloud.

I said nothing, however, and instead, stared at my brother's dispirited profile until he willed himself from the squall and turned my may. "So this Marino thing… we need to talk about it."

"I'm listening," I said, which was all the invitation Ethan needed to take the stage. Most of what he bandied about, however, was recycled information, having played out in the local news years ago. Let's see, there was reputed mob boss, Anthony Ricci, his son, David, who was gunned down by

Ethan's former client, Billy Maxwell, and Frank Marino, who was just a no-neck head-buster for the mob. About the only element to the story I had not heard before was that Ricci wanted the whereabouts of Billy Maxwell, which my brother had refused to divulge.

"And I'm not going to tell you either," Ethan said. "But that's for your own good."

"How do you figure that, since they already came after me once?"

"Because, it's just as you said before: if they really wanted to hurt you, Andrew, they could've done a lot more damage. What they did," Ethan suggested... he then wagged his finger at my face... "that was all just a message for me."

I fashioned a half-baked smile, which drew a curious look from Ethan, at which point, I said, "So the old adage, *don't kill the messenger,* is really a misnomer."

"What are you driving at?" Ethan asked, the curiosity in his eyes digging deeper.

"I'm not driving at anything. I'm just saying, according to your logic, the old adage, *don't kill the messenger* really oughta be, *don't kill the messenger, just fuck him up a little bit.*"

Ethan twirled the olive around his martini glass a couple of times, before pulling it out and setting it on a napkin. "If they can't double stuff these things with fresh anchovies, or at least pimentos and blue cheese, they ought to leave them out altogether." He then looked at me just as I took a swig of beer, and said, "That's not what I meant. And frankly, I'm sorry you got caught up in this thing."

"Okay, fine," I said, putting down my mug, "but at least tell me this... your old client, Billy Maxwell... you do know where he is then, don't you?"

Ethan nodded subtly.

"So why don't you just give him up, and be done with Ricci once and for all?"

Ethan inched his martini away from his mouth, but continued staring straight ahead, as though talking directly to the glass, and uttered, "Because I still may need a favor from Billy. He just doesn't know it yet. And it's not anything I'm going to discuss now. What I will say is, Billy paid me a lot of money to help keep him safe in prison – help keep him safe until he could leave the country." Then setting the glass on the counter, Ethan peered at me. "No, that wasn't a slip up on my part," he volunteered. "I figure you were bright enough to make the assumption Billy's out of the country."

"That would've been my guess," I contended.

"I also have a very incriminating conversation involving Ricci," Ethan continued, as though I had said nothing at all. "It's locked away, but Ricci knows it exists – knows if anything happens to me or my family, the recording gets released." Ethan then tipped his head toward me, saying, "Ricci only found out about it a few days back. Your episode with Marino happened what, about ten days ago? Sorry, but that's just bad timing, little brother. Point is, I believe the tape is strong enough to keep Ricci at bay, so I seriously doubt Marino will come back for more."

I dipped my head from side to side, as though balancing the weight of my brother's opinion, when he offered, "There's one more reason."

Indeed, there was one more reason. Yet, it wasn't the reason I knew to exist, anymore than it was the reason Ethan intended to open up about. No sir, according to the scuttlebutt Mickey's had occasion to hear, and share with me, some kind of investigation was going on regarding the untimely death of Judge Richard Beckett, payoffs the judge allegedly received from an unsubstantiated source, otherwise known as Anthony Ricci, and the lawyer who stood between them both... my brother, Ethan Rivers, who no doubt planned to use the situation as leverage against Ricci. But as I said, that wasn't something Ethan was prepared to discuss just yet. Instead, he nonchalantly shrugged his shoulders, and offered his other reason as, "I just don't like other people telling me what to do, Andrew. Ricci included. I had more than my share of that shit growing up with mother."

"Ricci's not mother, Ethan. He's a mafia boss, and a violent, dangerous man."

Ethan looked at me without expression on his face, or enthusiasm in his tone, and said, "Mother makes Ricci look like a saint."

# CHAPTER 22

Simply put, having a conversation with Gene Baxter proves that evolution didn't take with all people. The worst part is, I could've avoided talking to him altogether had I just looked at the number flashing on the screen when my phone went off. Given that I was knee deep in thought on the probate dispute with my parasitic mother, however, I didn't pay it any mind. As a result, I got to hear a day in the life, as told by *Early Man*. Interestingly enough, when Gene finally did shut up, I still wasn't sure if he spoke a complete sentence, or grunted a mouthful of incoherency. The only thing I could say with any degree of certainty... Gene was one seriously angry Cro-Magnon.

"Okay, now that you've got whatever that was out of your system, let's start over," I suggested. "And try and keep the decibel level tolerable, other-wise I'm hanging up."

Once again, Gene rumbled, stumbled and bumbled his way through the English language, but instead of launching into the great unknown, this time he managed to absorb enough oxygen to stay grounded, and say, "Sonny Marx has been sleeping with my wife. I take the no good son-of-a-bitch off the street... I give him a job, money, you name it, and he pays me back by sleeping with my wife."

"How do you know?" I asked, the question jumping out of me like a reflex.

"How do I know?" Gene repeated, his tone simmering. "How do I know?" he asked again, his tone inching higher. "I'll tell you how I know," he shouted seconds later. "Cause I caught 'em in bed together, Ethan! That's how the fuck I know! Is that a good enough reason for ya?!"

"Yep, that'll work," I muttered underneath my breath, followed by a definitive, "Okay, I understand Gene. But if you don't calm down, you're going to have a coronary."

"Calm down, nothin'," Gene growled. "That son-of-a-bitch can rot in hell for all I care. And that trial you're representing him on… the one I've been paying the legal fees… that party's over, starting today. The piece of shit's probably guilty anyway."

"Hold on, hold on, hold on," I countered, as my chair fell forward, leaving me a workable distance from my desk. "Let's not get crazy, Gene. Sonny Marx didn't suddenly rape two women because he's been having an affair with your wife."

"Affair? I didn't say anything about an affair. You think they're having an affair?"

I shrugged my shoulders, and replied, "I just assumed if they were sleeping together Gene, they might be having an affair. They wouldn't be the first."

"Goddamn him, I'll kill the slimy bastard!" Gene snapped, and in that moment I could picture my neighbor sitting in the office of that piece of shit building he calls a bar, spewing threats as fast as his bald head spews sweat.

"You're not going to do anything of the kind," I calmly assured Gene. "What you are going to do is take a step back and look at the bigger picture here. There are consequences to everything you do, Gene. Remember that."

Gene took the next several moments to settle down, a process that not only consisted of resolute, albeit heavy breathing, but one that also emitted the glorious sounds of his wheezing. Finally, he managed, "Yeah, so like what kind of consequences? Because the only consequence I see is that he's gonna have to fend for himself here on out."

"Let's think about that, Gene. What would Sonny's first inclination be if you threw him out on the street? Think he might start squawking about those sex dungeon parties you throw?" Gene's contemplative silence was my invitation to continue, so I followed up with, "What do you think Holly

Robertson would say? Or better yet, her police chief of a husband? Think ol' Pete would be surprised to learn his wife is not just a regular at your parties, but according to you, someone who's skilled with a whip? Think that'll go over well?"

I then reminded Gene about State Senator, and mother of two, Patsy Dunleavy, whose proclivity for blindfolds, leather getups, and gangbangs with African American men, might just upset the bible-belt portion of her constituency (which she drives three hours to get away from just to attend one of his parties). As if the good senator wasn't enough, I then brought up, Father Lucas Perry, who apparently comes to the parties wearing his traditional garb, only to discard it for women's underwear, which, after a little drinking and dancing, he takes off to get tied up and tickled. "Think that'll make the church laugh?" I asked. Before Gene could reply, however, I said, "Then again, what about that ex-NFL football player, Monty Simms, or that college coach… what the hell's his name? Ah, no matter. The point is, if the sex doesn't involve chain bondage, they won't play. And if none of that's enough, how about the local business leaders who frequent your basement just to watch a bunch of strange women play with all those mechanical toys you've got down there?"

"Okay, okay, you've made your point," Gene finally cut in.

"And those are just a few of the things you've told me. Can you imagine all the crap Sonny's been witness to?"

"I said okay, you've made your point," Gene anxiously repeated. He then wheezed what seemed like a never-ending sigh, before adding, "So what do I do?"

"You mean besides going to a doctor for a checkup?"

"What?"

"Nothing," I replied. "You do nothing."

"What do you mean, do nothing? If you think I'm carrying that rat bastard forever, you've got another thing coming," Gene snarled.

"I didn't say forever. Just wait until his trial is over," I countered. "After that I don't care what you do with him."

"Yeah? And how long is that gonna be?"

"We have a trial date about six weeks away. It may get delayed, though, depending on some other stuff I've got going."

"Oh, so the length of my attachment to Sonny depends on your big, bad schedule? Fuck that. Who the hell are you?"

"Then fuck you, Gene. You want to turn him loose, have at it," I said. "Just remember, you're not my client, and we don't have a privileged relationship. Understood?"

"Yeah, but I'm paying the freight," Gene touted.

"Well I wouldn't start pounding my chest just yet," I returned.

"What the hell does that mean?"

"It means, you cut him loose before his trial is over, and I'll tell anyone I goddamn well please all about your little playground. It means you could be ostracized by every one of your neighbors. It means your wife might divorce you because she's too embarrassed to stay married. It means you'd likely lose visitation rights to see your kids, never mind sharing custody. It means the authorities might not be willing to turn a blind eye to your sex parties anymore. It means your bar could shut down, and your other businesses, who knows, they could go down the tubes, as well." I steadied myself with a deep breath, then, "Shall I continue?"

Gene remained silent far longer than it would normally take him to rummage through his inventory of words in search of a response, prompting me to ask, "You still there?"

"You'd do that to me?" he finally posed, his somber tone flirting with disbelief. "You'd really do that to me?"

"Only if I had to," I asserted.

"Jesus, after all the years we've known each other – our wives, our kids. You'd really do that to me?"

"Only if I had to," I reiterated.

"And what if you lose?" Gene asked.

"Lose what?"

"Sonny's rape trial. What if you lose? Am I still prone to you telling people about the bar... my bar?"

"No. It's like I told you, Gene, once the trial is over, I don't care what you do with Sonny. And at the end of the day, I really don't care about your damn bar either. But leverage is leverage, so until the trial is over, you're on notice."

"Then I hope you lose," he said.

"It's certainly possible," I confessed.

"Well I hope it happens. And then I hope you die," Gene stated, his words lingering long after he hung up the phone.

# CHAPTER 23

Before Ethan and I parted ways the other night, I asked how he helped keep Billy Maxwell alive in prison, figuring the answer would really be little more than one of his typically inflated, if not altogether, self-indulged declarations. Still, I was curious enough to ask, to which Ethan surprisingly answered without a hint of pomp or circumstance. He merely said, "If you're that interested, do your homework."

"What does that mean?"

"It means, if you do some research on Knox State Prison, where Billy did his time, and an inmate named Curly Joe Baker, you'll figure it out. And what you can't figure out, you'll let me know then."

Joseph (Curly Joe), Baker was a 6' 4", 250 lb. block of concrete, who was also responsible for singlehandedly killing three armed men with his bare hands. Yet, his story is hardly that simple, or maniacal.

A graduate of Southeastern University with a degree in sociology, Curly Joe was unwittingly cast into the role of guardian at the age of twenty-three when his parents were killed by a drunk driver, and he was left to care for his younger twin sisters, Jaclyn and Juliette. Although his initial plan had been to move directly from college to Washington D.C., where he had been offered a job in the Department of Urban Development, Curly Joe was, nevertheless, forced to scrap that idea, and instead find work in the Detroit vicinity so he could move back into the family home, and his sisters could finish high school.

Finding steady, if not desirable employment, proved difficult, however, and Curly Joe spent almost two years bouncing around before concluding that a job in the field of sociology was not in his future. It was at roughly the same point in time when Curly Joe caught wind of a martial arts competition, with the winner taking home upwards of five thousand dollars. But money wasn't the motivating factor behind his decision to enter. Rather, it was the chance to renew his commitment to a sport that saw him earn a 3$^{rd}$ degree black belt in Jiu Jitsu by the time he was nineteen.

As it turned out, Curly Joe didn't just enter the competition. He breezed through it with such stunning flair, the win reestablished his reputation as a premiere force in the martial arts community, allowing him, in turn, to open, what would become in a short matter of time, the most successful karate dojo in the Detroit metropolitan area.

After his sisters graduated high school (and despite Curly Joe encouraging both to attend college out of state), they enrolled in City College, where they pursued teaching degrees in special education. Along the way, the girls found steady boyfriends (pre-med students Curly Joe would later describe in court as, "Decent little cats"), while Curly Joe found love with Ariel Waters, a woman he would describe in the same court proceeding as, "A magnificent soul," before concluding, "She completed the circle. And for a while we were all happy again – for ourselves, and each other."

Life would take a drastic turn, however, when after a night of pizza and beer, Curly Joe & Ariel would return to the Baker home, while Jaclyn, Juliette, and their boyfriends, would head off for a night of dancing, never to return again. Three armed men would shoot the boyfriends dead, and then take Jaclyn and Juliette to an abandoned farmhouse where they would be mercilessly beaten and raped for days on end, before being tossed into a ditch beside a lonely rural road.

Upon hearing his sister's decimated bodies had been found, Curly Joe walked into his bathroom and shaved his head, preserving only the long ponytail his sisters implored him to grow in the first place. "That's when people started calling me Curly Joe," his court testimony read. "They thought they were being funny. But I didn't care. I didn't even pay it any mind. Walking around with just a ponytail... for me, it was a way to pay homage to my sisters. So was killing the scum who killed them," he asserted; a statement his attorney (my brother, Ethan, it turns out), would later use so brilliantly in his closing argument to drive home Curly Joe's primary defense of temporary insanity.

From everything I've read, however, particularly the trial transcripts, Curly Joe Baker was more concerned with telling his story than he was in having my brother maneuver bits and pieces of it around in order to aid in his defense. In fact, at one point he told the judge, jury, and what I can only assume was a packed courtroom, "Once the police identified the three men as persons of interest, I went head hunting. Not to hurt, or torture them like they did my sisters. Just to kill them for taking my sister's lives, and to make sure they could never harm another person."

"But at the time you confronted these men, you weren't even certain they were guilty of the crime," the prosecutor charged.

"Oh no, I was quite certain," Curly Joe maintained.

"And how was that, Mr. Baker?" the prosecutor asked. "How was that?"

"Because, as soon as the one guy pulled out a gun, I kicked it from his hand, and then snapped his arm. Once he started screaming like there was no tomorrow, the other two started blaming each other. I knew right then."

"I thought you said you didn't torture them?" the prosecutor responded. "You don't call snapping a man's arm in two a form of torture?"

"No sir. I call it snapping a murdering scumbag's arm in two," Curly Joe returned, whereupon my brother stood, and said, "Your Honor, good people of the jury, let the record reflect, forensics has already established the gun pulled on my client was the same gun used to kill the boyfriends of Jaclyn and Juliette Baker. Any reasonable person would therefore conclude they were the same three men who brutally raped the Baker sisters. As to how my client came by the information, and whether his approach was proper... that's wholly irrelevant to these proceedings."

"Is that an objection, Mr. Rivers?"

"Of course it is, Your Honor."

"Then it's sustained. Keep your questions on point," Judge Moreland instructed the prosecutor.

"Will do, Your Honor," the prosecutor replied, followed by, "So tell us, Mr. Baker, how, exactly, did each of these men die by your hand, anyhow?"

"Objection, Your Honor," my brother submitted once more. "My client has never been to medical school. He is not a doctor, has never worked for a doctor, does not perform autopsies, has never assisted in an autopsy, has never witnessed an autopsy, and to my knowledge, has never worked for a medical examiner. Therefore, any conclusions as to how the victims died, is pure speculation on my client's part... not to mention highly inflammatory toward him."

"I agree, Counselor," Judge Moreland said. "This information would be better suited coming from someone in the medical examiner's office."

"I snapped their necks," Curly Joe announced anyway.

"What was that?" the prosecutor asked.

"I snapped their necks," Curly Joe repeated.

"Your Honor, I'd like to renew my previous objection," Ethan asserted. "My client's answer should be stricken from the record as he does not have the medical expertise to testify as to the victims' cause of death."

"Yes I do, Ethan," Curly Joe remarked. "Their neck bones were soft like chicken bones, and when they snapped, I could feel them crunch in my hands. No way they could survive."

"Your Honor, I'd like to request a short recess so I can confer with my client," Ethan said. "Obviously the strain of this trial has been an extension of the madness that first took his mind when his sisters were so brutally and senselessly murdered."

"Your Honor, please instruct Mr. Rivers to quit preaching to the jury. He'll have plenty of time to make his case when the prosecution rests."

"I'm not preaching anything to the jury, Your Honor. I'm merely pointing out that my client has suffered an immeasurable loss, which most, if not all of us, cannot begin to comprehend. The fact he continues to be plagued by the darkness of his sister's murders is just an ugly reality that Mr. Prosecutor is going to have to deal with. Then again, since he may not have siblings, Your Honor, he may not understand the gravity of my client's loss. Do you have siblings, Mr. Ward, or were you an only child?"

"You don't have to answer that, Mr. Ward," Judge Moreland said.

"Thank you, Your Honor, I had no intentions of it."

"It doesn't matter if he answers anyway, Your Honor," Ethan piped in. "It's already perfectly obvious Mr. Ward was an only child. That's the only way anyone can effectively explain his heartless approach to my client's pain and suffering."

"Okay, well for your information, you're wrong. I have a sister," Mr. Ward countered.

"Then that makes your attack on my client all the more pathetic," Ethan returned, and in that moment I knew my brother was laughing on the inside. Not only had he managed to put the prosecutor on trial, so to speak, he'd taken control of the courtroom with a single, but deft sleight of hand.

Curly Joe did not get the death penalty the prosecution had pushed for. He didn't even get successive life sentences for the three men he killed. Instead, Ethan managed to get him a sentence of twenty-five years. Meaning, Curly Joe had a shot of getting out in twenty, so long as he stayed out of trouble while doing his time, the one element I sensed as the connection between Curly Joe and Billy Maxwell.

Before scanning the prison records to solidify this connection, however, I jumped on Billy Maxwell's transcripts. I was curious to see if the remarkable courtroom acumen my brother exhibited on behalf of Curly Joe was on display in Billy's murder trial as well. A couple of hours later I finally looked up from the mound of documents I had been reading, and thought, never ruffled, never caught off guard, incredibly eloquent, on point, and laser sharp, my brother had been two steps ahead of the prosecution at every turn.

"In fact," I said to Mickey later that evening, "there wasn't one page I read where Ethan wasn't flat-out compelling. And that's what makes his representation of Sonny Marx so damn weird. I mean, mentally, it's like he's not even there half the time. And when he is, it's as if he can't wait to leave."

Mickey put down her glass of wine, and then studied my face a couple of moments, before saying, "Maybe all the stuff going on with your mother and the estate... maybe that has him sidetracked."

"Uh-uh," I uttered, shaking my head. "From what I've seen, he's been that way from the moment he took on Sonny Marx as a client. The estate stuff, that's all pretty recent."

"Well then, maybe it's because Ethan doesn't feel like anything significant has happened in the rape case yet. Or maybe it's because he doesn't have an audience yet," Mickey offered, her eyes popping wide as she hunched up her shoulders.

"I thought of all that, too," I responded. "But he was on top of every motion and hearing he attended for Curly Joe and Billy Maxwell. Even the boring procedural stuff, which he could've skipped altogether and no one would've batted an eye. No, something is going on."

"Don't take this the wrong way, sweetie, but maybe you're overthinking it a bit," Mickey proposed. "Maybe Ethan knows that Sonny Marx is really a guilty lowlife, and just doesn't care what happens to the guy."

"Why? He knew Curly Joe was guilty. He knew Billy Maxwell was guilty. Didn't seem to matter in those cases." I then tossed up my hands, before adding, "And besides, Ethan is representing Marx for the notoriety the case will bring, first, and the money he'll get paid, second. He could care less about guilt. Truth is, sometimes I don't even think Ethan registers guilt."

"Then I don't know," Mickey said, after hunching up her shoulders again. "But whatever the reason is, it'll show itself. Sooner or later, it'll show itself." She then flashed an inviting smile, which I assumed was engineered to soften the scowl etched on my face, and said, "C'mon, I want to hear more about this Curly Joe character. Tell me what you found in the prison records."

After adjusting my ass in the chair, I said, "Okay, so you know how an inmate gets time off his sentence for good behavior?"

Mickey promptly nodded, whereupon I continued, "Well, Curly Joe isn't one of those inmates. In fact, any chance his 25-year sentence would get reduced for good behavior went right out the door the moment Billy Maxwell stepped foot in the prison yard."

I then proceeded to give Mickey a synopsis of what I'd discovered in the prison logs, prefaced with, "What you first have to understand is that Curly Joe Baker is widely considered the toughest, scariest guy in the entire prison population. And that's over 5,000 inmates. In fact, in a few of the prison guard reports, the guards actually refer to Curly Joe as the 'baddest dude they've ever seen.' They even make a point in saying they are afraid of him, and they're armed men, separated by metal bars and doors. That being said, there have been four instances where Curly Joe has faced disciplinary charges. Three came during the short time Billy Maxwell was in prison. And one just a year ago."

"What was that one about?" Mickey quizzed.

"Just the basic, new, young inmate wanted to prove how tough he was, heard about Curly Joe, challenged him one afternoon in the prison yard."

"And?"

"Broken jaw, broken nose."

"Oh, how pleasant," Mickey remarked, a hint of innocence dancing in both her tone and vibrant green eyes. Then, "Okay, so how about the other three times? What happened?"

"First time, some big guy by the name of Rufus Buck approaches Billy in his cell-block. The guy, this Rufus guy… and I'm paraphrasing here… is basically described in the report as a menacing 300lb Neo-Nazi, notorious for his hatred of Blacks, Mexicans, and stirring up trouble with anyone who doesn't feed on white bread. Anyway, menacing Mr. Buck approaches Billy, and says, 'Your name, Billy Maxwell? Cuz' if it is, I gotta message for ya.'

Before Billy could so much as utter a sound, Curly Joe, who was evidently within earshot says, 'Yeah, that's Billy Maxwell. And, for the record, I'm Joe Baker. Ask for him, you get me. Only I come bearing gifts,' whereupon he decimates Rufus from head to toe, though not before getting Rufus to admit Billy came to prison with a price tag on his head."

"What happened to him?" Mickey asked.

"Well, the nice version is that he ate his food through a straw for six months. The not-so-nice version is that the six months didn't start for about two weeks, because he first had to be fed intravenously. Mouth was too mangled for a straw, and throat was too swollen for liquids to pass. Curly Joe all but ripped it out."

When Mickey's only response was to posture a disconcerting look, I asked, "Do you want me to continue?" I then waited until she nodded her consent, before saying, "Okay, the second time, two men, Pepper Munson, nicknamed, The Hammer, and L.T. Slater, approached Billy in the laundry facility of the prison, which is where Billy worked. Unfortunately, neither of those guys realized Curly Joe had been magically transferred from kitchen duty to work laundry alongside Billy, so they weren't expecting to see him. But all it took was for this Hammer guy to pull out his makeshift knife, and say, "Someone on the outside wants your head," before Curly Joe introduced himself, and his foot, which he used to shatter Hammer's kneecap. As for L.T. Slater... according to the report, he grabbed a metal turnbuckle used to hang laundry bags, or some such thing, and caught Billy with it pretty good because he ended up with ten stitches in the back of his head. Unfortunately for Slater, he ended up with thirty-two, with all but six on the front of his face."

"Dare I ask where the other six were?" Mickey posed, her words spilling out tentatively.

"Earlobe," I replied. "Apparently Curly Joe bit a little piece of it off. Just enough to send a message to the rest of the prison world – you know, in case the other twenty-six stitches weren't enough."

Mickey stared at me in silence (the pensive look in her eyes now filled with disbelief), so I finally said, "And since there was a third attempt to get at Billy, obviously Curly Joe didn't send a strong enough message. But he must have the third time around because that put an end to the attacks."

"I'm almost afraid to ask what happened?"

"I'll just give you the broad strokes, how's that?"

"No, no, no," Mickey said, waving off my suggestion. "I want to hear the whole thing. Just hold the thought until I get some more wine. You want some?"

"No, but I'd love a beer," I replied.

"Bottle or mug?" she asked, squeezing my shoulder as she drifted by.

"Bottle's cool."

A few minutes later Mickey returned holding a mug. "They were frosted," she said, setting it on a coaster, "so I thought you might like one."

"Yes, thank you, that's great." I then waited until Mickey got reacquainted with her chair, before saying, "Okay, so the third time another two guys show up from some prison gang known as the The Mutts, which is essentially a gang of inmates not associated with any other gang because of race, religion, political affiliation… like that."

"So they call them, The Mutts?"

"Apparently so. And from what I gather, the guards consider them the most dangerous gang of all."

"How come?" Mickey asked.

I shrugged my shoulders, and said, "I don't really know. I think it's just because they get into the most trouble. Have the most fights with other inmates, the most confrontations with the guards, that sort of thing. What I do know is that anyone in the gang has a tattoo of the letter 'M' on each forearm."

Mickey struck a contemplative pose, and then quipped, "Maybe it stands for mother."

"I don't know. I think after I tell you about these two guys, you'll be more apt to say, motherless."

"I'm listening," Mickey offered, the palms of her hands face up and spreading apart, suggesting the floor is mine.

"Okay," I began, after settling on a mouthful of beer, "so one of the two guys considered by the guards to be the worst of The Mutts, is a man named Lucas Hoss. Born and raised in Detroit, he received his first prison sentence at the age of eleven when he was sent to some juvey hall for attacking an eight-year-old girl waiting for a school-bus, and his last about seven years ago when he received a life sentence for breaking into an old woman's house, and then bludgeoning her to death because she didn't have anything of notable value. In between, he'd been in and out of prison for a variety of criminal offenses, including armed robbery, burglary, and felonious assault.

The other guy, Contavious James Henry, simply known as Hank, was born and raised in Brevort, Michigan, by his father and stepmother, both of whom he killed when he was seventeen. Shot them at point blank range while they slept. At the time it was thought he was figuring on inheriting some money, but when he sat in open court, and said, 'I killed 'em cuz' I felt like it,' that thought went right out the window. He's been in Knox State Prison ever since. Almost twenty years ago to the day. But along the way, he's earned the distinction of being a nightmare for the guards, having attacked six of them over the years, as well as being the only inmate to successfully take on Curly Joe in a fight."

"How so?" Mickey queried, her eyebrows arching high as she proffered a look of surprise.

"Because, he also has a 1st degree blackbelt in Jiu Jitsu. It's not the 3rd degree Curly Joe has, but it's enough when you attack someone from behind."

"That hardly seems like a success story."

"I know. But when a guy like Curly Joe goes down after getting sucker punched in a crowded cafeteria, even if it's only for a couple of seconds, the story not only spreads, it gets wildly exaggerated. So, in this case, it likely elevated Hank's status as someone not to be reckoned with... deserved, or not."

"Which is what he wanted in the first place," Mickey threw in.

"No doubt," I said. "And from all accounts he used it to his advantage because there were a few instances where he was reported for extorting money from other inmates – the threat being the ass kicking he'd levy if they didn't come across. And that's why it was so ridiculous of him to go after Billy Maxwell. He had no place to go, but down. Then again, either Hank forgot his first fight with Curly Joe was broken up before anything bad happened to him, or he was delusional enough to believe he actually took Curly Joe the first time, and would do so again. Whatever the case, Hank and Lucas Hoss had a handful of their fellow gang members surround Billy in the prison yard one afternoon, only to taunt Curly Joe into coming to his aid. And, as you might expect, Curly Joe obliged them. But he didn't go after Hank or Lucas Hoss at the outset. First he got the group to disperse so they were no longer a threat to him or Billy."

"How'd he do that?" Mickey asked, leaning back in her chair.

I rolled the question around a few moments, when Mickey said, "What on earth are you smiling about?"

"I'm not smiling."

"Yes you are. You're smiling. You're getting a kick out of this."

"I'm smiling now," I confessed sheepishly. "But I wasn't smiling just then. I was just thinking about Curly Joe, and what he did."

"Uh-huh," Mickey uttered, the hint of her own smile taking root. "You're like turning into his biggest fan, aren't you?"

"No, I'm not," I countered. "But you've got to admit, violent, or not, the man has some set of skills."

"Okay, fine, he's got skills. Now how did he get the group to disburse?"

"Pirouette," I said, after rolling the question around another few seconds.

"Pirouette? As in the ballet?"

"Yep. I mean, that's not how it's stated in the report, but that's kind of what he did."

"Well what'd the report say?"

"Basically, that he planted his right foot on the left side of one guy's head, and then in the same motion, spun around and planted his left foot on the right side of another guy's head, pretty much dropping them to the ground simultaneously."

"Yeah, you're right," Mickey said. "Pirouette... caveman style."

"Whatever," I said, dipping my head side-to-side. "That's what the description made me think of. Point is, the group scattered like flies, leaving Curly Joe to direct his attention to Lucas Hoss and Contavious James Henry. As you can probably guess, neither man fared very well. In fact, they both left the yard on stretchers – although for what it's worth, Hank did get the added bonus of losing his hearing in one ear."

Mickey stared ahead in silence, and though the light on her face gave way to the room's simmering shadows, I could still see her expression dancing along the tightrope separating what she understood, and what she hoped to understand. Finally, she said, "So the connection... what is it? Where does your brother fit into all this?"

"In a word, everywhere," I replied. "From representing Curly Joe, and Billy, which gave Ethan an open line of communication to foster an alignment between the two inmates, to the less obvious, his longstanding friendship with the warden. But it's the friendship that made it possible to move Curly Joe around the prison so he was always in close proximity to Billy." I then shrugged my shoulders, adding, "As for Anthony Ricci putting a price tag on Billy's head… that was just the catalyst that prompted Ethan to put the other pieces together."

"I'm curious, how did you find out about the warden and your brother?" Mickey posed.

"Frankly, I just put it to Ethan."

"What do you mean?"

"Just that when I originally asked how he helped keep Billy alive, he told me to research the prison and the parties involved, and what I couldn't learn on my own, to call him. So that's what I did."

"And just like that he told you?"

"Well, for starters, Ethan and Warden Jaffe being friends isn't against the law, so Ethan admitting it, isn't a big deal. The real issue is how they became friends, and how they've stayed friends," I suggested.

Mickey postured a curious glare, but otherwise remained silent, so I said, "Ethan told me he once got an unsolicited phone call from the warden. An inmate needed a good attorney to help with his appeal. He asked if Ethan would be interested. Ethan, of course, told me he pounced on the opportunity, which meant he likely researched the inmate's case first, making sure it had enough cache before agreeing to anything. But then I started to think about it, so after I got off the phone with Ethan, I did a little research on the list of clients he's represented from Knox Prison. Fourteen times in the last ten years alone, I found my brother's name associated with a nice, splashy case. The kind that garners juicy headlines, and keeps his name front and center for all to see."

"Don't know that that's a crime, sweetie," Mickey proffered.

"Yeah, but there's more, babe. Knowing my brother the way I do, I'd be willing to bet he pays Warden Jaffee a handsome little fee for the service, just to make sure Jaffee doesn't look elsewhere. It's pick-of-the-litter cases for my brother, and a quid-pro-quo payment for Jaffee. It's all perfectly underhanded, and all perfectly Ethan."

"You really think he'd set up a deal like that?"

"Yep," I said with a perfunctory nod. "And for one simple reason… Jaffee never had to do it for free. He only had to pick the right attorney to play ball with. But the money flow doesn't stop there. In return for keeping Billy safe in prison, I'd be willing to bet Ethan sent… scratch that… Ethan sends money to someone of Curly Joe's choosing. Maybe that old girlfriend of his, assuming they're still in touch."

"Why do you say that?"

"Because, when I asked Ethan who he had to pay off to keep Billy in one piece, he laughed. And when he laughs, it's for one of two reasons: he thinks it's expected of him, or he thinks he knows something nobody else does."

"So Curly Joe's girlfriend?"

"His girlfriend, Aunt Gladys, some distant relative. Pick one, it really doesn't matter. The point is, someone is getting money because Curly Joe kept Billy safe. In fact, I'm sure my brother set it up so that Billy funded the whole thing. But even if he didn't, or the money now comes from Ethan, it's likely a chickenshit amount anyway. Yet, if it means something to Curly Joe, Ethan will still do it, because that way he gets to keep Curly Joe on a leash."

"And that's what he's after?"

I snickered. "Hardly. That's just an added benefit. Ethan just wants to control the situation. That's all he ever wants with any situation. It's like a game to him. He's the puppeteer and everyone else is a puppet. There's just one problem – sometimes the puppeteer can't keep up with his own web of shit, which puts other people, his puppets, at risk."

Mickey sighed. "Okay, now you're talking in riddles, Drew."

"What I'm saying is, Frank Marino and a couple other Anthony Ricci lackeys, are the ones who jumped me in the stairwell. The web of bullshit my brother spun to keep Billy Maxwell safe has only caused Ricci to harden his efforts to find him. And that means stepping up the pressure on my brother, the latest example being the obvious shit-kicking I took."

"How do you know?"

"Ethan told me. I didn't mention it before because I still had my doubts. But reading all this crap proved it out."

Mickey stared at me for several seconds before letting her gaze fall away. "Will they come back?" she finally asked, her voice quiet, her tone hesitant.

I shook my head. "No. I don't think that's part of their repertoire. I think they first see how fucking with me affects my brother, before moving on accordingly. Maybe to someone closer. Maybe his kids, his wife. I don't know."

Mickey brought the glass of wine to her mouth, but then inched it away, as though having seconds thoughts. "I don't understand," she said, her eyes now square to mine. "How can your brother do this to people, to his family? I mean, why does he think he can get away with it?"

"He doesn't know any better," I replied. "He learned it from my mother."

# Chapter 24

Our law firm – my law firm – has had an executive committee in place from the time of its inception, oh so many years ago. Elected to three-year terms, the committee is comprised of seven lawyers, whose primary purpose, at least according to the company's bylaws, is to monitor the firm's economic performance, as well as to determine corporate policy and provide organizational direction. Realistically, however, if the policy determined, or the direction provided, does not morph into billable hours, there is a swift change to both, a measure I had propagated ever since I singlehandedly built the criminal defense department into one of the firm's annual financial juggernauts.

Generally speaking, the committee meets the first Monday of every other month, and though I had been unanimously elected the last three terms, I don't know that I've showed up for a meeting three times. Short of my own agenda, I just never really cared what the committee decided about anything, content, instead, to give my voting proxy to another member so I could go on about my day. But this afternoon would be different, since a court order was recently entered, giving my mother the unwelcomed ability to temporarily fill the seat left vacant by my father.

The judge, just as I had predicted, took the easy way out, saying, "Short of an agreement between your mother, yourself, and the law firm, this is the most equitable decision I can make at this time, Counselor."

I nodded my head as though I understood, when it was simply a prelude to questioning the judge's intellect, before laughing my way out of the courtroom.

Nevertheless, the ludicrous court order stood, so when the meeting convened at 4:00 p.m., I was already seated at the end of the conference table, one of six attorneys with incidental staff awaiting my mother's grand entrance. Fortunately, we didn't have to wait as long as I would have otherwise guessed, knowing my mother's propensity to dally at the expense of others. Unfortunately, her bejeweled arrogance was followed into the room by her boyfriend, and attorney, Connor Banks, prompting me to state, "Not a chance. He's out. Banks, get the hell out."

Banks maneuvered himself beside Evelyn, whereupon he shook his head, and said, "Sorry to rain on your parade, Ethan, but the court order stands."

"Jesus, Banks," I groaned, after an exaggerated eye-roll, "can't you even interpret a court order? It says my mother has the right to attend the meeting to insure her potential interests are adequately represented. That means, unless your name is Evelyn Rivers, you don't belong here."

Banks scoffed. "Don't give me that crap. You know as well as I do, the spirit of that order is to protect her interests, and that's just what I intend to do."

"You mean, your interests, don't you, Banks?"

"How dare you talk to Connor like that!" my mother snapped, the scowl on her face jumping at me seconds before her words even littered the room.

"People, people, let's all dial it down a notch," Jerry Mckay proposed, bringing his thumb and forefinger together as though pinching the air. He then veered in his chair to scan the glossy façade of Connor Banks, before glancing back my way, a subtle grin in tow.

"What was that?" Evelyn asked.

"What was what?" Jerry Mckay returned, his feigned innocence crashing into Evelyn's malevolence.

"That look you gave my son. What was that?"

"I didn't give him a look, Evelyn."

"You most certainly did. I saw you."

"You're imagining things, Evelyn."

"I'm imagining nothing of the kind."

"I think you're being a little too sensitive, Mother," I interjected. "Maybe you're just nervous."

"Nervous? Why would I be nervous?" Evelyn replied, her hands now glued to her hips.

I shrugged my shoulders, saying, "I don't know. It's just been my experience that people with lousy attorneys get nervous when they're put into compromising situations."

Evelyn could've stared at me for ten minutes or ten days and it wouldn't have made any difference. The contemptuous glare, the irreverent silence she once used to pump me full of guilt, had long since waned. As such, I simply stared back until she finally retreated to a burst of haughty laughter, which Connor Banks used as a segue, to say, "Don't think for a minute my client finds this a laughing matter. She is not here at your expense. And she will not be ignored, or ridiculed."

I spotted Banks a puzzled look. "What's your name again?"

Banks nodded his head and offered up a derisive grin, the grin disappearing shortly before the head-bob, at which point he set his briefcase down, tossed up his hands, and said, "Joke around all you want, Ethan, but my client is here because a court order gave her that right. And I'm here to see those rights are preserved."

"The only thing you're going to do," I said, while pushing myself up from the chair, "is go back the way you came – either on your own, or with a little help from me."

"Ethan, come on now," Ben Lilly chimed in.

"Stay out of this, Ben," I snapped without so much as glancing at my father's onetime friend and associate.

"Look," Ben continued, "all we have to do is call the judge and get his take on the order. It shouldn't be that difficult."

I pulled my eyes from Connor Banks, letting them settle, and then burn into the cherubic face of Ben Lilly, where they remained until Lilly tired of the glare, and hung his head. "Now then, as everyone in this room knows," I said, throwing my attention back to Banks – "everyone, that is, except you and my mother – any member of this committee can adjourn a meeting at any given time, and for any reason whatsoever. Therefore, I can assure you, before any judge is called, or any court order is further debated, this meeting will cease. So the choice is really yours, Banks. You can leave, my mother can stay, and a meeting can take place. Or, you can insist on staying and the two of you can have the room all to yourselves." When Banks and my mother traded looks, I promptly added, "Just remember, if you choose to stay, we're going to have to take an inventory before we leave."

Evelyn gave me the slow once over, before saying, "You stupid, stupid, boy." She then turned, filled the room with one final burst of haughty laughter, and disappeared out the door, leaving Connor Banks to dutifully bring up the rear.

# Chapter 25

Ever since I told Mickey about Frank Marino being the guy behind that little shit kicking I took in the stairwell, she's been a bit wary about the trials and tribulations otherwise known as, Ethan. I think she's got it stuck in the back of her head that if Ethan keeps yanking Anthony Ricci's chain, Marino's apt to pay me another visit. It's not an opinion without merit, since Marino is no more than a psychopath who likely drools at the prospect of inflicting pain wherever, whenever, and on whomever possible. Yet, it's not an opinion I necessarily share.

Either way, imagine my surprise when Mickey came into my office and announced that she wanted me to start an investigation into Marino's purported criminal activity. "Quietly," she said. "I don't want anyone else to know about it. Especially the Feds. I've already seen their handiwork in Judge Beckett's investigation. Right hand doesn't know what the left hand is doing. They find out we're looking into Marino, they could jump on the bandwagon and muck that up too."

"Okay, whatever you think. But why now?"

"What's the matter? I thought you'd like the idea."

"It's not a like, dislike kind of thing."

"Then what is it?"

I hemmed and hawed a few seconds, before settling on, "Well, you've recently been concerned about Marino coming after me, right?"

"That's correct. So?"

"So why would you have me investigate a guy you think wants to open up my head?"

"Because you don't think so. I'm just deferring to your instincts, and your repeated desire to go after him," Mickey contended, her words primed and painted, as though knowing the question had been on its way from the get-go.

"Then I guess I'm just surprised you're giving me the green-light so fast."

"I figured out how to free up the resources," Mickey responded. "Plus, I think the timing could be right."

"Not even gonna wait until I make you the beneficiary of my life insurance policy, eh?" I joked.

Mickey didn't laugh, however. In fact, she didn't even crack a smile. She simply locked her pointed sights on me, and said, "Listen, Drew, when Marino catches wind of what we're doing, which he will as soon as we spoon feed him the news, he won't be so quick to come after you. He'll know if someone so much as looks at you the wrong way, or breathes on you too hard, he's suspect number one. So actually, it's a defensive strategy that only appears offensive. The beauty is, the only thing Marino will ever know is the investigation is ongoing, so you should have all the time you need."

"Interesting," I mused, to which Mickey abruptly cautioned, "But there's more."

"Can't say I like the sound of that."

"You're not going to like the next part either, so I'm just gonna come out with it.

In order to do this, I have to take you off the Sonny Marx case."

Okay, so my immediate reaction was to jump up, and scream, *What the fuck are you talking about?* This was promptly followed by response number two… *That's a bullshit idea,* which ultimately gave way to response number three… the one, and only, "How come?"

"Because you give us the best chance at success with Marino," Mickey returned. "Which makes you the resource I need to free up."

"Oh, c'mon Mickey," I protested. "We have plenty of people who could pull it off."

"No," Mickey countered. "You're the best investigator around here by a long ways. That's why I can't have you focused on the Marx trial. It'll pull you in another direction. And when that happens, you'll end up delegating on Marino, even if you don't want to. And the more you delegate, the more people get involved, the weaker our case gets, and the less chance we have of keeping a lid on things."

I don't know if it was my prolonged sigh, the dispirited look that likely sat plastered across my face, or both, but before I uttered another word, Mickey shrugged her shoulders, and said, "Look, Drew, from where I sit, the Sonny Marx case is not particularly strong. It's largely circumstantial. So who knows what the outcome will be anyway. But this Marino investigation... we play it right and it could turn into something big."

After reluctantly nodding my head, I said, "Okay, fine. I get it. But what do I tell D.C.?"

"I'll tell D.C.," Mickey said. "He's been angling to sit first chair on a newsworthy case for some time anyhow, so I'm sure he'll be glad."

"What about my brother?"

"Ethan? Tell him whatever you want."

Turns out, it wasn't so much what I said, as what my brother didn't. In other words, after explaining to Ethan I was no longer on the Sonny Marx case, he mumbled, "That's not good, and hung up the phone. No, *How come?* No, *Really?* No, *Wow, what happened?* No, nothing. Just a garbled, "That's not good," followed by a dial tone of ambiguity.

# CHAPTER 26

Generally speaking, I don't watch the local evening news because, quite frankly, I've always found it to be a blighted mass of triviality. Besides, a few years ago, Olivia convinced me to try reading at night. She said it would help me relax. The problem with that concept, I spend a significant portion of my daytime hours reading legal briefs and whatnot. Therefore, picking up a book at night never seemed like a good way to rest the eyes, much less the mind. But then she handed me the John Steinbeck novel, East of Eden, promising me that if I wasn't hooked after 20 pages, she'd drop the subject altogether. She was right. Not only was I hooked, I was relaxed. Unfortunately, very few books have since held that distinction for me. As a result, while I continue to read, it's not uncommon for the television to be on at the same time, which means some local newscaster occasionally winds up chirping in the background.

With that in mind, every once in a while my ears perk up because I hear the statement, 'We have breaking news.' Sometimes the breaking news is as nondescript as a vacant building fire, other times as redundant as a multi vehicle accident due to inclement weather. Tonight was different, however, for tonight the breaking news was that a fifty-two-year-old man had been found dead in the trunk of a car. Details of his death, as well as his identification, were being withheld pending notification to his family. I assumed the man had been murdered, although beyond that rudimentary conclusion, the story held no real interest to me.

And then I picked up a newspaper the following morning, and saw the headlines, 'Treasury Agent Found Dead In Trunk.'

At that moment, I had to fight to hold my hands steady in order to read the story, though I couldn't fight off the sweat forming over my brows, or the gnawing pit in my stomach, when the article identified the fifty-two-year-old Treasury Agent as, Albert Ness.

Apparently, Ness had been killed by a single bullet to the back of his head, his tongue had been cut out, and his body stuffed in the trunk of his own car. And though I instantly knew Anthony Ricci was behind the murder, he made sure to confirm as much later that same morning.

Shortly before noon an envelope was delivered to my office. Inside was a bullet, with a piece of paper and the word, *Salute,* typed on it.

# Chapter 27

Over the years, I've tried to learn everything I can about the person I'm negotiating against before jumping in with both feet. Avery Forsyth, the Provo, Utah prosecutor I had been dealing with in my efforts to have Patricia Stevens' (aka, Nancy Sudwell's), record expunged, was certainly no exception.

Born to a family with five siblings, Avery, and his wife of 27 years, had six children of their own, the eldest, Avery Jr., once serving 45 days in jail for public intoxication, an excessive sentence likely orchestrated by dear old dad to teach sonny-boy a lesson. Beyond that, however, Avery Forsyth's family and professional life had largely been blemish free – the notable exception being his prosecution of Claudia Stutts, a sixteen-year-old high school student imprisoned for drug possession who hanged herself days after being incarcerated.

It was Claudia's suicide, however, that probably helped Patricia Stevens more than anything I could've done. I had gotten the distinct impression Avery lived under a perpetual cloud of guilt, believing his hardline prosecution of Claudia was likely the prelude to her untimely death. And though I never brought it up to Avery firsthand, I found myself reiterating the likelihood that Patricia would entertain the same fate if she were ever sent back to prison. Fortunately, Avery agreed with my prognosis and offered to draft the necessary documentation to formalize our understanding, before getting a judge to rubberstamp it. Unfortunately, he changed his tune at the last minute, and would not sign off on our deal until we had a face to face.

Apparently, Avery wanted to guarantee himself a cosmetic windfall in case the situation ever came back to haunt him during election season. Dousing the decades old record of a harmless prison escapee wouldn't look so bad if prosecutors traveled all the way from the Midwest because they needed his help in putting a serial rapist away. In fact, the tradeoff might just look pretty damn good.

So, a meeting had been scheduled, travel arrangements made, and then I got pulled from the Sonny Marx case, leaving D.C. to make the trip on his own. But D.C. was happy, even if he wouldn't say as much. And why not? He'd waited long enough to take the lead on a high profile case. If it also happened to be a bit circumspect... oh well. No case was perfect.

Meanwhile, I'd be lying if I said I wasn't somewhat relieved myself, knowing just how exhausting my brother can be in a normal setting, never mind the big stage and bright lights of a rape trial. In fact, the more I thought about it, the more eager I was to put some space between me and Ethan, and get after Frank Marino. As such, once I dropped D.C. at the airport for his midday flight, I headed back to the office to do some research, scuttling my previous plans to take the rest of the afternoon off.

Yeah, well, no sooner did I sit down with some old court records and newspaper clippings, when I had to push them aside to answer my cell phone, only to hear the angst riddled voice of my sister-in-law, Olivia. "The kids... they're missing, Drew! They're missing! I can't... I don't know where... they weren't waiting for me after school."

Turns out, my niece and nephew were last seen being hustled into a van by two men. The police had been called, an Amber Alert issued, and through it all, my brother was nowhere to be found – ergo Olivia's phone call to me.

"And where are you now?" I asked. "You still at the school?"

"Yes. The police left a few minutes ago. I'm with the principal. I don't know what to do. I can't find Ethan."

"Ethan's likely stuck in court, and can't use his phone," I replied. Then pondering the veracity of my own statement, I managed, "Are you okay to drive?"

"Yes. Yes, I can drive."

"Good. Go home and wait for me," I directed. "There's nothing more you can do at the school."

"But what if they come back here?" Olivia asked, her tone still walking anxiety's edge.

"The police will be in the area," I assured her, "so don't worry. But someone needs to be at the house. You need to be at the house. I'll be over as quickly as I can. I'm going to see what I can find out on my end first."

A little more than an hour later, I pulled into my brother's drive with two additional facts in tow. The security guard typically stationed at the school's exit was conspicuously missing at the approximate time my niece and nephew left the building, and the van matching the one used to drive off with my brother's kids had been found abandoned not three miles from the school.

"How do you know that, Drew? How do you know?" Olivia asked, her fingers clutching my lapel.

"Talked to one of my contacts in the police department, that's all."

"So, what does it mean?"

I gathered Olivia's hands in mine, and then feigned the same comforting smile I'd been offering random victims for years. "It means, the kids are going to be fine, Olivia. You'll see."

"No," she countered, pulling her hands away. "That's not good enough, Drew. I want to know what it means. I need to know what it means."

"Really, Olivia, it's too early to know anything for certain."

"No. Don't say that, Drew. You know something. You have to know something," Olivia insisted.

A few seconds later I shrugged my shoulders, and confessed, "Maybe... I dunno. But it's just a hunch."

"What? Tell me, what? They're my babies, Drew. They're my babies. You've gotta tell me," Olivia pleaded, her voice cracking from worry, her body trembling with fear.

I looked up, down, off to the side, but there was no escaping it – the anguish in my sister-in-law's eyes was filling the room like a dark and suffocating shadow. Even after I said, "Okay, fine. It means, I don't think this is about your kids, which is why I don't think they'll be harmed," Olivia continued to descend into the hollowed guts of agony. So much so, in fact, had I then explained the abduction was all a little too circumstantial, that Anthony Ricci was merely sending Ethan a message, that Leah and Liam would return home safe and sound, she wouldn't have heard me. Olivia, overcome with grief, had passed out.

By the time the gray February sky slipped into black, I had made no less than half-a-dozen phone calls. One to my doctor to discuss Olivia's fainting – one to Mickey to discuss my brother's unexplained absence – the rest to my contacts in the police department to get updates on my niece and nephew. Unfortunately, none of the calls amounted to a hill of beans. My doctor advised me to have Olivia lie down and stay calm (newsflash) – Mickey found the situation both strange and troubling, although she wasn't all that surprised (newsflash, part two) – and the police had nothing for me (the one newsflash I could've done without).

And then, bingo! 7:30 rolled around, and Ethan sauntered into the house like a man without a care in the world. "What the hell are you doing here?" he asked.

"Cleaning up after you," I muttered.

"What is that supposed to mean?"

"It means, the taped conversation you have about Anthony Ricci… that really scared him off, Ethan."

Ethan threw his weight forward, and his hands to his hips. "What the hell are you talking about? What happened?"

"Your kids, Leah and Liam… they were abducted by two men after school today. Something Ricci likely put in motion to get your attention. So, now does he fucking have it? Or you gonna keep playing games with him?"

"Ricci's got my kids? And all you can do is stand around twiddling your thumbs?"

I don't know if it was the nature of the question, the condescending manner in which it was posed, the entirety of the day, or just the ugly composition of our lives. All I know is, no sooner did the words leave Ethan's mouth, when I lowered my shoulder and charged forward, barreling into my brother with such force, we tumbled over the back of the couch, knocking over a lamp in the process. "C'mon, you n' me," I snapped, after scrambling to my feet. "You n' me. One time, Ethan. You n' me."

But my brother made no move toward me. He simply stood, tendered a mixed look of apprehension and concern, and said, "Are you okay?"

The question wasn't directed at me, however. It was directed at my sister-in-law, who had appeared from the other room, still visibly distraught. "Where have you been?" she asked, her tone, though shaky, simmering with enough pop, her anger was obvious.

"Andrew just filled me in. I don't know what to say, Liv. I would've been here sooner had I known. Are you... you okay? Can I get you anything?"

"So where were you?"

"I was in court all afternoon and couldn't use my phone," Ethan professed. "And then I had a late meeting at a client's office. But I saw your missed calls, and called you back as soon as I could. Twice, in fact. Both went straight to voicemail. I left you messages, though. Didn't you get them?"

Olivia met Ethan's question with silence, prompting Ethan to posture a dubious glare, and then nod his head slowly, deliberately. "Your ringer was turned off again, wasn't it? I bet it's still off now."

Olivia's sad eyes suddenly widened, pried open by an unexpected truth. "Oh Jesus," was all she could muster before hanging her head to cry.

It was roughly 9:00 o'clock before another word was uttered in my brother's house, and only then because I received the phone call we had all been hoping for. My niece and nephew were found wandering the streets, hungry and cold, but safe and unharmed.

"And you know who brought 'em in?" Sergeant Willow asked.

I went along with the sergeant's apparent surprise, and said, "No, idea. Who?"

"You heard of Anthony Ricci, right?"

"You mean the mob guy?" I returned.

"One and the same."

"He brought 'em in?"

"Yep. Apparently, he saw 'em walking down the street and had a feeling they might be lost. So he asked them. And sure enough, they were. The kids said something about driving around in the back of a car for a while before the car pulled over and the driver told them to get out. They weren't able to give a description of the car, or the driver though, because they had been blindfolded. And before that, the only thing they remembered about the van was that it was black. But we impounded it as soon a we found it abandoned, so if there's some evidence to get from it, we'll find it."

"Oh, I'm sure you will," I said, keeping the brunt of my sarcastic tone under wraps.

"Just lucky for those kids Mr. Ricci happened by when he did. Don't you think?"

"Absolutely," I said, promptly followed by, "and where is Mr. Ricci now? Probably left the station already, eh?"

"Yeah. He gave us a quick statement, his contact information in case we needed anything more, then hugged each kid and left. The kids are doing fine, though, so not to worry. Mr. Ricci stopped off at one of the fast food joints and fed 'em, so they're not hungry. But they look tired, and ready to go home."

"Good. Their father will pick them up. He should be there in the next twenty minutes," I said. I then thanked the sergeant, hung up the phone, looked at my brother, and said, "Yeah, that recording you have about Ricci… great insurance policy."

# Chapter 28

Anthony Ricci might have spooked Andrew – he might have spooked Olivia and the kids, as well. But I knew I could put off dealing with him until I was finished with my mother, which my good sense told me was in the foreseeable future.

That being said, according to Jack Francis, Connor Banks had been seeing, in addition to my mother, a thirty-year-old woman named, Riva Edmonds. Apparently it wasn't an everyday occurrence, since Jack had only been successful photographing Banks leaving her house in the wee hours of the morning three times in as many weeks. Then again, over the course of that same time frame, he photographed several men leaving her house in the wee hours of the morning.

Nevertheless, from everything Jack had been able to stitch together, Riva Edmonds was a licensed real estate broker, working for a company that specialized in reselling bank-foreclosed houses. Still, he made it abundantly clear that selling houses was her daytime job only. Before I presented the information to Evelyn, however, which I assumed she'd find most troubling, I decided the time was right for a little get together with her boyfriend.

"If he stays true to norm, he'll be at the Uptown Bar about 4:30," Jack had told me earlier in the day. "His preference is a stool at the end of the bar, closest to the waitress station."

"What's he drink?"

"Why?"

"Just curious."

Jack snickered, before responding, "Whatever you're buying."

Sure enough, at approximately 4:30 p.m. Connor Banks strolled through the bar like a peacock strutting its colors. Although he looked in my direction a couple of times, he was apparently too preoccupied with the happy-hour crowd to take much notice. A couple of handshakes here, a few finger-points there – if Connor Banks didn't know the names of those scattered about, he truly pretended otherwise. In fact, the affable smile painted across his face didn't disappear until he reached the bar, and realized I was leaning against it.

"Ethan... hey," he offered, his tone, like his expression, jolted by my presence.

"Didn't catch you at a bad time, did I?" I asked.

Connor Banks hung his coat over the shoulders of a bar stool, before responding, "Not at all. Just didn't expect to see you here."

"Hell, Connor, I'm full of surprises."

After studying my face a few seconds, Banks arched a single eyebrow, and said, "That's the rumor."

I smiled, and responded, "Rumor nothing."

"I don't mean to be rude," Banks said, after he pushed himself between two stools, "but I know you're not here by accident. So what do you want?"

I shrugged my shoulders, and then feigning surprise, asked, "What, you're not going to offer to buy me a drink?"

"Looks like you already have one," Banks replied, after glancing at the bar.

Without looking away from my hairspray-smelling, spit-and-polished adversary, I snatched my glass from the countertop and drained the contents. Then setting the glass back down, I said, "Not anymore."

"Very funny, Rivers."

"Wasn't trying to be funny. Was trying to get a drink out of you."

"Yeah, whatever," Banks grumbled, whereupon he looked over his shoulder, caught the attention of the bartender and ordered a shot of Jack Daniels. He then turned back toward me, and asked, "What do you want?"

"You mean, to drink? What do I want to drink?"

"No. What do you want? Why are you here?"

I took a deep breath, the air streaming from my nose for what seemed like a long weekend, before responding, "What I want, is for you to take a walk." I then reached inside my suit coat, and pulled out the photographs Jack Francis had taken. "They come in nice 8x10 glossies too," I said, tossing them on the bar. Before Connor Banks retrieved them, I added, "I'll cut to the chase, Banks. The photos are of you leaving Riva Edmond's house. And mind you, I know how she makes her money. Disappear from my mother's life and she never sees, or hears about the pictures." I then hunched up my shoulders, and asked, "Shall I continue?"

"Frankly," Banks replied, his tone perfectly calm, his expression perfectly contained, "whether you continue is completely up to you. Either way, you can go fuck yourself."

"Gee, that's not a very nice thing to say," I replied, tongue-in-cheek. I then waited as the bartender brought Banks his shot of whiskey, whereupon I snatched it from the counter and promptly drank it down.

"You're an ass," Banks said.

"Indeed," I responded. "And you drink cheap whiskey."

"Like I said, go fuck yourself."

I grinned, and said, "Have fun explaining the pictures." I then turned and walked out of the bar.

I didn't anticipate talking to my mother for at least another day, hoping in the interim that Connor Banks would change his mind and lower the boom on their charade of a love life. What I received, however, was a phone call from Evelyn not one hour after I left Banks standing alone at the Uptown Bar.

"I warned you, Ethan," she said, clearly angry.

"Warned me about what?"

"I told you I was happy. I told you not to interfere with my life."

"Happy, my ass. Your situation is comical," I countered.

"You... you just can't let well enough alone. You, who thinks he knows everything."

"I certainly know a conman when I see one. Something you apparently don't."

"I warned you," Evelyn repeated.

"Yeah, you already told me. So what?"

"Here's so what," Evelyn stated, the edge in her voice picking up steam. "I don't care what kind of pictures you think you have. Connor isn't going anywhere. But you, my dear, are."

"Oh really?" I returned, the edge in my voice also picking up steam. "And just what the hell does that mean?"

"It means you're finished."

# CHAPTER 29

Thank God my mother was an only child, because the only thing that could possibly be worse than Evelyn showing up at my apartment unannounced, would be if she had a twin sister and they showed up together.

That still doesn't change the fact, if I could have fooled her into thinking I wasn't home, I would have. Such was not the case, however, since I have no doubt Evelyn knew my whereabouts before making the jaunt over. The bigger question was how? And yet, since her popping over was such a rare occurrence, nails on a chalkboard notwithstanding, it wasn't something I was going to lose sleep over. Therefore, when she announced her presence, I opened the door.

"We need to talk," she declared, blowing by me like a waft of hot air.

"And what, pray-tell, do we need to discuss, Mother?" I asked, turning to see her backside stroll into the living room where she deposited her animal over the back of my couch, before saying, "Wine. Do you have any wine? Red, of course, and a dry cabernet, if at all possible."

"There's an open bottle on the counter. Knock yourself out," I replied, though it wasn't until I heard the words myself, that I thought how nice it would be if they actually came true.

"Where on earth do you buy your wine?" my mother asked moments later.

"At the store, Evelyn, like the rest of the masses. But hey, if you don't like it, don't drink it."

"No, no, no," she said, her haughty tone billowing like smoke. "It's fine. It's not my preference, but it's fine."

"And you showing up here isn't my preference either, but you don't hear me bitching about it."

Evelyn walked back into the living room, offered me a derisive grin, and said, "And who's fault is that?"

So there it was. I was now standing face to face with the woman who treated me like an intruder in the very house I grew up in, a woman who bristled at the mere sight of me just as often as she dismissed me as an afterthought. And yet, she now wanted to take the refuse of her misgivings and dump it in my lap. How utterly fucking perfect, I thought. There was just one problem: I stopped giving a shit about having a relationship with her so long ago, the memory of wanting to had died of old age. Nevertheless, Evelyn wasn't going to leave until she said what was on her mind, which is why I met her faded beauty with a derisive grin of my own, and grumbled, "What do you want, Mother? Get to the point."

"The point... what is the point?" Evelyn remarked, after pulling the glass of wine from her mouth.

"I don't know, Mother, what is the point?"

"Your brother, I suppose, is the point."

"Ethan has been the point from the time I was an infant, Mother, so if that's all you have, maybe we can call it a night. What do you say?"

"I say, you need to hear me out, Andrew. For your own good, if nothing else."

"So, then, coming over here has nothing to do with you? Wow. And here I thought just the opposite. Shame on me," I replied.

"Don't get cute," my mother cautioned.

"Or what? You gonna come after me the way you've been threatening to go after Ethan? Ooh, I'm scared," I said, my hands doing a little shimmy-shake for good measure.

Evelyn didn't seem to hear, or see me, however. In fact, she suddenly looked lost in thought, gazing at the walls in my apartment as though adorned with expensive artwork, when, in reality, they were covered with little more than white paint. Finally, she tilted her head and peered at me, asking if I knew what it was like to control someone? "Have them in the palm of your hand," was how she coined the phrase. She then balled her hand into a fist, and added, "It's powerful," grinning as the assertion spilled from her mouth.

I responded with a perfunctory head-bob, and said, "So, how's that wine?"

But Evelyn was having none of it, saying, "You know there's no such thing as coincidence, right? Events happen, situations occur. They just don't happen by chance. There's no such thing as coincidence."

I sighed. "Is there a point to all this, Mother, or what?"

Evelyn glanced at me and looked away all in the same motion, though not before depositing her contemptible glare atop the colors of her painted veil. "It was no coincidence a woman was raped not ten minutes from where your brother lived shortly after graduating law school. Just like it's no coincidence two women were raped in Chestnut Hills, not ten minutes from where he lives now."

Evelyn then walked toward me, her half-empty wine glass dangling from the fingers of one hand, while the index finger of the other was pointing at me, and said, "Just like it's no coincidence Ethan agreed to represent Sonny Marx."

"Okay, Mother, you're talking in riddles. If you have something to say, how about you just say it?"

Evelyn continued to point at my chest until she was close enough to actually stab it with her finger, which she did, while responding, "Like everyone else, I read the details of the Chestnut Hills rapes in the newspapers. Unlike everyone else, I know things about your brother. And let's just say the things I know about your brother, and the details of the two rapes, are eerily similar."

"Okay, stop with the finger," I asserted, pushing my mother's hand away before she poked me again. I then backed away until I was out of range, and asked, "Are you telling me Ethan is a rapist?"

Evelyn fashioned a patronizing smile. Then, "I'm simply telling you there are details that are eerily similar."

"Has Ethan ever been accused of anything before?"

Evelyn revved up what was left of her patronizing smile, but otherwise remained silent until I hunched up my shoulders, and said, "What? C'mon, what?"

My mother sipped her wine (purposely slow, I might add), before saying, "I don't know that he's ever been accused of anything before, and if he has, I'm not aware of any charges being brought against him."

"Then what the hell are you talking about? And what does it have to do with Ethan representing Sony Marx anyway?"

"Your brother is representing Sonny Marx because he needs a fall guy for the rapes. He's going to lose the trial to guarantee it. He's likely planned it that way from the beginning."

"Do you realize what you're saying, Mother? Do you realize how ridiculous this whole thing sounds?"

"Call it what you want," she returned. "Call it a story straight out of the rumor mill. Call it the ramblings of a crazy woman." Evelyn paused to drink the rest of her wine before handing me the empty glass. "Call it, a mother's intuition," she then added, her tone suddenly callous, her eyes suddenly lifeless. "Call it, mother knows best. Just don't call it a coincidence."

After my mother left my apartment, the ominous shadow of her words staying behind, I found myself walking the tightrope separating fact from fiction. There was Evelyn, of course, whose mere presence provoked malevolence and disdain. And on the other side there was my brother, whose indifference to everything not named Ethan, coupled with his circumspect demeanor, often times carried an undercurrent of secrecy. Still, I had sensed something tangible in the words Evelyn fed me. Maybe it was the look in her eyes, which, like her tone, had been unequivocal. Maybe it was realizing Evelyn had nothing to gain by concocting such a story, for the intimation Ethan was involved in the rapes was not something, short of his confession, anyone could likely prove. In other words, what did my mother have to gain by implicating Ethan? Was she now going to have the inside tract to my father's interest in the firm? Doubtful, if not altogether comical.

Nevertheless, I couldn't get beyond the need of confronting my brother, if, for no other reason, putting my mind at ease. Therefore, I punched his number into my cell, and the instant he answered, said, "Ethan, we need to talk."

"Yeah fine. We can talk later."

"No, we need to meet somewhere and talk now," I countered.

"Now? It's Friday night," he replied, amid the background noise of a restaurant. "I'm busy."

"Then very soon. And somewhere private."

"Why, you want to make me a plea offer in the Sonny Marx case?"

"I'm no longer involved with the case. I told you."

"Well then, what is it?"

"I'm not talking about it on the phone, Ethan. But I wouldn't be calling you like this if I didn't think it was important."

"Okay, have it your way," Ethan said, after a moment of silence. "I was planning to be at my office tomorrow anyway, so why don't you meet me there... say about eleven."

"Fine. See you then."

After spending a restless night planning, if not altogether agonizing over the conversation I wanted to have with my brother, the last thing I expected was sitting in a chair opposite his desk, not sure how to proceed. And yet, somewhere between shaking Ethan's hand when I first entered his office, and gazing at a desktop photograph of him, our father, and me, I found my clarity of thought suddenly compromised.

In fact, it was only when Ethan said, "Why do I get the sense your visit has something to do with Evelyn?" that I regained my footing. "She came to see me last night," I offered. "Showed up out of the blue."

"Now there's a good way to ruin an evening," Ethan cracked.

"And she did, too," I said.

Ethan leaned back in his chair, and then threw his feet up on his desk, before saying, "What'd she do now?"

"It's not what she did, Ethan. It's what she said."

Ethan sighed. "Okay, what'd she say?"

"She said it's no coincidence you're representing Marx."

"What do you mean? Why wouldn't I represent him?" Ethan queried.

"She also told me she knows details about you that are, in her words, 'eerily similar' to the details of the Chestnut Hills rapes."

Ethan pawed at his forehead a few seconds, before saying, "Okay, now you're talking nonsense, little brother. Say what you came to say. I have a lot to do today."

I took a deep breath, which did little to quell my angst. Then, "Did you ever rape anyone?"

Ethan let his feet drop from his desk, and his chair lurch to an upright position. "Is that what was so important that you had to rush over here today?"

"Yeah, that's what was so important. So what's your answer?"

Ethan remained silent, but I could no more glean innocence from his reaction than I could indignation, so I added, "Did you?"

Ethan shook his head, saying, "It's such a ridiculous question, it's not worthy of an answer."

"You owe me an answer," I stated.

"I owe you an answer because your mother's lost her mind? I don't think so," Ethan responded emphatically. Then resting his forearms on the desk, he continued, "But I will say this... it's apparent she's upping the ante in our fight over the firm. It's also apparent she's using you to do it. I'm surprised you can't see that."

Ethan and I then stared at one another long enough for an uneasy silence to settle between us. Finally, I said, "If you have something you want to tell me, now would be a good time."

Ethan shrugged his shoulders. "What is it you'd have me say, Andrew? You come to my office and ask if I'm a rapist... what, because our mother has decided to go off the deep end? Sorry, but I don't have to answer for her."

"How about answering for yourself?" I countered.

Ethan sighed, saying, "I thought I just did." Then before I could respond, he added, "Ya know what, Andrew? I said I had a lot to do today, and I do. So I'd like to get at it."

"Meaning what?" I asked.

"Meaning, we're done here. Now if you'll excuse me," he said. Ethan then fixed his eyes on the door, obviously waiting for me to open it and leave.

By 11:30 in the morning I was back outside watching the snowfall, it's purity lost against a backdrop of nebulous gray.

# CHAPTER 30

*M*ary Atwood navigated *her way around the restaurant parking lot just how you'd expect a woman wearing high heals to walk when confronted by asphalt in desperate need of repair. Nevertheless, I followed every calculated step until she got in her car and drove off, with me trailing close behind.*

*Three weeks later, I still did not know Mary Atwood. I knew she was the assistant manager at a bank I was a one-time customer of. I knew she lived alone in a two story Tudor, in a neighborhood of old, but well maintained homes. I knew many older homes, like Mary Atwood's, did not have air conditioning, and were, therefore, cooled by summer breezes and the open windows that let them in. I knew she seldom left her house to socialize, preferring the quiet company of her two cats. And as darkness tightened it's grip on the night, I knew she was never going to open the door to a perfect stranger — for as I said, I did not know her.*

*What I did know is that I had been completely overrun by the sleepless hours of my incessant appetite to take her, and by what I saw as the inevitability of our encounter. As such, I had but two choices: either break in and hope to catch her by surprise, or remain crouched behind a tree, staring into the lifeless eyes of godless shadows.*

*Yet, in my angst to enter her house and quell, finally, this obsession, I failed to remember that older homes could be a tad finicky. Mary's, of course, was no exception, for just as I put my weight on the top stair, it saddled the still air with the lonely cry of desperation, causing Mary to call out from the bedroom, "Who's there? Is someone there?"*

*I did not answer, however. I simply burst into her room, beat her about the head until she submitted to my will, and then raped her. But I did not enter Mary Atwood personally.*

*I used a magic stick, thrusting it inside her until satisfied I could offer no more, whereupon I disappeared into midnight's wounded belly, leaving behind the instrument of what would become her eternal nightmare, and the beads of sweat that fell from my brow as I created it.*

*After Mary Atwood, it wasn't long before I turned my attention to Janet Whitmore, a self described nutritionist whose only real claim to the label was the shape of her body (which she routinely flaunted at the gym), and not a college degree. Like Mary, Janet was an attractive thirty-something-year-old blonde who lived alone, sans the part time company of her boyfriend, Larry Stooge – a name that decried further description of the person. Still, his occasional presence was an annoyance, if not an issue, as the first two nights I spent camped out in front of Janet's house, the sediment of my engagement with Mary Atwood having thoroughly settled, he was there. Fortunately, the third night was different. Not only was she home alone, she put on a faint porch light and stepped outside just as I stood poised to begin my deliberate walk up the cobblestone path leading to her door.*

*But Janet couldn't see me, for I remained ever mindful to keep my prowling body below the sight lines of the surrounding shrubbery.*

*Waiting... waiting... what was she thinking while staring into the dark abyss? Did the Stooge propose marriage? Did he break up with her? Did she accept? Did she even care?*

*Waiting... waiting... what was she looking at? Could she envision the future the Stooge promised her? Did she see herself in a four bedroom colonial with three children and a dog? Or was she drawn to the underbelly of her imagination? Did she want something she could not have? Something forbidden by the law and frowned down upon by the church?*

*Waiting... waiting... what was she staring at? What was she thinking?*

*Waiting... waiting... what did she want? What did she want no part of?*

*Waiting... waiting...*

*Boom! The wait was over. Janet turned to walk back inside and I made my move, rushing the house, and then tackling her from behind before she even knew what hit her, all but putting to rest any further need to subdue her.*

*It was another three months before I saw Janet Whitmore again, and only then because she showed up at the gym for what had always been her typical morning workout.*

*"Where've you been?" I asked her.*

*Janet's eyes promptly fell to the floor, as though shamed by her pending reply, before muttering, "I had an accident, and was laid up a while."*

*"Well, it's good to see you back on your feet," I returned. I then winked at her and walked away, laughing to myself every step of the way.*

*What probably infuriates me more than anything else is when they whimper. I never whimpered. So why do they? Why can't they just do as they're told? I did. Why can't they? I did. You want to scream? Not a problem. I can punch a screamer into silence. You want to fight back? Hey, go for it. In fact, I expect a little fight. But this whimpering crap... I mean, it sounds like a puppy locked up in a cage, and no matter how hard you try to quiet it, it just keeps whimpering. It drives me nuts. It also makes me violent. I just never realized how much until I came upon the likes of Anna Finch, my 7th dalliance in five years.*

*I first noticed Anna Finch standing in the checkout line at the grocery store – the quintessential trough for women. She was average height, but otherwise an attractive thirty-something-year old with shoulder length, light brown hair, and a thin frame, which magnified her sculpted breasts. I took an interest in her right away. So I followed her right away – first to her car, and then to her house, stopping in between so she could pick up her dry cleaning. It was, quite frankly, the perfect way to spend an afternoon. I had my target, my outlet, my foreboding vengeance, and now all I had to do was sit back and wait for that urge – that vehemence – that rage – to propel me blindingly forward.*

*As what typically happens, however, days turned into weeks, weeks into months, and though Anna Finch had become a dwindling thought, I could still picture her as if I'd seen her only yesterday, for I knew the tide would ultimately turn against her, pitting me but a breath away.*

*And there it was. The sleepless night that soon turns into one too many. The dark hours that stir the angst of the misbegotten, and open the hearts of wounded souls, setting fire to thought and deed until contempt burns, and the ensuing scars beg for deliverance.*

*Anna Finch moved from window to window and room to room as though gliding across the floor; a wisp of air that would soon blow my way, for just as quickly as her garage door opened, I was inside closing it, though not without first grabbing Anna by the hair, snatching away any possible escape. Yet, it wasn't until I pulled her back into the house and she reached for my ski mask, that I threw her to the floor, and first heard the dreadful sounds of her whimpering.*

*"Stop it!" I demanded.*

*But Anna didn't stop.*

*"I said, stop it! Now goddamn it, stop it! Stop that noise!"*

*Still, Anna didn't stop. Wouldn't stop. Couldn't stop. In fact, the whimpering got worse, prompting me to once again seize her by the hair. Only this time, I dragged her across the floor and into the bedroom, where I smashed her head into the bedpost until rendering her unconscious, and, more importantly, silent. It was only then, when my fury eased and I was able to rape her in the manner she had come to earn.*

*I sodomized Anna Finch with a magic stick.*

*I first met Sally Rutherford in the Fall, when the season's vibrant colors stood like a bouquet of flowers against a backdrop of the sky's ocean blue. I raped her, however, in the middle of the following summer, when humidity hung in the air like molasses, and the moon's pale light gave birth to muted landscapes and droopy shadows. The story might go back a few years, but it goes something like this: we were at a cocktail party, and I liked the way she looked, so I made it a point to ask what she was drinking, intending to fill her next glass. And why not? She appeared to be in her early thirties, had a slender build, an attractive face, even though it hid behind a curtain of wavy brown hair, and eyes both inviting and disinterested with every passing glance. And pass them she did, for every moment I spent talking her up, she spent twirling her hair, trying oh-so-hard to look cavalier by briefly looking the other way.*

*She was also, as I had come to discover, not only submissive, putting up zero resistance when I attacked her, but a bit peculiar, at one point suggesting I take off my mask. Unfortunately, she had the same penchant for whimpering as Anna Finch, so our visit, as it were, turned violent. That is to say, I ended up beating her with the same magic stick I put inside her. I beat her pretty good too. Truth is, I was surprised there wasn't more blood.*

*I was also surprised Sally went to the police. Sure, sooner or later one of the women was going to come forward. Of that I was certain. I just didn't think it would be someone with such an acquiescent demeanor. I mean, let's face it: if a woman is pretty much afraid of her own shadow, doesn't it stand to reason she'd be afraid of mine? Then again, maybe she didn't* have a choice, in as much as the welts I left on her face and body might've compelled her to see a doctor, who, in turn, compelled her to see the police.

I don't know, I try to be so artful with that kind of thing, too. I guess I just got carried away. But hey, shit happens, right?

Meanwhile, Sally Rutherford let the cat out of the bag big-time, for the police report turned into newspaper headlines, and the headlines instantly drew focus on every Tom, Dick and douchebag walking down the street after dark.

I suppose that's why it was good thing I didn't have anymore pressing needs, and could, therefore, concentrate on my work, and stay indoors for a while.

It would be several more years before another woman came forward (as most were obviously too ashamed, too afraid, or both), and yet, and as luck would have it, when one came, so did another. I suppose I'm somewhat at fault for that too, since more than a few of my targeted women were married, naturally bringing their husbands into the foray. They had the strength of their men to lean on. Unless, of course, their men didn't want the attention, or, in some cases, the embarrassment of their wives being taken right under their pretentious noses.

On the surface, Lauren Hill and Patricia Stevens had much in common. Both were in their early to mid thirties, both slender, attractive, had sandy brown hair, and carried themselves like debutantes all because they lived in the cozy confines of Chestnut Hills (although one could argue my presence changed the definition of the word, 'cozy.').

Anyway, for all they had in common, they had much apart. For instance, Lauren Hill came across like some prim and proper little Miss-goody-two-shoes, when all she was trying to be was a sophisticated lady about town. Patricia Stevens, on the other hand, didn't seem to give two shits about what people thought about her. Sure, she acted like a hoity-toity queen simply because she had a rich husband. But that was the reputation of Chestnut Hills women in general. When all was said and done, Patricia Stevens was more no-nonsense than bullshit, a quality I actually admired about her.

Maybe the biggest difference between them, however, one which might just exemplify their personalities best, is the way each one reacted after realizing they were about to be abducted. That is to say, when I snuck up on Lauren Hill, I growled in her ear, just as I grabbed hold of her hair. Yet, before I could subdue her properly, she'd almost fainted dead away from fear. But when I growled in Patricia Stevens' ear, she promptly elbowed me, *catching the side of my head. She wasn't finished either, for no sooner did I grab her by the hair, when she kicked, screamed, tried to break free, the whole nine yards. And I have to say, she was one tough little bitch, even though she was never going to get away. Hell, at the end of the day, I just spun her around and punched her senseless. Lauren Hill was obviously much easier. I probably could've gotten away with uttering, "Boo," to subdue her. Be that as it may, I decided to make use of the car she was standing next to, and banged her head into it a couple of times. Nothing serious, mind you. Just enough to take her from trembling fool to deliriously woozy.*

*Meanwhile, the trauma of being severely beaten and sodomized didn't stop either one from coming forward, which, not only put the cops on high alert, and sent the media into a feeding frenzy, it forced me to come up with Plan B in the process.*

*Here's the thing, though. Plan A, Plan B... hell, you can say, Plan C, and it won't matter. I'll always come back to the notion, it wasn't always like this, all the stuff with the women. In fact, in the beginning I would sit on my bedroom floor with my arms draped tightly across my knees, my spine pressed hard against the wall, and glare at the door until the anger beating at the walls inside me was finally muzzled by a competing and overwhelming sense of guilt – the long, strenuous battles oft times leaving me so mentally and physically drained, I was unable to leave my room, and only then after I was certain the ravenous shadows stalking my being would not wake before the morning's rising sun. I was sixteen years old at the time.*

*By the age of twenty-one, the anger would no longer recede as quickly, or with as much certainty, such, that by the age of twenty-five, the overwhelming sense of guilt that once stared down my rage with all the clarity of the north star, had been reduced to just another flickering light. Nevertheless, I championed that light until it no longer flickered and in its place stood the face of a hissing fuse. And then it was only a matter of time before I exploded.*

*Of course, once I did, and then once Lauren Hill and Patricia Stevens came forward all these years later, all anyone in the media could ask, was, "What kind of person would do these things?"*

*Ha! Leave it to the media to get it wrong once again. What they should've asked was, "Why? Why does a person do these things?"*

*Unfortunately, the answer isn't that easy to come by. In fact, I'm not even sure I know. Maybe it's because I was born this way. Maybe it's because I know how to get away with it. Or maybe, just maybe, it's because I like doing it.*

*Then again, maybe it's because of the suggestive way she talked to me when I was just a child — maybe it's because she started to touch me when I was 5 years old — maybe it's because she instructed me to touch her — maybe it's because of the way she kissed my mouth — maybe it's because she used to lick me with her tongue — maybe it's because she forced me to lick her with mine — maybe it's because she used to come into my room as often as five times a week and have me touch her with what she termed, "her magic stick" — maybe it's because when I was 7 she instructed me to put the magic stick inside her, which continued until I was 13 — maybe it's because she used to put the magic stick inside of me — maybe it's because she convinced me that everything she did, everything I was forced to do, was okay, even though I could never breathe a word of it to anyone — maybe it's because I was too ashamed to breathe a word of it anyway — maybe it's because the weight of her deeds and the weight of our secret was so utterly profound, I couldn't carry it anymore. If I didn't explode, I would implode. Maybe it's because I chose life over madness — maybe it's because the physical resemblance between Evelyn, when she did those things to me, and the women I now do them to, both ignites and releases my fury.*

*Maybe, maybe, maybe... that's a whole lot of maybes, when the only thing certain is, I've raped eight women in as many years, and another fourteen between the time I graduated law school, and Olivia gave birth to the twins.*

# CHAPTER 31

I f my mother is correct, and Ethan was planning to have Sonny Marx take the hit for the Chestnut Hills rapes, an assertion I can't seem to wrap my arms around (if for no other reason than because I just don't want to), my brother was going to have to find another fall-guy. Word has it, Gene Baxter is facing imminent charges for vehicular homicide in the death of his one-time pro-tégé. Apparently, Baxter ran Sonny over as he was crossing the street on his way to, *The Knight Owl Bar and Grill*.

It'll now be interesting to see what Mickey decides to do with the Chestnut Hills case. On the one hand, she can close the file because our suspect is dead. On the other hand, she may decide to keep it open to see what else might develop. In other words, if we've been dealing with a serial rapist, as many in my office believe, and Sonny Marx wasn't the guy, then the real per-petrator may get the stones to resurface. My guess is the decision will largely depend on the budget, and whether Mickey wants to devote resources to a case that suddenly has no end in sight.

From a personal standpoint, I hope the entire goddamn thing just disap-pears. I do not want to think... scratch that... I can't fathom a scenario that puts Ethan in the skin of a rapist. I know what my mother said, and I know how adamant she was saying it. But come on, Ethan a rapist? That can't be. He's got a wife, two kids, a beautiful home, a successful career – that can't be. Sure, he's unusual at times... even a bit strange. But most of that I chalk up to arrogance and a perverted sense of self-esteem.

So what if his compulsion to grandstand is to silence everyone's voice but his own? So what if it propels him forward with the strength and ease of a person in total command of his surroundings, even though his eyes tend to anxiously dart to and fro? In reality, it's all just a comingling of confidence and insecurity, common traits of a person smart enough to realize he moves through life as both predator and prey. And yet, wouldn't every average Joe gladly dance to the same beat if doing so brought them the riches my brother has earned? Of course they would, for at the end of the day, average isn't stupid, it's just... well, it's just average, so in the grand scheme of things, maybe they wouldn't.

Either way, the point is, nothing my brother has ever said, or done, has been precipitated by anything more than a man trying to make his mark the only way he knows how, and not, as my mother would have me believe, by something deviant, or sinister. In fact, I'll take it a step further, and say, I've been at my job long enough to recognize the most common traits of a serial criminal. And I don't see that Ethan possesses any of them.

He's never been a loner, unless locking himself in a bedroom to get some privacy can be defined as anti social. But what kid hasn't pulled that move growing up? He did not have an unstable family life, although I'm the first to admit, it also wasn't perfect. Then again, how could it be when Evelyn was our hedonistically driven matriarch? That said, show me a perfectly idyllic family and I'll show you life in a fairytale. He was not abused as a child, unless that somehow means he got far more attention than he wanted. By the same token, Ethan getting far more translates into me getting way less, which is nothing more than emotional abuse by attrition. And yet, I still turned out relatively normal. So why wouldn't Ethan?

So then, what's left? My brother suffering the ills of his evil genius? Frankly, I don't find that remotely plausible, because that would mean Ethan was a genius, number one, and he was cut from the same cloth as madmen like, Clive Howard, and Theodore Bundy, which I think is number two.

Days later, I was unfortunately reminded, of yet, one more common thread tying serials together. They have a fight versus flight mentality. As a result, when the earth beneath their feet begins trembling, such that the walls around them start caving in, they have an instinctive propensity to pick up and leave, particularly when the risk of staying put otherwise exposes them to probable guilt and incarceration. Because of Ethan's dogmatic stance in challenging my mother for control of the firm, however, the thought he would willingly takeoff never occurred to me – not even when my sister-in-law called to inform me, Ethan had vanished, as I immediately connected his disappearance to Anthony Ricci.

In fact, it was only when Olivia mentioned the note my brother left behind, that the light bulb in my head flickered to life.

# Chapter 32

The past few days had gotten so bad, so agonizingly bad, I'd fall asleep under a blanket of shear torment, only to wake up in a pool of sweat, with Olivia's ardent glare digging into me as she questioned the senseless mutterings of my lurid misgivings. "Nightmares. Some awful nightmares," I replied, relieved she hadn't deciphered a single syllable, much less a complete sentence. Nevertheless, it would only get worse. Sooner or later I was bound to say something incriminating, of that I was certain.

I was also certain I was beginning to choke, suffocate, in fact, from the burgeoning weight of Anthony Ricci's threats, the black hole Sonny Marx's death suddenly put me in, the unforgettable reality of life with mother (knowing full well her self-serving memories would soon beget those of my own, evoking a very disturbing picture for all the world to see), and, worst of all, the mounting fear I was going to abuse my daughter, Leah, much the way Evelyn abused me.

Suffice it to say, it wasn't a matter of figuring out what to do. Hell, I knew I couldn't stay and fight the sum of such overwhelming forces. Sure, I could keep Ricci at bay. All I had to do was give him the whereabouts of Billy Maxwell. But why bother if I couldn't shed the other issues staring me down? I was still going to have the Chestnut Hills dilemma, inasmuch as that moronic Gene Baxter couldn't leave Sonny alone, as I had instructed – though I'm really not sure it would've mattered anyway. My mother saw to that. She figures the profound trauma and endless humiliation I will face by reliving my abusive childhood will keep me quiet, knowing full well if it doesn't, and I expose every nook and cranny of what she did, it's still just a matter of *he-said, she-said.* Of course, Evelyn effectively stacked the odds in her favor regarding that issue as well, for the story she spoon-fed Andrew will ultimately force his office to shine the *rape light* on me. So in the end, who are they going to believe? Obviously, Evelyn's taking the wise gamble they'll believe her, whereas I don't have the luxury of gambling at all. I still have the glaring issue with my daughter, Leah, whose nighttime habit of running around the house in her nightgown now had me conjuring up different images – sordid images – images that had me peeking in her bedroom while everyone else slept.

No, it wasn't a matter of figuring out what to do. It was figuring out when to do it.

# CHAPTER 33

'*Olivia,*' my brother's note began, '*by the time you read this, I'll be a thousand miles away. It was never my intent, or desire, to leave you and the kids. But circumstances beyond my control, circumstances I'm not at liberty to discuss, have forced my hand, leaving me no choice.*

*While my sudden departure will no doubt come as a surprise, imagine the difficulty I faced once I realized what I was up against. Unfortunately, it all came at me like a tidal wave. I wanted to stop it. I tried to stop it. But I couldn't, no matter what I did, how hard I fought, or what sacrifice I was willing to make. The noose just kept getting tighter and tighter, and my prospects for success, smaller and smaller.*

*But understand something, Liv, I didn't do anything wrong. In fact, if I'm guilty of anything, it's been dealing with people who never cared about anyone or anything besides themselves, people who entangled me in their web of lies only to take advantage of me. They never stopped to think how my safety, my life, might've been undermined along the way. That's why I'm in this predicament.*

*The point is, I'm going away for a while. Maybe a long while. If I can send for you, I will. If I can come back without putting my neck in a guillotine, I'll do that too. Until then, if you need help with anything, my brother is only a phone call away. But understand, he doesn't yet know what you are finding out right now. I trust he'll help you, though, even if he disagrees with what I'm doing, or what I've done.*

*Two other things you need to know. I've set aside enough money to last you a lifetime, so don't worry. Just go to our safety deposit boxes at the bank and everything will become clear to you. The other — keep my mother away from the kids, at all costs.*

*Okay, Liv, I've got to go. Got a plane to catch. Remember, I'm sure my brother will help you in whatever way you need him, so don't be afraid to ask.*

*I'll be in touch as soon as I can.*

*Love you,*
*Ethan.*
*P.S. Give the kids a hug for me.'*

After reading Ethan's note a second, and then a third time, my disbelief still swelling from the first time, I pawed my forehead a few moments, as if that was going to rub some clarity into the mix. Finally, I peered into my sister-in-law's worried eyes, and asked, "Is it okay if I keep this, Liv?"

"What are you going to do with it?" she replied, her curiosity barely washing over her anxious tone.

"Probably read it another dozen times. But in the end, I'll get rid of it so no one ever sees it again. I don't want to take the chance it'll be used against him."

"Do you think Ethan did something wrong?"

"I don't know, Olivia. I really don't. What do you think?"

Olivia shrugged. "Ethan doesn't tell me a lot," she said, her gaze momentarily falling to the floor. "Sometimes, I think he lives in two worlds. Home and away. Home, I know about. Away, I don't."

"Well, if it makes you feel any better, I'm gonna try and find out, because I want to help him." I then sighed, before adding, "In the meantime, we have your kids to think about."

"God, what am I gonna do, Drew? What am I gonna tell the kids?" Olivia asked, her eyes welling up, prompting her to dab them with the hem of her sleeve.

"You're going to tell them their father is away on business," I replied. "You're going to tell anyone who asks, the same thing. That's all you can do, until we know more."

"Do you have any ideas?" Olivia returned, her voice still teetering. "Any place you might start looking?"

"Unfortunately, Ethan's never told me too much either, Liv. It's been like that ever since we were kids. So no," I said, shaking my head, "at this point, I don't have a clue where to begin."

Truth be told, I knew exactly where to begin – the link between my brother's two worlds.

# Chapter 34

The morning sky began as a whitewashed canvas – distant, subtle patches of blue discernable once the sun's splintered light slipped between thick clouds stretching north to south, stitching the mountainous terrain into seamless pools of green. It is a portrait I have seen painted every morning since my arrival. One that will change within the hour, and then change once more an hour, or so, after that, culminating in what would be a flawless blue sky but for a smattering of white streaks loitering high above, where they will remain until the warm, afternoon winds blow them out to sea.

Daylight notwithstanding, when I initially landed in Costa Rica, I was far more consumed with getting the lay of the land, than I was taking an interest in the color of the sky, or the direction of the wind. I spent my first few days finding a used, nondescript Jeep to buy, visiting the banks I had originally wired money to from the States, discovering the spirited streets of Jaco Beach, and purchasing a handful of groceries and clothes to better absorb the taste and feel of life inside a tropical rainforest. Admittedly, however, it's difficult, if not altogether impossible, to ignore the rugged brilliance of the countryside.

It had also become difficult to ignore the prevailing calm and solitude that ensued, particularly when I sat on the balcony of my hotel room and watched night fall, it's slow, systematic descent like darkness being dripped from an hourglass, turning the ocean below into a sheet of black glass. Oddly enough, it was only then when I thought about Olivia and the kids, and only for a few minutes at that. It's not that I wasn't concerned for their wellbeing, because I was. I truly was. It's just, from the moment I got here, I've been basking in the premise, I was free of the masquerade – free of the smoke and mirrors that defined my past. Never mind if they continue to oblige my future. It's still tomorrow's shadow digesting the sins and trespasses of yesterday's, an evolving fate I was happy to accommodate.

Billy Maxwell's boat was docked in Los Suenos Marina, the midway point between Jaco Beach and Herradura, a seaside village that made Jaco look like the downtown streets of Manhattan. It was remote, and far less crowded, serviced only by a two-lane road that zigged and zagged its way from mountaintop jungle to the ocean below. It was plain to see why Billy chose the area as his place of refuge.

Although quite a bit of time had come and gone since I last saw my old client, recognizing him wasn't going to be a problem. The problem was going to be figuring out which fishing boat was his since there were quite a few of them bobbing about. But there weren't going to be too many with a Detroit Tigers baseball hat dangling from a fishing pole. So when I saw one some ten minutes after I started walking the marina docks, I had a strong sense the boat was Billy's. The fact it was also named, *The Gypsy*, only added to my belief. "Captain Billy Maxwell," I called out, "you have a fisherman waiting for you."

Two... three... four, and nothing, so I repeated, "Captain Billy Maxwell, you have a fisherman waiting for you."

Two... three... four, only this time, Billy appeared from the galley, grin in tow, and said, "Hell, Counselor, I've been expecting you ever since you sent your boy-scout to come and find me. What took you so long?"

I didn't want to laugh. I didn't even want to smile. And yet, I threw out some combination of the two, before responding, "Just waiting for you to get a boat worthy of taking me for a ride." I then shielded my eyes from the sun's glare, perused the boat from stern to bow, and added, "And it looks like you did."

"Then get your ass on board," Billy commanded. "I need a first mate."

"First mate nothin'. My boy-scout, as you refer to him, told me you had a first mate. Said she had a great pair of legs too."

"She did… she does," Billy returned, his ponytail dancing atop the back of his neck as he nodded his head. "But now she's pregnant with my kid, so her time on the boat is limited."

"Well, then, congrats to you," I offered.

"Thanks, we're both happy about it." Billy then smiled, and added, "Now you commin' aboard, or not?"

A few beers and a half-bottle of rum later (or just about the time our reminiscing hit a dead-end), Billy pulled his eyes from the shimmering blue water, looked at me, and said, "Don't take this the wrong way, but you didn't come here because you want to be friends, Ethan. You're not that kind of guy. And I know, because I'm not that kind of guy either."

I studied Billy's sun-drenched face a few moments (the rigidity he once proffered having since eased), before responding, "I had some trouble back home. Needed an escape route just in case. Unfortunately, just in case became a reality."

"I know better than to ask what the situation is about."

"I wouldn't tell you on a bet."

Billy winked. "That's why I know better than to ask."

"You're better off not knowing anyway," I suggested.

"Just tell me this… does Anthony Ricci have anything to do with it?"

"He's a small part of the equation."

"Then that means he's been on you because he still wants to find me."

"Well, you didn't really think he was going to stop looking for you, did you?"

"Nope. Not at all. Doesn't mean I wouldn't have preferred you telling me he fell off a cliff, though."

"Not to worry. I've thrown him enough curveballs."

Billy turned his attention back to the open water, which he scanned in silence for several moments, before saying, "I owe you a lot. I haven't forgotten."

"That's okay. Assuming I can trust you, then I know how you can pay me back," I returned.

"What do you mean, assuming you can trust me?" Billy countered. "You're the only thing standing between me and Ricci. I don't do right by you, then it's my ass on the line."

"Okay," I said, flashing Billy the palm of my hand. "Just making sure where you are in all this. You can't blame me for that."

"I don't," Billy said, his tone quickly settling. "Just tell me what you need me to do."

"Drive me to Panama City."

Billy squared his eyes on mine. "Panama City, as in the country of Panama?"

"One and the same," I replied.

"If you don't mind me asking, why Panama City?"

"Because, I want to stop there on my way to South America. Going to Brazil. The way I see it, if they can hide a bunch of Nazis after World War II, they can hide an ugly American now."

"I've been there. Don't know anything about any Nazis, but they sure do have a lot of good lookin' women."

"No blondes," I muttered.

"What's that?"

"Nothing. Just talking to myself. So will you do it?"

"You do realize it's like a 12 hour drive, don't you?"

"It's about 320 miles," I replied. "It's also another layer between me and the trouble I left behind. I could fly, but there's no record of anything between me and Panama if you drive me there. It'll be like creating one big blank spot. Makes for a better detour, if you know what I mean."

"Understood," Billy said. "I just didn't know if you realized it's a slow drive. Lot of winding mountain passes, that sort of thing."

"That's all right. That's why I bought the jeep, which you can keep, by the way, after you drop me off."

"Bullshit. I have a Range Rover. It'll be a lot more comfortable. You can leave the Jeep at my pad." Billy then dropped his hands to his thighs. "So, when do we leave?"

I shrugged, saying, "A week. Maybe ten days. No need to be overly hasty. Want to make sure I'm not missing anything. I also have to clean up some banking issues. Besides, I have to at least stay here long enough to miss my return flight back to the States. New York, to be exact."

"Okay, so you want to keep everyone guessing. I get it," Billy declared. "But it's not like the airline won't know you're not on the flight, Ethan, no matter where you're supposed to be flying to."

"I can't control what I can't control, Billy. But I can still check-in like I'm going and thereby create an element of doubt. Same thing with the hotel. If I checkout on the day of my flight, the immediate assumption will be that I left town. And even if I don't, the assumption will linger, perpetuating the doubt."

"And sending everyone on a wild goose chase in the process," Billy offered.

"It's at least something," I said.

"So when is the flight back?"

"Five days. And yes, before you say anything, I realize that conflicts with me leaving here in another week, or so."

"Okay, so what's up with that?" Billy queried.

"Let's just say I ran into a few issues I didn't anticipate." I then shrugged my shoulders, adding, "Chalk it up to doing business in a third world country."

"Believe me," Billy said, nodding his head, "I know how ass-backwards this place can sometimes be. Meanwhile, you're still gonna need a place to stay after you check out of the hotel."

"I'll find something," I said.

"What's to find? Just stay with me," Billy proposed. "Or stay on the boat." Billy then twisted around in his chair, rolled out his arm like he was introducing a stage act, and said, "I mean, look at the damn thing. It's forty-five feet of pretty goddamn nice. Two bedrooms, two showers, full kitchen, the works."

"Yeah," I said, looking over my shoulder, "it's quite obvious you didn't blow all your drug money."

Billy snickered. "Are you kidding? I made a fuckin' pile."

# CHAPTER 35

Let's see now, first my mother hurls rape allegations against Ethan, then Ethan disappears, and then my sister-in-law, Olivia, alludes to his strange behavior, saying she thinks my brother lives in two worlds. As if that wasn't enough to make my head spin, I then wait for Evelyn to go out on one of her hoity-toity dates, and go search the house, hoping to find something, anything, in fact, to undermine her credibility and silence her rape allegations, paving the way for Ethan (wherever he is), to return home to his wife and kids.

And then I remembered the floor safe that sits in the corner of my mother's overblown walk-in closet, behind some clothing. The safe's always been there, just like the key to open it has always been buried under some sweaters on the top shelf. Evelyn probably figures I never knew about the safe, and after opening it, I wish I hadn't. The truth is, however, I've known about the damn thing since childhood. Just like the kitchen table, couch in the great-room, or desk in my father's home office, it was there, so I never thought anymore about it, let alone being curious enough to look inside.

But now I was. So I did, promptly finding some naked pictures of Ethan when he was, I don't know, seven, eight, maybe nine-years-old. I'm not just talking Ethan in the buff either. I'm talking, Ethan blindfolded, Ethan tied up, Ethan holding what looks like a dildo. Hell, there were even a bunch with my mother, some showing her partially clothed, others not. Yet, in each instance, she was either straddling my brother, or touching some part of his naked body; cementing the fact that Evelyn choreographed my brother's horrifying childhood in ways I cannot begin to fathom; cementing, too, that she was obviously insane.

I know I vomited. I know I cried. I know I screamed at the spineless complacency of my dead father. I'm just not sure how long I remained in the murky confines and treacherous embrace of our blighted house, our sunset house, before my mother and Connor Banks returned from their evening out, their savage noise spiraling up the stairs, sending a chill through my otherwise numb body.

I grabbed the pictures, taking as many as would fill my pockets, leaving the remaining few strewn about the floor, and barreled downstairs.

"What are you doing here?" Evelyn barked the instant she saw me.

I ignored the question, and instead, seethed at the inhumanity of the face it fell from.

"I said, what are you doing here?"

I charged forward, grabbing my mother by the throat and then driving her backwards until her body slammed hard against the wall. "I found the pictures, you fucking cunt! I found the pictures!"

"Hey, hey, hey… what are you doing? Stop! What are you doing?" Connor Banks bellowed. He then grabbed me from behind, pulling at my arms until I let my mother go, whereupon I turned and drilled him between the eyes, his knees crumbling as he dropped to the marble floor, at which point I drilled him again to keep him there.

Gasping for air, my mother inched backwards, though I quickly swallowed the space between us. I didn't latch onto her throat, however, notwithstanding my raging desire to choke every ounce of life out of her. Rather, I seized her by the hair, drew her head back, and spit in her face. "You fucking animal," I growled. "You fucking pig. You utter a single word about Ethan to anyone… you make one more move against my father's law firm… you so much as look or breathe the wrong way, and so help me god, I'll see that you rot in hell." I then pushed her from my grasp and left her cowering in the corner.

I've met Jack Francis twice in my life – once at a party my brother and sister-in-law hosted a few years back, and the other time, just recently. I was in

Ethan's office discussing a motion he wanted to file in our probate dispute with Evelyn, when Jack poked his head inside to say hello. The point is, I didn't know much about him, other than he was a private investigator employed by my brother's firm. Olivia says it would not be unusual for them to speak several nights a week, however. She seems to think they're pretty close friends. "Or," as she pointed out, "as close as Ethan lets somebody get." Either way, it was reason enough to see if Jack had some insight into my brother's whereabouts.

Having said that, I did not want to cold-call him. I did not want to schedule a meeting with him either, as that would merely give him cause for concern. No, I wanted to see his face and hear his words, measure his expression and gauge his tone, for the topic of my runaway brother was sure to draw a reaction, even from the most disciplined.

Yeah, well, the joke, so to speak, was on me, because after I showed up at his office unannounced, and told him Ethan was not away on business, but had, in fact, disappeared, Jack had no reaction whatsoever – not when I indicated Ethan may've committed a serious crime, and may be in trouble as a result – not even when I said, "But I can't help him if I can't find him."

He simply proffered a look of indifference, and replied, "Sorry, Andrew, but I don't know anything about it, so there's really nothing I can do."

"Well, if something comes to you, or you have a sudden change of heart," I said, my smirk and caustic tone nipping at his irreverence, "you'll know where to find me." I then put my card on Jack's desk, never figuring he'd call a few hours later, asking to meet the following morning.

9:00 a.m. didn't come soon enough. The sun was out, the temperature was fairly mild for late February, and I had grown tired of my couch, where I had been sitting since five o'clock in the morning, my mind a jumbled mess.

Do I stay quiet about the twisted perversions of my mother? Do I tell Olivia, knowing she'll then have to cope with the horrors Ethan endured, not to mention, live with the fear he may one day inflict those same horrors on his own children? Do I tell Mickey, knowing she'll forever wonder if I too was abused, yet judging my every move as if I was? Or do I just go to the police with pictures in hand and let the system run its course? The thing is, if I do that, I'll be forced to watch it run over my niece and nephew as well, since the situation will do nothing but expose them to unlimited ridicule and embarrassment, likely forcing Olivia and the kids to move away.

Then, of course, there's still the unsettled matter of the Chestnut Hills rapes. Sure, the pictures I found pretty much blew-up any chance someone would believe my mother, let alone the prosecutors in my office, or a jury of her peers. But that still doesn't mean it hasn't crossed my mind. Was my brother guilty, or wasn't he? Did he have a monster lurking within, or not? Could Evelyn, despite her polluted mind, be telling the truth, or was she simply throwing Ethan to the dogs before he did the same to her? Were her actions preemptive, premeditated, or a precursor of things to come?

I supose I could go on and on, but what would be the point? At the end of the day I wasn't kicking up any dust until I first found my brother anyway.

"Jaco Beach."

I looked up from the menu. "What?"

"Jaco Beach," Jack repeated, as though he'd just read my mind. He then took a seat in the booth opposite me. "Sorry I'm late. Traffic."

"That's okay," I said, waving off the apology. "Now what were you saying?"

"Jaco Beach. I think that's where Ethan is."

"Where in the hell is Jaco Beach?"

"Costa Rica."

"So what makes you think he's there?" I queried.

"It's not what, it's who," Jack responded.

"Okay, who?"

"Billy Maxwell. I assume you've heard the name before."

I nodded. "That would be a safe bet."

"Then, can I also assume you know about the connection between Billy and Anthony Ricci?" Jack asked.

I waited until Jack's coffee was poured and the waitress lumbered away, before replying, "You mean, the connection, as in, Billy Maxwell killed Ricci's son, David? Yeah, I know all about it... right down to the welts on my face.

Ricci sent one of his goons to kick my ass in the hopes it would spook my brother into giving Billy up."

"That was probably Frank Marino," Jack advised.

"Ethan said the same thing. Unfortunately, I never got a look at him so I wouldn't know him if he walked in the door right now."

"I've never seen him either. I've heard plenty of stories, though," Jack remarked. He then stirred some sugar into his coffee, before adding, "It's interesting, though."

"What's that?"

"You getting roughed up. Your brother never mentioned it to me. I would've thought otherwise."

"That's vintage, Ethan," I stated. "He gathers information. Doesn't matter who you are. He only gives it out if he thinks it'll help him."

Jack tipped his head from side to side. "I don't know. I never thought about him that way. You're probably right, though. You know him better than me."

I sighed. "Unfortunately, Jack, I'm not sure I know him at all. But I do need to find him."

"And that's why I wanted to meet with you," Jack returned. "I can help."

"Why the sudden change of heart?" I asked.

"Listen," Jack said, hunching up his shoulders, "when you came to my office and said you needed to find him because he might've done something wrong, I was skeptical. I mean, after all, you are a prosecutor. Then I thought about it some more, and came to the conclusion, you're his brother first. So yes, it would only be natural for you to want to help him. The thing is, so do I. He's done a lot for me."

"Thanks for the offer, Jack. But no," I said, shaking my head. "If he's in Jaco Beach, I'll find him myself."

Jack snickered. "There's more to Jaco Beach than surf and sand, my friend. It's a place where people go to get lost, not found."

"I see. And you know this how?" I asked, a dubious grin in tow.

"Because, I've already been there." Jack asserted. He then leaned forward, his jawline growing taut, his dark eyes narrowing, and added, "Your brother sent me to find Billy Maxwell. But it was Billy who found me. The point is, you're brother was cooking up an escape plan back then. He knew trouble might be brewing. I just never realized it until you told me he took off. But that's why I think I know where he's at. And since time is of the essence, which it always fucking is when trouble is involved, I'm going with you. Keep you from walking in circles." Jack let his shoulders fall back against the booth, and then calmly folded his arms. "Do you have a passport?"

I nodded.

"Good. When do we leave?"

# CHAPTER 36

The first thing I noticed was her hair. Long and blonde, it played in the afternoon breeze like the sunlight played upon the deep blue ocean she was facing. It wasn't until she turned and started walking toward the hotel pool, however, her whimsical gait that of a ballerina tiptoeing her way across the sand, that I got a sense of just how pretty she might be. So I left my 6th floor balcony and headed downstairs to see firsthand.

And she didn't disappoint. God knows, she didn't disappoint. Not too tall, and not too short, she stood at perhaps the most perfect of heights – one that allowed her slender frame to slip between statuesque and flat-out adorable with effortless grace. Better still, the way the sunbaked-bronze accentuated her taut, vibrant skin as she moved.

Then, of course, there was her face, which I meandered to the other side of the pool to get a better look at – finding a lounge chair to fill when I was ten, maybe fifteen yards away. Close enough, though, to see the seamless stitch of her brows, and how they sat above the almond curve of her eyes. Close enough to see crisp cheekbones define a delicate nose and tapered jawline. Close enough to see the luster of her smile jump from rose-tinted lips. Close enough to see the slight curve of her tender neck, and the narrow shoulders it melted into.

Close enough to see that she was, I don't know, maybe ten years old.

Fortunately, I was checking out of the hotel to go stay on Billy's boat, dodging my lurking temptation for at least one more day.

# CHAPTER 37

Given that I'd kept Mickey in the dark about the recent events surrounding Ethan and my mother, I didn't think now was the time to bring her up to speed. On the one hand, there was no sense telling her where my brother may be hiding, when doing so could expose her to the perils of Anthony Ricci. On the other hand, I didn't feel like hearing her tell me I was going on a fishing expedition.

Therefore, I lied. I'm not talkin' some mamby-pamby little white lie either. I'm talkin' bullshit of epic proportions. Meaning, the *business trip* Ethan really wasn't on, was now taking place in Miami (my jumping off point to Costa Rica). He and I were looking to buy an office building with some of the money we would be receiving from the old man's estate. Ethan had traveled ahead of me to scope out various properties. Having now located one, he wanted me to come to Florida and see the building before negotiations started heating up.

"No, I'll have zero idea what I'm looking at," I said, when Mickey questioned my real estate acumen. "But the seller doesn't have to know that."

I'm not sure if Mickey believed me, and heaven knows I wasn't going to put it to a test. The way I saw it, I had little choice in the matter anyway. I mean, if I didn't go chase after my brother, what was going to happen? Nothing good, that's what. Absolutely nothing good.

Obviously, dealing with my sister-in-law was a whole different matter. For one thing, I didn't have to lie. I simply had to explain, Jaco Beach might not bear fruit – that Ethan could, in fact, be anywhere. For another thing,

I didn't have to worry. Olivia knew the ramifications involved. She understood, silence was tantamount to vigilance. What worried me was her sudden indifference to Ethan's wellbeing. Had anger at my brother finally set in? Or was she simply masking her emotions in an effort to appear strong? Sure, I could've asked. I just didn't think it was any of my goddamn business, so I didn't. Besides, once we said our goodbyes, I was at a complete fucking loss anyway. Let me put it like this: an obligatory hug, a peck on the cheek, maybe even the side of the mouth, I get it. But an inviting embrace, followed by a lingering kiss on the neck, and a nuzzle to the ear, now that's a different story altogether – especially when Olivia inhaled deeply, as if drawing in my scent, and then whispered, "You come back to me safe." Letting me go only when I promised to do so.

I think it's fair to say, Jaco Beach was beckoning at just about the right time. Although the flight, now that I could've done without. I mean, between the turbulence blowing the plane around like an empty beer can, and the fact all service had been cut off (can you say, no cocktails?), we got off to a pretty rocky start. Once we landed, however, Jack was familiar enough with the area to get us from airport to hotel without a hitch. In fact, midway there he even turned into Mr. Travel Guide.

"We're approaching the Tarcoles River Bridge," he announced. "It's commonly known as Crocodile Bridge because not forty feet below is the largest concentration of crocodiles anywhere in Central America."

"So that would explain all the cars pulled off to the side," I remarked.

"Yep. The tourists want to see them. I'm gonna pull off too. It's worth a look," Jack said, as he maneuvered our rental accordingly.

Yeah, well, three things became abundantly clear as I was standing on the bridge. One, it was designed by third-world engineers from a third-world country, meaning two, I wanted to drive over it as fast as possible, because three, while the largest concentration of crocs might've been lounging below, it would only take one to swallow my ass whole. Point being, as soon as the foot traffic cleared, I said, "Let's get out of Dodge."

Hotel de Luz was tucked along a hillside on the northern end of town, not too far from the docks of Hermosa Beach, where Jack thought we might find my brother. Had there been much daylight left, I might've been tempted to continue our trek, but Jack assured me, once the pending dusk settled, the winding jungle roads would be difficult, if not altogether too dangerous, to navigate – the operative term being *jungle* – the relevant concept being *crocodile*.

"Yeah, tomorrow will be soon enough," I said. "Besides, I could use a drink."

Jack concurred, so after we checked into our respective rooms, we headed to the hotel's outdoor bar, which, despite its expansive setting, filled up in a hurry. Nevertheless, we managed to snag a high-top, where we spent the next few hours consuming the local fare. The only problem, somewhere between all the rum and coke, I heard, *that voice* – the one who found my beating in the stairwell so goddamn entertaining – the one I said, I'd never forget. Well, I didn't, and there it was, hovering over the bar like the very humidity that hung in the night air.

I casually looked around, and yet, saw nothing out of the ordinary, though I'm not really sure what I expected to see. I mean, what does a Mafia hench-man look like in the tropics? It's not like he was going to be standing around in some shiny silk suit. No, he was going to be dressed like every other typi-cal moron who hasn't seen the sun in god knows how long. Maybe it was my imagination, I told myself. Maybe the liquor was getting the best of me. Either way, I looked at Jack, and said, "Did you happen to hear that… that deep, raspy voice?"

Jack proffered a quizzical look. "Can't say I have. But I've pretty much been tunin' out the noise. Why do you ask?"

I leaned toward him. "Because it's the same fucking voice I heard the night I got jumped at my apartment."

"You're certain?"

"It's awfully goddamn similar, Jack. Like too close for comfort, similar."

Jack nodded subtly. "You think it's Marino?"

"I don't know. I've looked around a few times, but I don't even know what the cocksucker looks like, so it hasn't done me a whole lot of good."

"I wish I could help you there, but I don't know what he looks like ei-ther." Jack rubbed at his stubble a few moments, before adding, "Did you see anyone looking back at you when you were scanning the joint?"

I sighed. "Nothing out of the ordinary."

"It wouldn't be out of the ordinary, Drew."

"Still, I can't say as I did."

"Well if you do, take note of it. But don't let your imagination run wild either."

"You think he could've been on our plane?"

Jack polished off his shot of Centenario, and then flagged the waitress down and ordered two more. "I'm gonna go take a leak," he muttered. "When I come back, we'll kill the shots, and then head to our rooms like it's just another day. We'll get an early start tomorrow. In the meantime, I'll try and think of something, just in case."

"Okay," I responded, not realizing Jack's idea of an early start was to call my room at 5:30 the following morning.

"What's up?" I asked, snapping up the phone before my head exploded from the sudden blare.

"Nothin'," Jack returned. "Shower and get dressed. We'll grab some breakfast. After that I've got an errand to run."

"What kind of errand?"

"I'll see you in the lobby in an hour," Jack replied, before clicking off.

Ninety minutes later we were sitting in Pepino's Taco Bar, eating Gallo Pinto, a traditional Costa Rican breakfast mainly consisting of rice and beans. It was not my first choice by any stretch, but Jack insisted I try it. "Had it here my last trip," he said. "It's definitely worth a try."

Okay, so either I was really hungry, or the food was really good. All I know is, once breakfast was served, not another word passed between us until we got to that last coffee warm-up, and I asked him again, "So what kind of errand do you have to run?"

"Gonna pick up a gun," he replied, his tone as nonchalant as the rising temperature outside.

"Gun? For what? Who you planning to shoot?"

"No one." He then smirked, adding, "Unless someone pisses me off."

"Seriously, why the gun?"

Jack shrugged, saying, "Because, I don't want to be caught flatfooted, Drew. That's a rule I try and live by. It comes in handy in my line of work. No reason to change it up now."

"So you think that was Marino's voice I heard last night, don't you?" I asked, the question falling out of my mouth as I perused the restaurant, the early morning crowd a sparse mix of tourist and local alike. "You think he's here, don't you?"

Jack waited until my fidgety gaze settled back on his own, before responding, "No, he's not in the restaurant having breakfast, if that's what you mean. But if he followed us... if he's really in Jaco Beach, my guess is we're gonna see a couple of guys sitting in a car in the parking lot. Just sitting. Just waiting."

"Great. Fucking great. So what are we supposed to do?"

Jack smiled. "Pay the bill and leave."

"C'mon, Jack. Spare me the bullshit."

"No bullshit," Jack returned, his smile quickly fading. "We're gonna pay the bill and leave. Then we're gonna walk outside, get in our car, and drive away. It's business as usual, so don't make it a point to look around. If Marino's waiting for us, a car will pull out of the parking lot a few seconds after we do."

"That's it? Walk outside and don't look around? That's the big plan?"

Jack smiled again. "Don't worry. I've got something else brewing. But first we've got to see if Marino's actually out there. Otherwise, it won't matter."

Yeah, well, long story short... Marino was... so apparently, it did!

# CHAPTER 38

Carlos Felipe was orphaned when he was eight-years-old, and his sister, Luisa, was five. With no other family to take them in (unless you consider an uncle who'd spent half his life in prison), they were sent to the *San Jose Orphanage*, where they lived happily as brother and sister until bureaucracy deemed it necessary to split them up, moving Carlos Felipe to Tambor, a small town in the southern Nicoya Peninsula, about a day's ride away.

Five years would pass before Carlos and Luisa would see each other again, and only then because their respective schools scheduled a joint field trip to the midway point of Antonio Manuel National Park. Yet, in the time apart, Carlos Felipe had become embittered, hardened, his incessant glare a reflection of his gnawing anger. It was their short, tear-filled reunion, in fact, that convinced Carlos to leave his orphanage in the middle of the night, and carve out a path all his own. Bureaucracy would not look for him if he did, and nothing would be gained if he did not.

By the time Carlos turned fifteen, life on the street had become a series of criminal activities, each designed to line his pockets and enrich his status such, by the time he was eighteen he had entrenched himself as leader of a burgeoning, and feared street gang, aptly named, *Calleja Diablos*, or, *Alley Devils*.

Through it all, Carlos Felipe stayed in touch with Luisa, often sending her letters detailing how life would change for the better once she turned sixteen and was free to leave the orphanage. True to his word, it did too, for

Luisa moved into Carlos' two- bedroom, one-bath clapboard house, and for the first time in her life Luisa had her very own bedroom, not to mention, no longer having to share a bathroom with eleven other girls. It was the beginning of a ten-year period that would see Luisa grow into a beautiful woman, Carlos grow his criminal enterprise, and the two of them grow their sibling affection for one another – a bond tested when Billy Maxwell moved to Jaco Beach, walked into a café one sunny afternoon, and promptly locked eyes with Luisa. A chance encounter to be sure, it also marked the start of a relationship Carlos wanted his sister to abruptly end. "Before you're disrespected!" he snapped.

When Luisa refused to obey, even going so far as to parade her affection for Billy through the downtown streets of Jaco, Carlos became so enraged, he threw Luisa out of the house. It was a situation Billy rectified, however, with a prompt and heartfelt apology; a simple gesture that served as the catalyst, for what would become, an endearing friendship.

As a result, it was not at all difficult for Jack Francis to put his hastily conceived plan in motion.

"So you're just going to lead Marino right to Billy's doorstep? Is that what you're telling me?"

"That's what I'm telling you."

"And you came up with this plan when, over your morning dump?"

Jack sighed. "Actually, this was all planned last night after you and I left the bar. You went to sleep. I went to see Carlos."

"And what about my brother? What's Ethan's part in all of this?"

"No part."

"Okay. So when does all the fun begin?"

"Tonight."

"When tonight?"

"When it's dark," Jack returned, his steely expression and abrupt reply a clear indication he was focused on navigating terrain outside our conversation.

"Well it gets dark about 6:30," I remarked.

"Nine o'clock," Jack countered, peeling his eyes from the road to look at me. "Nine o'clock."

"So Ethan already knows we're here, doesn't he?"

"I would assume Carlos has told him by now, yes."

"How well you know this guy anyway? Carlos Felipe, how well do you know him?"

"I met him by chance last time I was here. Billy introduced us. Why?"

I shrugged my shoulders, saying, "Just curious."

"Listen, I don't have to know him well," Jack declared. "If Billy trusts him, that's good enough for me."

"Billy Maxwell went to jail for killing Anthony Ricci's son in cold blood," I asserted. "He now lives in Jaco Beach, where, for all I know, he's running guns and drugs with Carlos Felipe, who's nothing more than a local thug. So tell me, how does that suddenly make him, or his opinion, the gold standard?"

"What, I should put my trust in Frank Marino?"

I cast my eyes on the passing scenery. "Touché," I muttered.

"What's that you say?" Jack queried.

"Fuck off, Jack. And by the way, where are you driving to?"

"I don't know. But we've got some time to kill, so I figured I'd lead that fucking idiot on a wild goose chase."

"You don't think Marino's figured out that we're onto him following us?"

Jack snickered. "Listen, from everything I've heard, Marino is a few fries short of a happy meal."

"Even so, you don't think he knows you're playing with him right now?"

"At this point, Drew, it really doesn't matter what he knows. His goal is to get to Billy. If he thinks I can help get him there, he has no choice but to follow me. Besides," Jack added, as he glanced my way, "it's a nice afternoon for a drive."

It hadn't been all that long since I last saw Ethan, and yet, the angst I was feeling as the car wound it's way up Billy's drive made it seem like it had been a year. Who knows, maybe I was just nervous about the inevitable collision with Marino? Either way, I found myself at a loss for words once Jack and I walked into Billy's house and I saw my brother leaning against the far wall, probably locked in that position ever since he saw the flicker of our headlights. "You shouldn't have come here," he said, his expression taut, his tone rigid.

"Nice to see you too," I replied.

"Seriously Andrew, you shouldn't have come here. Jack, you shouldn't have brought him."

"Where? Here, or Costa Rica in general?" Jack wondered.

"Costa Rica."

"Sorry Ethan, but I tagged along with Drew, not the other way around."

"Doesn't matter, he still shouldn't have come."

"I came because of your wife and kids. Remember them?"

"Billy?" My brother suddenly called out. "I think it's showtime. Another car's coming up the drive. Billy?"

"Yep, I got you," Billy said, as he entered the room, what I hadn't noticed until then to be an open, airy setting of tropical colors and tall, green plants. "Jack, nice to see you again. Andrew, I presume. I'm Billy," he said, offering his hand, and then pulling it away in almost the same instant I took it. "Now if you would be so kind as to go stand next to your brother."

I looked at Jack, who nodded his head, saying, "Floor space is limited. You're better off over there."

"Whatever," I mumbled, before making my way across the room, Ethan watching my every step.

"Everyone in place?" Jack asked Billy.

"Yep. They've been here about an hour."

"You ready?"

"Yeah," Billy replied. "It'll be nice to put this to bed once and for all."

In what was probably another 30 seconds (but felt like an hour), there was knocking at the front door. "C'mon in, door's open," Billy called out, as though expecting his neighbor.

And just as Jack had predicted earlier, in walked Frank Marino and some other goon, with guns drawn.

"Well, well, well," Marino uttered, his ominous glare scanning the room, before landing squarely on Billy. "It's been a long time you little scumbag. Bet you didn't plan on seein' me again?"

"Wow, you mentioned the voice, Drew, but you never said how ugly he was," Jack quipped.

"Hey, keep it up scumbag lover, and you'll be the first to go," Marino warned. He then motioned toward Ethan and me, and said, "Put a gun on those two over there, Joey. They're lawyers, and I don't trust lawyers."

"Oh, how rich," Ethan remarked.

"Shut your trap, Rivers."

"Go fuck yourself, Marino."

"Hey, watch your tongue, pretty-boy, or I'll cut it out," Joey said.

"You can go fuck yourself too," Ethan returned.

"Shut him up," Marino directed.

"With pleasure," Joey responded. Before he took a step toward my brother, however, the front door opened again, only this time Carlos Felipe and five *Calleja Diablos* walked in, three holding shotguns, two handguns, and Carlos Felipe carrying but a wink and a smile.

*"Hola, mi hermano,"* Carlos said, as he walked over to Billy for a quick man-hug. He then turned to face Marino, and said, *"Dejar caer tu el arma."*

"What the hell?" Marino countered.

"He said to drop your weapons," Billy advised. "I think you better listen."

"I'm not dropping shit."

Billy tipped his head from side to side, as though contemplating Marino's statement, before saying, "Actually, you're probably gonna do that too." He then motioned to the *Calleja Diablo* closest to Joey, at which point the butt of a shotgun cracked the side of Joey's skull, dropping him like a two-hundred pound bag of dirt.

*"Tomar un duradero la respiracion,"* Carlos Felipe said.

"What the fuck does that mean?" Marino grumbled, as a *Calleja Diablo* stripped him of his handgun. "Can't your fucking monkey speak English?"

"It means, take a lasting breath," Billy advised.

"Or in your case," Carlos Felipe added, "it means you're gonna die," whereupon a dull thud filled the room, Marino falling over after a shotgun butt kissed the back of his head.

"*Tomar los fuera la espaida,*" Carlos Felipe promptly said to his fellow gang members. "*Quitar los de su la ropa. La corbata los arriba bueno. Entonces somos la partida a dejar caer los encima de el cocodrila Puente.*"

"How about a little translation," Jack suggested, before I could utter the words myself.

"Carlos told his guys to take them out back. Strip them of their clothes, and tie them up good. Then we're going to drop them over the crocodile bridge." Billy smiled, before adding, "By morning, any evidence of their pitiful existence will be long gone."

I took a deep breath, and then blinked.

My brother, on the other hand, glanced at me, and said, "Interesting."

I spent the next few hours drifting between the violence I had just witnessed, and the crime I was now a party to. Ethan didn't see it that way, however. He simply accepted Marino's fate as part of Marino's destiny. Then again, he magically dismissed leaving behind his wife and kids as little more than a matter of his own destiny.

"And the pictures I found of you and mother when you were just a child… what would you call those?" I asked.

Ethan gazed at me for several moments, the clarity in his eyes slowly giving way to a contorted mix of agony and anger. He then turned away in silence.

The rest of the night was no more settling. While Jack, Billy, and his merry band of pirates, were busy feeding the goon squad to a bunch of hungry crocodiles, Ethan and I watched as the black sky segued from purple to violet, before giving way to a hazy mix of gray and blue; the face of the early morning sun methodically climbing above the tree line, exposing Billy's mountaintop as the lush and rugged green terrain it was, and not just the shadows it wore at night.

Along the way, I spoon fed him pieces of our deeply troubled mother, crippled dead father, and the law firm he fought so hard for. Yet, in each instance, Ethan said very little, as if subdued by the words and the painful memories they carried. Hell, even when I threw Olivia and the children at him, all he did was nod his head.

In fact, it wasn't until I stood to stretch my back, when Ethan muttered, "I've got to go," whereupon he slipped out the front door.

"Where?" I called out after him. "You've got to go where?"

Ethan stopped dead in his tracks, and without turning around, responded, "Home. I've got to go home. I'm going to make a deal with Ricci."

"A deal? What are you talking about, Ethan? What kind of deal?"

"I'm going to give up Billy."

"Now? You're going to give him up now?" I countered. "After all this?"

"No. After Ricci kills mother. I'll give him up then." Ethan then turned my way, and added, "Evelyn needs to die."

Seconds later my brother disappeared into the sinister undergrowth below.

97900265R00130

Made in the USA
Columbia, SC
19 June 2018